SAPPHIRE

Blood Stones Novel 1

Bunny Brooks

Copyright © 2023 Bunny Brooks

All rights reserved

The characters and events portrayed in this book are fictitious. Any similarity to real persons, living or dead, is coincidental and not intended by the author.

No part of this book may be reproduced, or stored in a retrieval system, or transmitted in any form or by any means, electronic, mechanical, photocopying, recording, or otherwise, without express written permission of the publisher.

CONTENTS

Title Page
Copyright
Blood Stones: Sapphire
Chapter One 1
Chapter Two 9
Chapter Three 16
Chapter Four 23
Chapter Five 30
Chapter Six 37
Chapter Seven 46
Chapter Eight 53
Chapter Nine 63
Chapter Ten 72
Chapter Eleven 79
Chapter Twelve 86
Chapter Thirteen 94
Chapter Fourteen 102

Chapter Fifteen	109
Chapter Sixteen	118
Chapter Seventeen	125
Chapter Eighteen	133
Chapter Nineteen	140
Chapter Twenty	148
Chapter Twenty One	156
Chapter Twenty Two	168
Chapter Twenty Three	175
Chapter Twenty Four	186
Chapter Twenty Five	195
Chapter Twenty Six	201
Chapter Twenty Seven	208
Chapter Twenty Eight	215
Chapter Twenty Nine	223
Chapter Thirty	231
Chapter Thirty One	238
Chapter Thirty Two	245
Chapter Thirty Three	253
Chapter Thirty Four	262
Chapter Thirty Five	269
Chapter Thirty Six	277
Chapter Thirty Seven	284
Chapter Thirty Eight	292

Chapter Thirty Nine	302
Chapter Forty	309
Chapter Forty One	317
Blood Stones: Citrine	325
About The Author	327

BLOOD STONES:
SAPPHIRE

This is the beginning of a new erotic reverse harem series. Please note that some of the actions of these fictional characters are not acceptable out of the realm of a fiction novel. Readers should be 18+ due to the mature nature of the material.

CHAPTER ONE

Vannah

I stood above the grave site, dirt in my leather glove, and tried to feel something. Anything. Grief? Heartbreak? Relief? Sadness? But, I didn't feel anything but numbness. I was cold and empty and there was no sun that could break the clouds of my anguish. The dirt in my hands held heavier than my heart.

"Vannah" a male voice prompted me. I turned to see my twin brother, Gio, standing at my side. But, it was my father behind him that had spoken my name. His expression was tight but his eyes pressed me to get on with it.

I raised my hands above the grave – the metaphorical double grave – and let the dirt down into the casket. The thump it made beat louder than my heart. Gio put his arm around me, as I dusted off my hands, before leading me away from the grave side. The priest, Father Thomas, began to speak through the final prayer.

I didn't listen, fuck God honestly, and let Gio walk me to the car.

Two hours later, I was at the wake. I stood by the door, shaking the hands of every person that came in – the family members kissing my cheeks and giving me their love. I lost track of how many people gave me their condolences and their gifts and their food. My father, and Aldo's brother, stood either side of me.

I turned to my father, "I think...I think I'm going to go lie down".

"Of course, darling". He glanced into the room before making eye contact with Gio – my brother came over to us almost instantly, knowing my father wanted him even just from the look. "Take your sister up to one of the guest's rooms and ensure she has a lie down".

My father gave my cheek a kiss and I gave him a sad smile. Gio led me upstairs silently. My parent's house was too big, and was different to the one we had grown up in, so I was glad to have his lead. Gio found the largest guest room and waved me inside.

My twin was silent as I kicked my heeled pumps off, and pulled my black blazer off before discarding it carelessly on the floor. The bed was high as I climbed onto it. Gio picked up my jacket, folded it, and placed it on the couch as he watched me get under the covers. He stood staring at me for a few seconds.

"I wish there was something I could say to make you feel better" he whispered.

"Tell me AJ is alive again" I deadpanned, staring at the ceiling. "That is the only thing that will make me feel better".

"AJ?" Gio asked delicately.

My hand went down and pressed against my flat stomach. "That was what Aldo and I called the baby. Aldo Junior". I took a deep breath, tears dancing in my vision once more. "It was stupid, as we didn't know if it was a boy or a girl, but we started calling it AJ".

Gio took a seat on the bed next to me. I looked up at him as I tried to ground myself. My brother's dark hair was swept backwards with gel, diamond studs sparkled in his ears and his brown stubble was trimmed neatly. Only the dark circles under his eyes gave his stress away.

"Get some sleep". He pressed a sweet kiss to the top of my head. That made me smile because usually my brother and I argued like cat and dog. He must have known how truly broken I was to have lost my baby...as well as my husband.

"Gio?" I called, as he got up to leave. He turned back to me with a raised eyebrow. "What happens to me now?"

He was silent for a long moment, running a hand over his face and chin. The scratchy noise of his stubble echoed through the room. "Dad has already lined up a suitor for you".

I gave a humourless laugh, "I'm literally at my husband's wake and he's already playing matchmaker".

He shrugged, "you know Dad".

"Let me guess? Forty years old, balding head, a massive gut and looking for a second wife to give him a son".

Gio shook his head, "not this time. One of those was enough for you, I made sure of that. This time we've got someone else in mind. Someone young, and attractive and strong enough to protect you".

I snorted, "oh yeah, what's the catch?" Because, I knew there was a catch. In a mob family there was always a fucking catch.

"The catch, Giovannah, is that Dario requested you".

I sat up in the bed so fast I was surprised I didn't give myself whiplash. "Dario? As in Dario Conti?" I put a hand to my throat. "As in Dario Conti, out of Vegas?"

Gio smirked, "the very same. He heard about Aldo's murder and told father he was looking for a respectable wife with a name. He made it clear he was interested in giving you the life that we all want for you. Your children will just bear the Conti name rather than the Bianchi name".

For the first time in a month, the numbness inside me began to dissipate. With it came a wave of emotion, from the information that Gio was telling me, that broke through the numbness inside me. "I...do I have a choice?" I swallowed deeply.

"Conti is a good fit for you, Vannah, trust me. I've looked into him and I think you'll like him better than you liked Aldo. Plus, as much as the Bianchi and Conti call each other partners, it is about time we had a marriage to solidify that bond".

I didn't say anything else. What could I say? It was decided, I was to marry Dario Conti and move to his territory in Vegas.

✝

A month later, I sat in front of a vanity as Melanie curled my hair and Brianna finished my makeup. Originally Melanie had been doing my makeup and Brianna my hair, but after Melanie began to slap on foundation orange enough to be sponsored by Fanta, I got them to switch. And, to be fair to her, Brianna was going my makeup well.

"Dario Conti" Melanie giggled, "you're so lucky. I heard he's like Brad Pitt hot". She pretended to fan herself.

Brianna rolled her eyes, "ew, Brad Pitt is old and crusty".

"Fine, then he's Ryan Reynolds hot". The two women, I think they were technically cousins to me, giggled together. "Have you actually met him, Vannah? Dario, I mean?"

"Once" I replied softly. As nice as Brianna and Melanie were, I was not in the mood for chatter and giggles. It was my wedding day – my second wedding at only twenty six – and I was nervous as hell. When I had married Aldo I had been scared, but also excited. This time? I was just straight up terrified.

I had met Dario, my future husband, before. When I was nineteen and young and full of hope. I had been wearing a white dress that day too. Because the one and only time I had met Dario Conti, was at my first wedding.

Weddings, funerals and birthdays were big in the mob – mainly because the women held the celebrations while the men used the excuse to meet up and discuss business. When I had married Aldo, the Conti family and the Bianchi family had just formed an alliance. It had been the first celebration that had had former rival mafias joint together as one. Ironic that the next step in joining the two syndicates was by this marriage.

There had to be some sort of irony in that. Meeting my second husband at my first wedding. But, that was the way in our world. Ironic that most of the family was catholic, because they climbed over each other like mating rabbits.

"Do we think a red lip is appropriate?" Brianna asked, as Melanie finished my hair.

"Hmm, maybe not for a wedding" her sister replied.

"I want a red lip" I cut in. "My flowers are white and red roses and I have a red sash on my dress. So, yes, red lip and if we can add some red to my eyeshadow that would be great. Not too much, it's not a Christmas party, but just a hint".

"Oh, sure" Brianna blinked – shocked at my directness. Despite these girls being part of my family, they didn't know me well. As the daughter of the head of the family, I had been isolated and protected. Then, when I became the wife of the consigliere, I had to be isolated and protected. My entire life I had spent entertaining myself and being surrounded by gun-wielding bodyguards.

Brianna and Melanie shared a look at my directness, not expecting it as I was aware I gave off a very 'sweet' vibe, but they did what I asked. And, well, I was sweet. I tried everything in my power to be kind and caring and considerate to others. But, it didn't mean I couldn't stick up for myself.

When the girls were ready, and left to go to the church, I admired myself in the mirror. My snow white pale skin was flawlessly made up, my natural black hair was half pinned up with the rest curling down my back. The dress was simple; A-line with long lace sleeves and a red sash that pulled in my delicate waist. I had had a princess style dress for my first wedding, but I had opted for a more timeless silent movie star look the second time.

A knock came on the hotel door and I turned to see my father walk inside. "Giovannah, you look so beautiful" he smiled softly. He wore a black suit, his greying black hair gelled back and a large pinkie ring on his finger. Walking into the room, he picked up a corsage of red and white roses and attached it to his jacket. "You ready to do this?"

I smoothed down my dress again before nodding at him. "Yes. I'm ready to become a Conti".

CHAPTER TWO

Salem

I took a drag of the cigarette - it was a hand rolled tobacco mixed with a small amount of weed – and passed it over to my oldest friend. Dario took it without pause and took an even longer drag. Despite what he told me, he was damn nervous. I hid a smug look as he handed the cigarette back. But I was obviously not very good at hiding my feelings.

"Wipe that damn smirk off your face" he grumbled at me.

I snorted a laugh, "it's sweet to see you so nervous". I pinched his cheek like his grandmother used to do.

He slapped my hand away with a look of pure

murder. "Keep it up, Matusalemme, and I will shove my gun so far down your mouth that when I pull the trigger, the bullet with come out your asshole".

"Ooh creative". I smoked the last of the cigarette, before dropping the end and stepping on it. I probably shouldn't have been smoking outside a church, but hey I wasn't sold on the whole 'sky daddy' situation anyway. "It's fine to be nervous, D".

"I'm not nervous just..." he trailed off, not finding the right words.

"It's your wedding day, every groom gets a little bit of cold feet. It's the natural part, especially when you barely know the bride". I gave him a sarcastic look, which he returned with another murderous glare, before a car pulled up in front of the church and a familiar family were dropped off. "Get ready to suck up to the in-laws" I whispered teasingly to Dario, as they approached us.

Emanuele Bianchi did the button up on his jacket, brushing lint of his suit as he walked up. The Mafia don was beginning to fill out in his stomach; the slightly stretch of his old suit hinted it was a recent development as he began to slow down and pass the reigns to his son. The son in question, Giovanni, cut a slender figure in his own three piece suit. He was Vannah's twin brother.

Dario's new mother-in-law, Lucia, followed her husband and adult son quietly. She was pretty, with permed blonde hair and large blue eyes, but her skin was showing the beginning of wrinkles despite her obvious Botox regime.

I'd noticed that women in the Bianchi Mafia were either one extreme or the other. They were either loud, screaming, fight you on everything types or the complete opposite good catholic wife type. Lucia was definitely the second, as was her only daughter Vannah.

"Dario" Emanuele greeted, shaking hands with my oldest friend. Dario greeted him back firmly, before shaking hands with Giovanni and kissing Lucia's cheek. The Bianchi's all wished him well for the wedding, before nodding their heads to me in greeting. "We'll see you inside".

"You're not walking Giovannah down the aisle?" I asked – the words out my mouth before I could stop them.

Emanuele gave me a once over, like he was trying hard to remember who I was, before giving me a small smile. "Giovannah has been married before; I have already given her away. It seems redundant to do it again".

"Of course" I replied, giving him an innocent smile, "I forgot about her being previously married". They said their good lucks again, before slinking into the oversized catholic church. Once they were gone, Dario gave me a dangerous look. "What?" I asked with fake confusion.

"Don't push it, Salem. Whether we liked them or

not--"

"Not" I interrupted.

"--we still have to work with them. The Bianchi filter the cleanest product through the states, and unless we want to start making our own, then we need their contacts. Otherwise we'll lose control of the market back home and the Cartel will smell a weakness".

I groaned, but I didn't push it. Even within the life of organised crime, cartels were considered the worst. The mob may have been monsters, but at least we were monsters who had honour. We'd never kill children, or an innocent bystander, or even a cop if we really didn't have to. *You do wrong, you die.* We'd never kill someone who didn't *do wrong* as the saying went.

So, Dario was right. If we wanted to keep control of Las Vegas – including the gambling and prostitution – we needed to watch over the other things we didn't deal in. Mainly the drugs. Bianchi's men worked the drugs to us and without them a cartel would sense a gap in the market and turn the streets into a full gang war.

So the Bianchi's were the lesser of two evils…plus it meant we got to have Giovannah Bianchi to ourselves.

When Dario had first made the alliance with the Bianchis, his uncle had told him to marry one and have a child with her to seal the agreement in blood.

Dario had agreed, as much as he didn't want to get married, that that was a good idea. So, when he had been invited down to a wedding of Emanuele's daughter, he'd agreed in order to see all the females within the family to pick one he wanted to marry as a pretty little trophy wife.

The problem was that the one Dario decided that he wanted...was the one getting married. Yeah, not ideal.

Dario had taken one look at, the then, nineteen year old and decided that she was the wife for him. He'd thrown the idea of a having a trophy wife out instantly and decided he wanted a proper marriage...but only to Vannah.

And there started his obsession with Giovannah Bianchi. An obsession that he had dragged myself and Vincenzo into.

Seven years later and he was finally getting his wish to marry her.

After the first few years of Dario being weirdly obsessed with Vannah – despite only meeting her the once – Enzo and I decided that we needed to take over the business with the Bianchi family. So, when a funeral for one of their elders happened, and Dario was invited, I went in his place.

Bad decision. Because at the wake afterwards, while all the old farts sipped whiskey and talked business, I snuck out to the garden. And I saw the most beautiful little twenty two year old woman, playing tag with two little children. I looked at her and my dick got instantly hard. Plus, I loved watching her be such a good mother...until the real mother turned up and thanked 'Vannah' for watching them. The sadness in Vannah's eyes, at obviously not being a mother, was hard to see. I had to physical stop myself from grabbing her and putting my baby inside her.

I was hooked from that moment on.

Enzo got annoyed with me. I was supposed to go the Bianchi's to get in between Dario and his obsession. However, I just made it worse when I came back with stories of Vannah for him to obsess over more.

Last year was the true turning point for us though. Because that was when Enzo finally met Vannah. There had been a mass Interpol investigation into the Amalfi branch of the Bianchi's – so a group of the syndicate here had gone over to Italy to clean things up. Enzo had agreed to go in Dario's stead, as neither of us thought that Vannah would be there.

But, we were wrong. Vannah was not only there, but her and some of the other top women used the excuse to have a vacation while their husbands worked. Enzo was sat next to Vannah, whose husband Aldo had gone ahead days before, on the plane over and had apparently sat with an erection for the entire ten hour flight. Enzo was the strongest of us, mentally, but apparently two weeks of seeing Vannah in a swimsuit, and an unhappy marriage, was enough to get him on the 'we want Vannah bandwagon'.

And we were finally getting what we wanted. Our patience had paid off big time.

Giovannah Bianchi was about to become Giovannah Conti and live with us back in Vegas. She may have thought she was marrying Dario, but actually she was marrying all three of us.

CHAPTER THREE

Vannah

The car door opened and the driver offered me his hand to take. It was time. It was time to get married. I took a deep breath and let him help me out. I stood outside the church, smoothing my dress down before stepping inside. At the entrance, my mother was waiting for me. "Beautiful" she commented, brushing a hand over the red sash to get rid of a crease.

She gave my hand a quick squeeze, which was as close to affection as we got within my family, before she headed down to take her seat. I wrapped my hands tightly around my flowers, as the music started. Taking a moment to compose myself, I let out a long breath. Then, I began down the aisle.

I got half way down before I looked up from my feet to the alter. A single step of mine faltered, as I saw who waited for me. Dario Conti was more than I remember. Holy shit, he was way better than I remembered him to be.

He stood at least six foot five, a large muscled figure that had been stuffed into a designer suit, glossy black hair that was shorter at the sides and gelled back in the middle. His blue eyes were piercing. He looked like he had just stepped out of a magazine. Tall, sexy and a hint of danger.

Comparing him to Aldo was like comparing champagne to beer. Completely pointless because they were different categories.

My mouth dried in lust as I reached him – Dario stood at least a foot taller than me, so I was glad for my red high heels. I swallowed deeply as I stood in front of my nre husband, looking up at him. He looked down at me and his eyes darkened.

Dario took my hand and kissed the back of it. My cheeks went as red as the roses in my bouquet. He leant forward and whispered into my ear. "Vannah, you look a vision".

I could feel his breath tickling my neck and it went straight to my pussy. Which was very unusual for me – I wasn't one for undulated lust. But, Dario was like a beacon of sexual energy. "I'll apologise for the dress now" he breathed out.

"Apologise?" I asked breathlessly.

"The moment we are alone I am going to rip it off you". He pulled back, smirking softly as I held in my gasp. We were in a church, standing next to a damn priest, and Dario was making my underwear wet. If there was a hell, Dario was going to drag me there wet and lustful. And I was welcoming it.

The priest cleared his throat, and I tried to remember the entire church of people watching us. Dario nodded to the priest and the man then began the ceremony. The words went in one of my ears and straight out the other. I was too busy staring up at my soon to be husband and wondering what my life would soon be like.

Finally came the vows and we both got through the 'I do's' quickly and almost robotically. Then came the exchange of rings. My father had told me that Dario had chosen the rings, so I was surprised when I was handed a black ring.

It was cold to touch, Black Zirconium I assumed, with a gold layer inside. Within the ring sat a small single ruby. It was a beautiful, yet masculine ring. I took it as Dario held his hand out to me. With shaking hands, I carefully slipped it onto his finger. His hands were warm and soft but with rough knuckles that told me he was a fighter.

Dario was then given two rings. The first was an engagement ring – platinum and dainty with a giant ruby stone. I couldn't help my smile. Red was my favourite colour, not that he knew that, and I loved it more than my first boring diamond engagement ring. It fit perfectly as Dario slipped it onto my finger.

Then came the wedding ring. Like his it was black, but it was V shaped so that it hugged the ruby ring. The ring contained three small gemstones – a blue sapphire, a green emerald and a yellow citrine. Three stones within the one ring.

I admired the ring before smiling up at Dario, his eyes were sparkling with something that was almost like mischief. The priest broke the moment by declaring, "you are now husband and wife. Mr Conti, you may now kiss your bride".

Before I could even contemplate what was about to happen, Dario's arm was around my waist and he tugged me to his body. I gasped, but a second later his lips were on mine. I responded eagerly – lust and warmth spreading through my body. He tasted like danger and felt like sin.

He pulled back and smirked at me, the kiss ended too soon. I was shocked to see the same thoughts mirrored on Dario's face. It was nice to know the lust was going both ways. People began to cheer, as Dario took my hand and we turned to face the crowd.

As we took a step down, to walk the aisle as Mr and Mrs Conti, a shout echoed through the room. Everyone was clapping us, but something about the yell made Dario go rigid. We both turned to see someone from the front row, one of Dario's men, rushing towards us.

It took me a second to realise he was screaming for me to 'get down'. I frowned in confusion before turning to see Dario's wide eyes on my chest. I glanced down to see a tiny red dot on the chest of my white dress. For a second I thought it was lipstick, then it moved an itch towards the left. Towards my heart.

The screaming man ploughed into me, and Dario, before I could work things out in my head. The second we hit the floor, a loud gunshot ran out and the priest screamed. I hit the ground with a grunt of pain, as the unknown man covered me.

With strong arms, he grabbed me under my armpits and dragged me behind the front pew. People in the church started screaming, and more gunshots rang out, as we took refuge behind the wooden blockage – Dario right beside us. My brain caught up a moment later. Someone had just tried to shoot me. That red dot hadn't been lipstick, it had been someone lining up a trajectory to my heart.

I turned to the man who had saved my life as both he, and Dario, pulled handguns from under their suits. It didn't surprise me – mafia were always mafia, even on their wedding day. The gunshots silenced, but the noise of running and screaming people didn't.

Dario turned to me and cupped my face. A shiver of

lust went through me at his touch, "are you hurt, my love?"

"No" I shook my head.

He nodded and turned to my saviour, "keep Vannah safe and get her back to the hotel. I don't know what the fuck that was but I want out of here immediately".

"I'll get us on a flight home this afternoon" my saviour growled, "I don't know who the fuck the Bianchi's have gunning for them, but they crossed the line targeting a Conti".

"Agreed" my new husband growled, "Vannah stay with Salem no matter what happens". He gave me one last look, before disappearing with his gun raised into the chaos of the church. I watched him go with baited breath.

"Don't worry, Dario will be fine" my saviour reassured me. I took him in for the first time, hating that I couldn't help but also be attracted to him. Salem was six foot, with wavy brown hair and a short precise beard. Tattoos covered his entire body, from his neck all the way down to his fingers – only his face was uncovered, although I noted little designs inside his ears. When he spoke a piercing shone from his tongue.

Whereas Dario looked like a quintessential mafia heart throb, Salem looked more fitted for a biker gang. But, I couldn't help but feel lustful as I looked over him. Dario was my normal type but I could see the appeal of a man like Salem. I felt bad for the lust though, I had just married Dario. There was something wrong with me.

Salem took my hand in his and gave it a squeeze. "Beautiful" he whispered – his voice gravelly and strong, "I will protect you and take any bullet that comes our way".

Not knowing what to say, I blurted out "I'm Vannah". It was a face slapping moment if ever I had had one. I was honestly a fucking idiot.

Salem chuckled, "I know who you are, beautiful Giovannah". He raised my hand to his mouth and kissed the back of it – just like Dario had done. I blushed, oblivious to the chaos and mayhem around us. "Now, let's get you somewhere safe".

And, with his hand in mine, he did just that.

CHAPTER FOUR

Vannah

Salem got me out of the church fairly easily, having slipped out the back way and back alley. I could still hear the distant sounds of shouting and even a very far away siren. I assumed someone on the street had called the cops, because it sure as hell wouldn't have been anyone in the Bianchi or Conti family. But my father could deal with the cops easily enough if he needed to.

"We should catch a cab" I suggested.

"Nope, got a better idea" Salem said, before tugging on my hand. In my heels I struggled to keep up with him, even though he was barely jogging. A little part of me was wary, as Salem was a stranger to me. But, if Dario trusted him then I assumed I was fine. I didn't know Dario well, but I doubted he would risk anything happening to his new wife.

Salem jogged through the streets, before we headed into a parking lot. We came to a stop beside a hot red sports car. "Is this yours?" I asked in confusion, as Salem took his suit jacket off.

"Nope" he grinned, wrapping the jacket around his arm and smashing it through the window. I cringed, but before I could even be shocked, Salem was inside and hot-wiring it. Within less than two minutes, the engine was running. He leant over and pushed the passenger door open. "Let's go, Princess".

I dubiously climbed into the car, making sure the skirt of my wedding dress was tucked in, as he put the car into the drive. We drove for a few minutes in silence, passing the church and all the chaos that surrounded it. As we did, the adrenaline began to wear off. I had almost been shot...at my own wedding.

"Thank you" I finally whispered, turning to Salem as he drove. "You saved my life".

He gave me a sincere smile, "there is nothing to thank. I'm just glad you're alright".

"If you hadn't seen the red light..."

"I wouldn't have missed it. I couldn't take my eyes off of you".

His words made me blush – he was obviously friends with my husband but it almost seemed like he was flirting with me. Weird, but then maybe I was reading it wrong. It wasn't like I had a lot of experience with men.

"I'm sorry your wedding was ruined" Salem said, after a few more minutes of silence.

I shrugged, "the important bit was over".

"Well it'll be something to tell the grandkids one day" he winked at me. I didn't say anything else, as I was finding it awkward how much he was flirting with me...and I didn't like that I was enjoying it so much. I was married to Dario and I was attracted to Dario, that was all that mattered.

Salem pulled up on the side of the road and killed the engine. "Our hotel is just up here, but better dump the car before we get there" he explained. We both climbed out and Salem took my hand again as we walked down the road.

A woman stopped us a few hundred yards later, smiling and telling us congratulations. It took me a few seconds to remember I was wearing a wedding dress and Salem was in a suit. I opened my mouth to tell her we weren't married, but Salem spoke first. "Thank you so much. It's the happiest day of our lives". He gave my hand a squeeze and we walked on.

"What was that?" I hissed, when we were out of ear shot.

He raised an eyebrow at me, "I don't know what you're talking about, beautiful".

"Stop flirting with me. I'm married to Dario. You're not my husband".

"Oh really?" he smirked. He raised our conjoined hands so that I could see our fingers. My finger had the new rings on and Salem also had a ring on his martial finger. The ring was black with a single ruby gemstone – identical to Dario's. "Tell me, Vannah, if I'm not your husband, then why am I wearing a wedding ring?"

I just stared at him in confusion as he winked at me, before pulling me further up the street to the hotel. He whisked me through the large lobby, into the elevator and to the suite at the top. My stomach was churning nervously the entire time. I was confused and scared.

The suite was beautiful, but generic, with a large lounge area and its own little kitchenette "Do you want a bottle of water?" Salem asked me, heading to the mini fridge and pulling two bottles out. I nodded and he threw one to me. I caught it before going over to sit on the couch.

As I sipped my water, reflecting on the day, Salem was on the phone chatting. I first heard him updating Dario, before speaking to someone named Enzo and then booking flights to Las Vegas for three people. Once he was done, he came and sat on the other sofa opposite me.

"Dario is cleaning up things with your father, he'll be here shortly" he informed me.

"What did you mean earlier?" I demanded, crossing my arms over my chest. "When you showed me your ring. It's the same as Dario's".

Salem watched me for a moment, before giving me an almost manic grin. "I was just teasing you, beautiful. All Conti men have the same wedding band".

"Oh. So you're married?"

"Yep, sure am". He leant back in his seat and smile. "She's is beautiful and sexy and I am one of the luckiest men in the world. Her smile lights up a room and her laugh is the most magical thing I've ever heard. She is kind and caring and I knew the moment I saw her that she was the love of my life".

His words made me smile, "that's beautiful. I hope she knows that".

"Well I've told her, if she believes me is another thing" he shrugged.

"Do you have children?" I asked. I was hoping that Dario was on the baby train as much as I was, but it would at least be nine months before I had a baby – so it would be nice if others in the higher rankings of the Conti Family had children I could fuss over in the meantime.

"Not yet" Salem replied, looking into the distance with a smile on his face. That was truly a man in love. "But she really wants one and I'm going to waste no time putting one inside her".

"You sound excited by that. It's nice to find a man as excited to have a baby as the woman".

"Yeah, well, I'd give her anything she wanted if it made her happy". He paused looking at me closely – too closely for a married man. But, again, maybe I was reading things wrong. He was flirty but the way he spoke about his wife was with overwhelming love. So, perhaps I was just being cautious. "Do you want a baby?" he asked me.

I smiled warmly, "there is nothing I want more in this world".

"Then I'm sure your husband will happily give you one" he winked at me. I didn't say anything else on the matter – it was something to discuss with Dario in private. Salem seemed like a nice guy, flirting aside, but he wouldn't really know what Dario did and didn't want from our new marriage.

About thirty minutes later, Dario arrived at the hotel – his gun back under his jacket like before. "Are you alright?" he asked me, as I stood up to meet him. I nodded as he cupped my cheek. I couldn't help the shiver of excitement at his touch. If the cocky look in his eyes said anything then the smug bastard knew it too.

"What happened? Who tried to shoot me?"

"I don't know" he admitted, "we found the perch

he was shooting from but he had gone by the time anyone got up there. Your father has some of his people going through the streets to see if anyone knows anything".

"Why her?" Salem questioned, "why Vannah?"

Dario shrugged, "dramatics? To hurt Emanuele? Who knows. But the most important thing is that we get the hell out of dodge".

"I've got us a flight booked. But, only for the three of us. The others will have to fly back tomorrow like planned".

"Perfect, grab our things and we'll head to the airport now" Dario nodded, before turning to me. "Did you pack your bags? I told your father we were leaving the day after the wedding, so he said your bags would be packed before the wedding".

I nodded, "my stuff has been in bags since Aldo died. They are at my brother's house".

Dario grinned at me, "good. You ready to see your new home, wife?"

CHAPTER FIVE

Dario

She gave a soft moan. The sound breathy and gentle, naturally erotic and sexual. The erection in my pants hardened even more...which I hadn't thought possible. I clenched my hands together, as I looked over the top of Vannah and to Salem across the seat aisle. We shared a look, both of us brimming with sexual fantasies of our girl, before we looked back at her.

Vannah slept beside me, her beautiful face scrunched up adorably as she mumbled and moaned in her sleep. She had traded her wedding dress for a knee length red dress, but had kept her wedding makeup and hairstyle. Vannah was beautiful, reminding me a little of a fifties Hollywood starlet, and I couldn't help but love her.

She changed a bit since the first time I had seen her. When she'd walked down the aisle towards that fat, sweaty, man seven years ago – I had almost murdered half the church in rage. I had seen her floating down the aisle, wearing a white puffy dress, and had had to control myself not to put a bullet in Aldo Bianchi's head and marry her myself.

But, as I looked at her now, I was glad I had waited. Her marriage to Aldo had been unhappy and unfulfilling for her – but during that time she'd matured and gone from Daddy's Princess to a mature capable woman. At twenty six, she was not a girl anymore, she was a woman who was finally ready for a man. Or, well, three men.

Vannah moaned softly in her sleep again and I gripped the arm rests to stop me from reaching over and touching her. I looked past her to Salem, who was also watching her intensely. "She's mine tonight" I told him – words quiet enough not to wake Vannah but loud enough that he heard.

He narrowed his eyes at me, "who decided that?"

"I did. She doesn't know the situation yet, but she understands that she is my wife. With me, she'll enjoy sex. But with you, even if she does enjoy it, it will confuse her and make her feel guilty".

Salem grunted, but he did see my point. "Fine, but first thing tomorrow morning we're sitting her down, all three of us, and explaining the situation to her".

"Maybe not the Aldo thing though".

He cringed, "agreed. She doesn't need to know about the ugly stuff. But, she needs to know about Enzo and I".

The rest of the flight went quick, with Vannah waking a few minutes before the seatbelt sign came back on. Realising she had fallen asleep, she shot me an embarrassed smile and blushed. Her reaction went straight to my dick, just like everything she did.

In the airport we quickly collected all the bags, before piling it all in the car that Enzo had sent for us. Vannah was watching everything out the window as we drove – it was evening and the lights of Las Vegas were a sight. She smiled as she took it all in.

We weaved through the glittering streets, before travelling towards Country Club Hill, near 'Billionaires Row' but a little more secluded. The car rolled up to the large iron gates, decorated with a large C for Conti. Our head security guard, Johnny, greeted us before scanning the car for explosives and letting us through the gates.

"The house in beautiful" Vannah commented, as she took in the large sandy coloured mansion. The large pillars holding up the porch were pure marble and seemed to shine in the beginning of moonlight. As we collected the bags out the car, she admired the entrance.

Once inside the house, I let Salem take her bags to her room as I gave her a quick tour of where everything was. She was a little overwhelmed, but she'd have time to explore going forward. "This is Salem's room and--"

"Wait? What?" she cut me off. "Salem lives here to? I thought this was our house?"

"It's complicated" I replied slowly – not tipping my hand about sharing her with my two best friends just yet. She wasn't quite ready for that. I'd tell her in the morning...after we'd consummated the marriage. "I'll explain a little more in the morning" I replied truthfully. "Enzo will also be living with us. His room is the second on the left".

"Enzo?" she frowned, "was he at the wedding?"

"No I left him in charge here. As much as he wanted to be there, I couldn't leave the business completely unmanned. You have met him though, he went with your family to Amalfi last year".

Realisation clicked in her eyes, "oh, right, of course. Vincenzo, I remember him now. We didn't see much of each other, but he seemed...nice". Her words had me hiding a smile. She may not have seen much of Enzo, but Enzo had not taken his eyes off of her. I also found amusement in her struggling to describe Enzo. Because she was right, he was anything but nice.

I took her down to the room next to mine, "this will be your bedroom". I pushed inside and showed her the bedroom that Enzo had designed for her. It was different shades of beige, with pops of bright red – our girl liked her red. Salem had put her luggage in front of the large closet. I showed her around, including her en suite, but she was quiet. "You don't like it?" I asked.

She blinked in shock, "oh no, it's beautiful. It's exactly how I would want my bedroom to be".

"But?"

"But, I'm wondering why I have my own room". She raised an eyebrow at me, "as husband and wife are we not going to…share a marital bed?"

I took a deep breath, keeping my lust at bay and praying my erection wasn't obvious. "You can sleep in any bed in this house, including mine, whenever you want. But I thought you might want a place of your own. Especially if I'm working late in one of the casinos, I wouldn't want to wake you up when I come in and out all night".

So nervously wet her lips, "so you do…want to share a bed with me? Right?"

Damn she was killing me. "Of course I do, Vannah. You're my wife and I would love nothing more than to have you in my bed every night". I knew that Salem and Enzo would have something to say about that, but fuck them they weren't there then.

"I see". She glanced around the bedroom once more, before asking what she really wanted to. "Can I see your room then?"

My cock was so hard it was almost painful. I wasn't even touching her and I was ready to cum in my pants like a twelve year old boy. But, I had been fantasizing about Vannah for seven years. I was more than ready to act some of those out. I took her hand, noticing how dainty her fingers were, and led her from her bedroom and into mine.

The entire room was shades of grey and metal – a little bit more masculine than I was sure her tastes ran. At face value it looked a very normal room and as long as Vannah didn't dig too deep, she wouldn't be disturbed. It would definitely freak her out if she looked in the shoe box under my bed or the safe in the closet.

Turning to her, I took in her beauty. She really was a picture of perfection. Vannah smiled shyly at me, as I walked over and cupped her face. She looked up at me with large bright eyes. "Do you want a baby?" she blurted out.

I paused, but I shouldn't have been surprised. Vannah wanted a child but that was between her and Salem for now – but I couldn't explain that to her just yet. "We'll use a condom tonight, my love" I smiled, "we need a little time to get to know each other better first".

She pouted slightly, "but you want a child right?"

I chose my next words carefully. "If you want a child then your husband will give you as many as you want". My words had her grinning, as I ran my thumb over her prominent cheek bone. "You really are so beautiful, Giovannah".

Leaning down I finally kissed her like I had always wanted to.

CHAPTER SIX

Vannah

Dario Conti, my *husband*, kissed me like he was about to die. His arms wrapped around me, anchoring me to him, as his lips possessed mine. There was nothing gentle or sweet about the kiss. It was hot and lustful and almost bruising with strength. But I loved it. My entire body lit up with desire.

My hands rested on his chest, which I could feel was tight and hard underneath his shirt. His heart was pumping just as fast as mine was. Dario's tongue slipped into my mouth and I couldn't stop the little moan I made as his tongue explored my mouth. He pulled back after a moment, leaving me panting and desperate. "I've never wanted anything more than I want you right now" he told me.

I grinned up at him, "well you've got me".

My words caused an almost feral look to enter his eyes. Then his lips were on mine again, his tongue exploring once more, as his hands ran over my body. One hand travelled down my back, skimming my ass, while the other moved up the front. My nipples were hard and I shivered as his hand glided over them through the material.

Dario quickly unzipped the back of my dress, before pushing it off my shoulders. It fell to the floor around my feet – leaving me in nothing but my underwear and my red high heels. He pulled back and groaned almost painfully. "Vannah, you are going to kill me". His eyes roamed over my white lacy lingerie – it was a bridal set but I hadn't gone for the garter as I hadn't been sure on what Dario and I were going to be like together.

His hands went around my body again, as his lips found mine. He was bending down, due to our height difference, so he quickly picked me up so he was upright once more. I kicked my shoes off and my legs wrapped around his waist as our tongues continued to lick and play. Carefully, he walked us over to the large bed.

He placed me down in the centre of the bed and climbed on – his body covering mine as we continued to kiss. From this position, I could feel his erection pressing against my core through his pants.

He was hard and, from what I could feel, large. My underwear was soaked as he began to grind himself against me.

A breathy moan came from my mouth, as the bulge in his pants rubbed against my clit. More wetness seeped from my cunt. I wasn't sure I'd ever been so turned on in my life – and we had done nothing but kiss and rub up against each other a little. I couldn't wait to have him inside me.

Without breaking the kiss, I began to unbutton his shirt and pulled it out from where it was tucked in his pants. He'd taken off his suit jacket and gun holsters before giving me a tour. Under his shirt, his golden coloured skin was smooth and flawless but soft dark hair sat on the top of an amazing set of abs. Dario groaned in my mouth as my hand ran over his skin.

I pushed the shirt off his shoulders, and he pulled back enough to get it off. A few tattoos were scattered over his chest and back. He threw the shirt across the room uncaring, before he was back kissing me once more. His hands ran up the length of my body, skin on skin burning, before he cupped my breasts. I moaned again as he tweaked my nipples through the bra.

My hands began to fiddle with his belt, desperate for both of us to be naked. I had never felt so desperate in my life. I couldn't undo his belt, so with a grunt Dario pulled away from me. Standing beside the bed, he kicked his shoes and socks off before removing his pants. I swallowed deeply as he stood in nothing but his grey boxers – his erection obvious.

Climbing back on the bed with me, he pulled me up slightly so he could unclasp my bra. He threw it away before laying me back down. We kissed again, my hands getting tangled in his dark hair, as his hands continued to run up and down my body. Dario then spread the kisses over my neck and down my chest.

More moans came out of me as he took one of my nipples between his lips. "Fuck" he groaned around my nipple, as his tongue teased and played. My legs wrapped around him, my feet crossing under his pert ass as I pressed myself to his erection. I was desperate for the friction.

Dario worked his kiss away from my nipples and down my stomach. His lips vibrated against me, almost like a growl, as he reached my panties. Hooking two fingers in them, he pulled them down. I raised my hips up, allowing him to remove them. Once I was naked, Dario sat back on his thighs and looked over me.

"Fuck me, Vannah. You are a fucking goddess". He made a noise of almost pain again, before he put his hands on my thighs and pushed them apart. He kissed his way over my skin, making me pant and moan. Then his tongue licked over my labia, slightly parting my lips to touch my cunt. I almost came off the bed in shock.

But, before he dove in like he was about to, I put my hand on his head and pushed him up. "What?" he asked, looking up at me from between my legs. "Is something wrong?"

"You don't..." I trailed awkwardly, "you don't need to do that".

He frowned in confusion, "what give you head?"

"I know guys don't like doing it. You don't need to impress me, we can just have normal sex".

He raised an eyebrow, "going down on my woman is 'normal' sex, Vannah. Plus, I like doing it. I can literally smell your cunt from here and it's almost making me cum in my pants. I'm going to make you cum on my face, wife, and I'm going to love every fucking second of it".

His words had me shivering with desire, as he tongue went back to my centre. He licked through my slick folds, dipping into my cunt, before swirling over the sides. It was the most amazing thing I had ever felt. The noises I was making were completely involuntary. I felt like a woman possessed as I jolted and squirmed in pleasure.

Dario's arms clamped around my hips, holding me in place, as he continued to fuck me with his mouth. His tongue continued to play before he sucked on my clit. I almost cried I was so overwhelmed with pleasure. He sucked on my clit for a few minutes, making a violent orgasm slam into me.

I screamed as my head tilted back, my legs snapping shut around Dario's head and my wetness gushing over his face. I couldn't form words or thoughts, as his mouth continued to pleasure me – rolling the orgasm on and on, until I had to physically push him away.

Dario gave a dark chuckle as he looked up at me. My chest was heaving, as his lips and chin glistened with my arousal. He kept eye contact with me as he licked his lips suggestively. "You taste exquisite darling" he purred.

He moved up my body once more, kissing me deeply – allowing me to taste myself on him. My stomach was still softly clenching and unclenching as his skin glided over mine. With a groan, Dario pulled away from me and leant over to his side table. He pulled a condom from the top draw.

Sitting back, he tore his boxers off and his erection sprung up. The tip of him was wet with precum – his shaft large and veiny. He ran his hand up and down over his erection a few times, biting his lip as he looked at me. "God, I can't wait to be inside you" he whispered. Even though I had just had the best orgasm of my life, his words still had wetness seeping from me.

Dario carefully put the condom on, rolling it down while looking down hungrily at my soaked cunt. When it was on, he nudged my legs further apart.

"Open up further for me, my love" he commented. I did so, spreading my legs completely open. "Shit" he swore, as he settled in between my legs.

Holding himself between my legs, he ran the tip of his cock over my folds and circled my clit. I whimpered, biting my lip. Slowly, Dario edged himself into me – gently and inch by inch. "Vannah, my love, you feel like heaven". He pushed all the way until he was seated inside me. He paused for a moment; eyes closed as he cussed under his breath.

"What? Is something wrong?" I asked.

He gave a snorting sort of laugh. "I'm just trying to picture a naked grandma so I don't cum right now like a virgin". He let out a long breath. "You are so fucking tight around me".

"I'm sorry".

He laughed again, "do not apologise! It a great fucking thing, so good in fact I want to cum already". He opened his eyes and looked down at me. Dario lowered himself so that he was pressed back on top of me, capturing my lips again. He kissed me deeply, keeping still inside me, before he slowly began to move.

His cock rocked back and forward gently, as he travelled his kisses down my throat. His teeth scrapped against my skin, forcing a shiver down my spine. Slowly, as he kissed me, Dario began to increase his thrusts. I felt him against my walls, filling me up so completely I almost wept with joy.

This was what sex was supposed to feel like.

Before long he was thrusting fast and hard, both of us moaning and cussing as our bodies slapped together. Sweat lined both of us, as our teeth clashed and our hands gripped each other. My legs wrapped around him, forcing him as deep as he could.

It changed the angle just enough that I could feel him hitting my clit from the inside. A scream of pleasure forced itself from my throat, as my legs squeezed him tighter to keep him in position. But, Dario wasn't going anywhere. He continued to fuck me like a professional, hitting my walls with speed and strength.

Another orgasm hit me, as my nails dug into Dario's back, my entire body spasming underneath him. "Oh fuck, baby, you're gripping me so tight. Jesus, fuck, you feel so good" he panted. Dario gave a roar, before his mouth fell open and he came inside of me. He pumped himself in and out a few more times, riding out his orgasm, before resting our foreheads together.

"Wow" I whispered, as we both caught our breaths. I didn't know sex could be like. I had never felt so good and so free in my entire life.

"Holy fuck" Dario breathed, gently kissing me. He pulled back and slowly slipped himself from me. I couldn't help the soft moan as he glided out of me, my arousal gushing out with him. He stood up from the bed and carefully pulled the condom off himself.

"I'll be right back" he told me.

He slipped into the en suite bathroom before coming back a few seconds later all cleaned up. He climbed back onto the bed, glancing at the liquid covering my thighs. I blushed, "I'll go get cleaned up. I don't want to dirty your bed".

Dario gave a dark laugh, the sound dangerous and lustful. "You don't need to get cleaned up, my love". He pushed my legs apart and settled back between them. "I was just thinking about how delicious you looked right now".

I blinked in confusion, "I don't understand. We've had sex already".

He leant down and peppered kisses over my stomach. "We've had round one. I'm just getting you ready for round two". He gave me an evil look, "we're going to be going all night, wife".

And with that, his face dived straight back down into my cunt once more.

CHAPTER SEVEN

Vannah

The day after my wedding, I woke up truly happy for the first time in years. My body hummed with previous pleasure and a little sting in my vagina reminded me of the countless orgasms Dario had given me. If this was day one of our marriage, I had good feelings for the rest of the days.

I stretched in the bed – Dario's bed – and my body groaned and clicked. I turned to Dario, but he was gone and his side of the bed was cold. There was a small piece of paper at the end of the bed. I grabbed it to see a little note from my new husband. *'Had some work to do. I miss being inside you already'*.

His note had shivers going through my body. I had never had sex like that before – again and again and again. I was sure I had had more orgasms in one night than Aldo had given me in our entire seven year marriage. The fact that Dario wanted more sex? Thrilling.

I folded the note and slipped out of the bed. I pulled on my dress, before heading back to my bedroom where my bags where. I didn't think of it as my bedroom, and if Dario kept giving me orgasms like that then I wanted to spend every night with him.

I was about to shower but decided to wait until after breakfast, as the smell of cooking wafted from downstairs. I dressed in a pair of yoga pants and a t-shirt, braided my crazy sex hair, before heading down. I hoped it was Dario cooking for me – although, I wouldn't have been surprised to find out we had a chef. The house was big enough and I doubted he had time to cook for himself.

When I got down to the kitchen, there was a man cooking eggs with his back to me. At hearing me enter, he turned to see me. It was Vincenzo – or Enzo as Dario called him. I vaguely remembered him from the vacation to the Amalfi Coast, but so much had happened that vacation that I didn't remember much about him. Nothing but the fact that he had been very intense and had stared at me a lot. But he'd been sweet one night when he had found me crying.

Enzo was massive; both in height and stature. He

had to be at least six foot seven, every part of his body bulged with muscles – even his neck was bigger than my thigh. He had a dark buzz cut with a large scar that ran down the left side of his face. He wore a pair of jeans and a white t-shirt; his arms were tattooed and a few peaked out from the neck of the t-shirt. He was intimidation personified.

I was living with three very attractive men.

"Giovannah" he smiled, putting the spatula down and making his way over to me. "I'm sorry I missed the wedding, despite what happened". He reached me, his dark eyes shining as he looked me over. "I watched it, you looked as beautiful as ever". His words made me blush.

Before I could reply, Enzo cupped my face and leant down and kissed me. I squealed in shock against his lips, as his other arm went around my waist. I didn't move for a long moment, then my lips responded. Suddenly, I remembered who was kissing me and I pulled away.

"What the hell are you doing?" I yelled, pushing away from him.

Enzo frowned at me, "I'm kissing my wife".

"I am not your wife. I am Dario's wife". I gave him a look, wondering if he was crazy. Hearing my raised voice, two sets of footsteps sounded before both Dario and Salem rushed into the room. They looked between us in confusion.

"What happened?" Dario asked.

I moved over to his side and leant into him. We may have only been married for a day, but after our passionate night I felt close to him. "He kissed me" I exclaimed, pointing at Enzo.

Enzo gave me a look of annoyance, "I am allowed to kiss you. You're my wife".

"Fuck" Dario muttered, under his breath as Salem shook his head at Enzo. "We hadn't…we hadn't explained anything to Vannah yet".

Enzo frowned, "why not? Why do you get her?"

"Get her?" I squawked, "he's my husband".

"So am I!"

"Alright, alright" Salem said, holding his hands up and silencing everyone. He turned to Enzo and nodded to the cooking eggs. "Why don't you dish us up some breakfast and we can explain everything to Vannah?"

There was a tense moment, before Enzo turned back and began to dish up the eggs and bacon he had been cooking. I looked up at Dario in confusion, but he just gave me a reassuring smile. "Take a seat" he smiled. He leant down and pecked my lips, before helping me onto one of the large stools at the kitchen island.

Salem sat opposite me, as Enzo began putting the plates down. "Where is your wife?" I asked him, as Dario sat beside me and Enzo beside Salem.

"Now I'm the confused one" Enzo muttered, glancing at his friend.

Salem cringed, "I may have told Vannah a little white lie yesterday".

"So you're not married?" I was super confused what was going on.

"No I am...but I am married to you". Salem gave me a grin, and a flirty look, as Enzo just stared at me intensely. I frowned, assuming this was some weird prank, before turning to Dario. I expected to see my husband laughing, or smiling, but he looked at me seriously and apologetically.

"So everyone in this room thinks they are married to me?" I asked sarcastically. Someone must have had a video camera or something on me. Because I had no idea what the fuck was going on, but it couldn't be real.

"We don't think. We are" Enzo said. He held his hand out to me – like Dario and Salem, he also wore a black wedding ring with a small ruby stone. "The ruby is you, Giovannah, and the three gemstones on your ring is us".

I looked down at my own wedding rings. One large ruby engagement ring, and three gemstones on my wedding band. A sapphire. An emerald. A citrine. Three stones, three men.

I turned to Dario in confusion. "I don't understand. What the hell is happening?"

He took a deep breath, before speaking. "I wanted you to be my wife the moment I saw you back when you married Aldo. Salem wanted you when he saw you at the wake for your grandfather. Enzo wanted you after your vacation together last year. We all wanted you more than anything".

My heart began to beat so fast I was worried it was going to burst from my chest. I opened my mouth, but no words came out. Salem took over explaining for Dario. "The three of us are best friends and we are very close. We agreed that rather than fight for who got to have you, we would share you. It was decided that you would legally marry Dario – because he is the head of the family – but that you'd be actually married to all three of us".

"You can't...I can't..." I stammered. I took a deep breath and ran a hand down my face. "One person can't be married to three people".

"Who says?" Enzo raised an eyebrow at me. "Yeah, maybe it's not what the average Jane and John Doe do. But, it will work for us. We all care about you and you will come to care about us. Polygamy is just as natural as monogamy".

My mind and thoughts were blank, as my heart was beating like crazy. How could they possibly think this? How could they think it was fine just to all be married to me? They were insane all of them.

I turned to Dario, hoping he would disagree and tell me that he just wanted it to be me and him. But the look in his eyes was begging me to understand. "This is going to work, Vannah, we've been talking this over for a very long time. We're going to take care of you and love you and--"

"And we'll have a baby together" Salem added. He reached over and took my hand over the counter top.

I snatched my hand away and jumped to my feet. "You're all insane. I would never bring a baby into this fucked up house". I turned and ran out of the room.

Inside my new bedroom, I locked the door and collapsed into a heap against it. I had woken up happy, but it had quickly been soured. I should have realised. I was stupid to think I would ever be happy. Happiness had never been a part of my life...and it still wasn't.

CHAPTER EIGHT

Dario

I parked my car in my parking space behind Conti Capital – the largest of my four casinos that decorated the Vegas strip. I also had several night clubs, a handful of restaurants and one arcade. But the four Conti's casinos – Gold, Deco, Raw and Capital – were where I ran the majority of my less legal business from.

The Conti Group, my business empire, was completely legal. I paid my taxes, had perfect health and safety and paid all my employees well. It brought just as much money in as my 'family' business. But, it didn't have all the perks of owning half the damn city.

My grandfather had started the Conti Group back when Vegas was exclusively run by the mob. But, times had changed and I had gone 'legit'. Or, at least, I had taken the less legal side of my business underground. As far as most people were aware the Conti Group was a profitable, slightly charitable, organisation who just happened to have an old tie to a mobster.

I climbed out my Jaguar, trying not to think about Vannah, before heading through the back entrance. I did most of my less legal business out of Conti Capital because it was just off the main strip and the atmosphere was very different. The other three casinos were all themed.

Conti Gold was a black-tie Monte Carlo feel place; mainly for high rollers and people that were putting thousands down for fun. Conti Deco was based on the roaring twenties; with gold sparkly cocktails, showgirls and flappers. Conti Raw looked like an upmarket motorcycle bar, with leather dressed staff and live rock bands. But Conti Capital was for the ones who wanted no frill, no thrills, just gambling and gambling hard.

It was still a nice, expensive, casino – but there were no pointless umbrellas in the drinks, no fancy uniforms for the staff and no dramatic wall decorations other than paintings. I walked through the main belly, the sound of slot machines and fruit machines whirling, as the tables were littered with gamblers despite the fact it wasn't even lunch.

The gamblers all looked dreary and sombre, as they bet their way into debt and more marital problems. I glanced around, getting a few nods from my security who were watching everyone carefully. I bypassed them and to my office on the top floor.

"Boss" a voice greeted, as I walked into my office. Davide, one of my high ranking members, was perched on the sofa in my office while my assistant, Isabella, was making him coffee. I greeted them both, as I put my briefcase down and Isabella poured me a coffee as well. "How was the wedding?" Davide asked.

"Fine until someone tried to snipe my wife the second I had gotten a ring on her finger" I replied. I was super angry that I had come so close to losing Vannah despite only just getting her. But the hours of sex from the night before mellowed me out a lot. Plus, I felt having her in my territory took the edge off – despite the bullets being aimed for my wife, I was pretty confident she had been targeted was because of her father not her new husband. So, the danger shouldn't have followed us from New York.

"Shit, boss, seriously?" Davide raised an eyebrow in shock. "I hope the new Mrs Conti isn't too shaken up".

"Giovannah is fine". I took a seat at my desk, as Isabella placed a pile of important documents on the edge of my desk. I thanked her, she welcomed me back, before heading out the office to allow

Davide and I to talk business. "I know Enzo has been watching everything on the business side, but any problems on the street?"

"Nothing drastic" he shrugged, "but the day you left there was a FED sniffing around Purple Satin".

"How do you know he was a FED?"

Davide shrugged, "if it walks like a duck, talks like a duck and quacks like a duck? Then it's probably a fucking duck". He took a sip of his coffee. "Cops are always trying to get into our business, but this guy? I don't know it felt different. The way he was asking the girls questions and eyeing up the entrance's security? It just seemed like recon work".

"And you're sure he was a FED and not a rival?" I asked, sipping my own coffee. "It wouldn't be the first time that other syndicates tried to test my hold on the city. The Eastern Europeans especially after I took care of their skin trade. I wouldn't be surprised if they have some other girls stashed somewhere and they're hoping to put them to work".

Davide snorted in disgust, "Boris wouldn't dare test you. Not after last time". He considered for a moment, "I was pretty sure he was a FED, but can't say for sure he wasn't just a street motherfucker who could pull off the FED look".

I grunted my understanding, "let all the madams know that if anyone shows up, at any of the boarding houses, to let you know. I want to speak to this Quiz Master myself or at least set Salem on him".

He snorted, "Salem would have him pissing his pants, the psychotic fucker". He laughed to himself, but we both knew he wouldn't dare take on Salem either. "Where is the lovable psycho today anyway?"

"He's watching Giovannah for me. I need to get some work done, and visit Raw to oversee the extension work, but I didn't feel right leaving her on her own just yet". We discussed a few more things as we finished our coffee. There were three tiers to the Conti Mafia – the top which was just myself, Salem, Enzo and now Vannah. The middle tier, trusted members of my organisation who took managerial roles and oversaw my operations. And then bottom tier, the street tier, were the ones who did the grunt work like move dirty money.

Davide was at the top of the middle tier and he was in charge of the streets. He was in charge of making sure things such as; the brothels ran smoothly, that the drugs were being delivered safely and all the lower level members were doing their jobs. I only truly trusted my best friends, and Vannah, but Davide was one step down from 'trust' – which in our business basically made us family. Which made sense because I wouldn't be surprised if we were brothers with the way my father was playing thirty years ago.

"I'll see you later, Dario" he clasped my shoulder. He walked towards the door, but paused and rocked on his heels. He awkwardly looked at me, running a hand over his face. He was debating telling me something – which was very unlikely him. Davide was very loyal, bordering on brown nosing.

"Something wrong, Davide?"

He cringed, "I saw something, not business related, but I'm not sure if I should tell you or not".

"Why wouldn't you tell me?"

"It is something that Enzo did". He cringed again, as I tried to keep my face neutral. Enzo was difficult at the best of time, but he was my oldest friend so I allowed for his 'quirks'. "Yesterday, I stopped by your house to drop off your marriage paperwork. I rang the bell, but there was no answer, so I used my spare key to go inside".

"And?" I prompted when he went quiet.

"Enzo was in your lounge and he was watching the live stream of your wedding". He went quiet again – I felt like I was pulling teeth.

"Davide, spit it out already".

"He was…pleasuring himself…as he watched your wedding". He grimaced, cheeks blazing like he wasn't a thirty year old man. Internally I was calling Enzo all types of names, but externally I was as cool as ever. "I've never known Enzo to be into girls, so I wasn't sure if it was about you or about your new wife. But, whatever the fuck it was, it was weird".

"It was about Giovannah" I assured him – I didn't need a rumour spreading about Enzo being gay for me. "Enzo has a weak spot for her. It's just a little crush and he'll get it out of his system soon, don't worry about it". I got up and clasped his shoulder, "Enzo is Enzo, just forget what you saw".

"Sure boss" he nodded. I showed him out, waving him goodbye, before closing the door and losing the fake smile.

"Fucking Enzo" I grumbled under my breath.

I was legally married to Giovannah and we weren't telling anyone outside of our household about sharing her. I may have been the king, but a king always had usurpers to deal with. I needed to appear cool, and strong, and impenetrable.

If people knew that my wife was having sex with two other men, I would be a weak laughing stock. I didn't need that and Vannah didn't need the slut-shaming that would come her way. What we did in the privacy of our own house was none of anyone else's business. I would need to remind Enzo and Salem of that, as I was sure they'd forget as they got swept up in their lustful hazes of Vannah.

Grabbing the documents on my desk, I went through and signed what I needed to before giving them back to Isabella. I then headed back out of Capital and drove down to one of my other casinos, Raw.

The atmosphere was vastly different as I stepped inside. Tourists were milling around; live bands were playing rock classics and sexy leather dressed staff walked around the betting tables and drinking vinyl booths. I glanced at one of the female servers, in her leather skirt and bra, and instantly wondered what my precious Vannah would look like wearing one.

Sexy, of course, but I wasn't sure if she could actually pull it off. She was a little too innocent for thigh high leather heels. Maybe after a few years, when the three of us had completely corrupted her, things would be different.

I went through a staff exit, before walking through the large building to the extension that was underway and closed off from the public. Marco was speaking to the contractors as I arrived, giving them very detailed orders. "Mr Conti, sir" the head contractor, Adam, tensed as he noticed me.

His greeting had Marco spinning on his heels to face me. Marco was pushing fifty, and grey was beginning to be the prominent colour in his hair now. His protruding gut wasn't helping his aging appearance. "Dario" he smiled, but there was wary in his eyes.

"Uncle" I replied coolly. Marco was on my shit list at the moment and, if the drip of sweat on his brow was any indication, he damn well knew it. "I see the constructions are well underway".

"Yes sir" Adam replied, taking over for my sweating uncle. "We're hoping to have the initial framing done by the end of the month, from there it should only be another two months to dry wall and put in all the bars and stages".

"Hmm" I considered. Enzo's birthday was in two months' time so that was pushing the time frame. "I need it done in two months. I want to have opening night on the twenty-seventh and I plan to hold a private party here on the twenty-sixth".

Adam gulped, "we'll try our best sir but a lot of my men are working on several projects at the moment so time is a little limited".

I levelled him with a cool look. It was a straight, penetrable, stare that held the whisper of danger. I had perfected the look by the age of twelve when I had first started seeing how badly my father was running things. Even seventeen years later, the stare was still good enough to make hardened criminals shit themselves.

"I suggest, Adam, you look about making sure that your men have their priorities in check, then. I'm sure you're as eager to get this extension done as I am".

"Yes Mr Conti, sir, of course I am". He was visibly shaking. "I will have it done in two months, you have my word".

"Good" I replied coolly, "I'll return in a few weeks for a progress update". Having dismissed him, I turned back to my uncle and clasped him on the shoulder. "Come on, old man, I have a job for you to get back into my good graces".

He paled like a sheep, "you want to give me a job? Dario, I'm a little old to be doing any heavy lifting".

We both knew he didn't mean actual heavy lifting – he was sliding towards retirement and we both knew his alcohol dependency had destroyed his shooting aim years ago.

"Don't worry, dear uncle, this is a job that is perfect for a little sneaky rat like you".

CHAPTER NINE

Vannah

Dario and Enzo were gone, leaving me alone with Mr Flirty and Tattooed. I took my time in my bedroom, showering and blow drying my hair – trying to avoid confronting the big elephant in the room. I had woken up feeling so damn smug and so damn excited, just to have the world crash around me. I had thought Dario Conti was my prince charming, but he was just another villain disguised as a hero.

After the intimate night we had spent together, where I had had several rounds of easily the best sex of my life, I couldn't believe he was willing to share me around like I was a breeding bitch in a kennel.

To him I was nothing but a common whore to line his sheets, who could fuck his friends when he was busy. They could fancy it up anyway they liked, calling themselves my husbands, but I wasn't stupid or a kid.

I could hear Salem moving around downstairs, so I spent a while doing a face of makeup. I had nowhere to go, and nothing to dress up for, but it gave me an excuse to stay in my room. I had been annoyed, at first, that Dario was giving me a separate room to his, but now I was so glad to have a haven to hide within.

Just as I was practising my winged eyeliner, my phone buzzed. I glanced at it to see a text from Salem. When the hell he got my number, or how his was saved in my contacts, I didn't know. Nor, I imagined, did I want to know. I looked at it on the home screen, not wanting him to see that I had read it.

Salem: You didn't eat your breakfast. Do you want to go somewhere for lunch?

A simple text but I ignored it, turning back to my reflection in the mirror. I did the other eye, and my phone beeped again.

Salem: I know you read my first message, little V. You keep ignoring me and you're going to hurt my feelings.

There was a winky face emoji and I rolled my eyes so hard I wouldn't be surprised if he heard me. But, I knew he wouldn't stop texting me until I replied or worse he'd come up and disrupt my peaceful hiding space. I typed back a quick message.

Vannah: Not hungry. No, I don't want to go anywhere with you.

His reply came before I had even but my phone back down.

Salem: Got it loud and clear. You don't want to go out with me...you'd rather stay in with me. Cheeky.

His text came with another winky emoji like he was a teenage boy. I shook my head and blocked his number. I was in no mood to try and navigate flirting with one of my 'husbands'. I was deep in denial and staying there.

I spent roughly another hour in my room, completing my makeup before curling my hair. I had dressed in a pretty red summer dress, and pulled on some strappy wedges. I looked at my reflection in the mirror and smiled. As much as I wanted to hide away from Salem, Enzo and Dario, I didn't need to hide away from the rest of Las Vegas.

I grabbed a little shoulder purse, before heading downstairs with my head held high. Salem heard me, or maybe he'd been waiting, and he met me in the large entrance way of the house. "Fuck me, you are so damn sexy" he growled out, as he looked me up and down. A shiver went through me – I tried to convince myself it was disgust, but I was lying to myself.

"I'm going out". I kept my voice even; despite the way my heart was pounding.

"Sure thing. I'll drive" he grinned.

"You weren't invited. I'll take a cab".

"Yeah, no". Salem moved and physically blocked the doorway. "You want to go somewhere, one of us will take you".

I raised an eyebrow, "so I'm not allowed to go anywhere on my own now?"

"Of course you are. But yesterday someone tried to shoot you and we still don't know who". He gave me a hard look and I cringed. Honestly, I couldn't believe that the shooting at the church had slipped my mind. I hadn't even spoken to my family to find out if anyone had been hurt. "When we find out who it is, and I put a bullet in their head, then you can have a bit more freedom".

"I won't be a prisoner" I growled. Salem grabbed me, shocking a yelp out of me, before spinning me around and pressing me up against the door. I gulped as his body moulded with mine, caging me up. I looked up at him and I hated that my body reacted. My nipples hardened through my dress and I felt a little jolt of excitement started in my pussy. I hated that I reacted like that.

"You are not a prisoner, Vannah" Salem whispered, one hand cupping my face as he forced our eyes to meet. "You are the single most important thing in my life. If anything were to happen to you, I would kill myself to be with you".

"You barely know me". My voice was barely a whisper.

"Wrong" he smiled, "I know everything about you. You are my wife, my love and my only reason to live. I have waited four years to make you mine and anyone that so much as looks at you wrong, I will kill and torture in the most brutal ways".

His words had a spike of lust running through my body. I was no stranger to danger, but I had never had someone say those sorts of words to me before. Because I looked into his dark brown eyes and I knew that he spoke the truth. But, I couldn't fall into his trap. Whatever these guys wanted, the only thing I knew was that I was a married woman. I was married to Dario and I didn't care if *he* didn't mind sharing me, but *I* didn't want to be shared.

"Fine" I relented, "you can come".

His body pressed tighter against me and he gave me a manic grin. "Oh I can *come* can I? Where abouts? Inside you? Or on your face, maybe your breasts… fuck, I'll come in my pants if you tell me right now".

I blushed like a beetroot and pushed him away. "You're a sex pest".

"Only for you, Little V". He grabbed my face and smacked a kiss on my lips – the kiss was instant and hard, like a goodbye platonic kiss. Even though it wasn't a sexual kiss, I still hated how much my body responded to him. "Now, let's go get some lunch. I know you said you weren't hungry, but you blatantly lied to me. I know a great little place to get some traditional pasta".

Salem dragged me to the garage, before opening the passenger door to a glossy black Ferrari. I was silent as he hopped into the driver seats and left the Conti estate. It was quiet for a few minutes, before he flicked on the radio. Trying his luck, he reached over and rested his hand on my thigh. I pushed it away and he gave me another manic grin.

Vegas looked different in the daylight. Less glamourous, less flashy and less impressive. There was also a stark difference from the extravagant strips, to the rundown housing around it, and then to the fanciest suburbs. I grew up in New York, I had seen the wealth gap, but it felt different in Vegas – like it was two sides to an ugly coin.

Salem drove us away from the touristy areas, past a small vineyard, and to a little area of cute cottage style European houses. It was very Italian, which was nice. In an ideal world, I would relocate back to Italy permanently. Maybe I would do that when I was old and my children had all grown up.

We came to a small family style Italian restaurant and Salem parked up. The inside of the restaurant was colourful and looked like it had come straight from Rome. The smell of roasting tomatoes, olive oil and slow cooked meat met me, as I opened the door. The host smiled up at me as I walked in, then her eyes widened as Salem appeared behind me.

"Mr Galluci" she stammered, standing a little straighter.

"Table for two. Ideally on the balcony" Salem replied coolly, giving her a casual but cold smile. She snatched up two menus, before leading us through the restaurant and up to the small second story. The balcony was obviously closed for lunch service, but she unlocked the doors and quickly set up a table.

"If there is something you want that is not on the menu, just tell me and the chef will be happy to make it for you" she stammered. "Would like a bottle of wine and some canapes?"

Salem looked at me, hinting for me to decide. I gave a smile to the host, "a bottle of your sweetest rosé and a jug of lemon water". She disappeared to get those instantly, as both Salem and I looked over the menu. I was glad to see all the options looked pretty authentic.

I had been born in Italy, unlike a lot of the American mafia, and my father had moved us over to New York when I was eight. So, I was very picky when it came to authentic Italian food – if I even saw someone putting cream in pasta, I was not eating it. My nonna would have slashed at me with a knife for daring to put something like that in my mouth.

A few minutes later, an older gentleman appeared

with our drinks and an older woman trailed behind him with some olives, bread and oil. They placed both on the table for us. "Mr Galluci, what a pleasure to have you here".

"I'm glad you think so, Pavanetto". Salem was very cool, very aloof and giving off vibes of pure danger. I wasn't seeing Salem then, I was seeing Matusalemme Galluci – a top ranking mafia member. I hated that it turned me on a little bit.

"Ma'am" Pavanetto tilted his head to me. He wasn't a direct immigrant if the lack of Italian accent was anything to go by. Not a good sign for my food expectations.

I held my hand out for him to shake, "Giovannah Conti". I introduced myself, a little bit to remind Salem that I wasn't his wife but Dario's. Also, I was interested in gaging their reactions. They both shook my hand, but they were both whiter than a ghost.

"Mrs Conti, I apologise, I was unaware of any female family members" he rambled.

"Giovannah is Dario's wife" Salem replied shortly. His face was calm but there were sparks of annoyance in his eyes. At his words, I thought the Pavanetto's were about to pass out. Deciding to end the awkward situation, I turned back to the menu.

"Do you make your carbonara in the traditional way?" I asked, speaking in Italian because I can be a bitch and I wanted to test their culinary knowledge.

They looked clueless, so I repeated the question in English.

"Of course" Pavanetto nodded, "egg yolk only, we do traditional here".

"Good, it'll take a carbonara small plate to start and then I'll have the Osso Bucco for main" I informed them. I glanced over at Salem, whose lips were a bit tight. I was pretty sure it was nothing to do with me and all to do with the Pavanettos.

But, he simply gave the Pavanettos a smile and handed the menus back. "I'll have the same". He turned to me and gestured to the olives, "have a drink, Vannah. Mr Pavanetto and I need a little chat about taxes first".

The Pavanettos shared a look, before they followed Salem back into the restaurant and around the corner to a private back area. Once alone I poured myself a glass of the rosé, took a black olive, and glanced over at the beautiful gardens around.

I may have not liked my current situation, but at least I had good wine and a good view for a while.

CHAPTER TEN

Vannah

Salem returned a few minutes later, looking as cool as a cucumber – despite having likely just been threatening the little old couple who ran the restaurant. As he walked back to the table, I couldn't help but admire him. He wore a light blue button down, that was rolled up to reveal his tattooed arms, and a pair of black pants that were tight against his muscled physique.

I may not have wanted three crazy killer husbands, but I couldn't argue that they were all ridiculously hot.

I tried my hardest not to check him out as he neared

the table – but given the small smirk that pulled at his lips, I was obviously not very successful. Which was odd for me, because I had never been one for all-consuming lust that melted away my common sense. Yet, here I was checking out my 'official' husband's crazy enforcer.

"Sorry about that, beautiful, I had to remind some people about late payments" he replied, giving me a bright grin. He took a seat opposite me and poured himself a glass of the rosé.

"They better not spit in my food now" I frowned.

"They wouldn't dare. You own their asses and half of this restaurant now that you're a Conti". He gave me a stupid wink, which I pointedly ignored by sipping more of my wine. The two of us drank our wine and ate the bread and olives silently.

A knock came on the closed balcony doors – no doubt Salem had told them to give us privacy – before a younger male waiter delivered our carbonara. He gave us both nervous smiles before disappearing once more. We both quietly began to eat. Their carbonara was good...but mine was better.

"Are you going to ask all of the questions that you're dying to know?" Salem smirked, putting a forkful of pasta in his mouth. I stayed silent, taking another mouthful of my own food. "Oh come on, Vannah, I can see all those questions in your eyes".

I swallowed my mouth, "how will I know you'll answer what I ask?"

Salem put his hand on his chest, "cross my heart and hope to die".

"Not good enough". I gestured to his wedding ring. "Give that to me. If you lie to me or I don't like your answers, I won't give it back".

He raised an eyebrow, "and how will you know if I'm lying?"

"My father taught me a very clever way, but I can't tell you how or otherwise you'll change your behaviour to deceive me". There was a long moment of silence, as I just stared at him with my hand out. Finally, Salem sighed and took the ring off. I closed my fist around it the moment the cool metal touched my palm.

"Alright, ask away" he grumbled, finishing up his pasta.

"Dario said you'd talked this all through together, which meant you must have discussed what you all envision our future together. Tell me what you see".

"I see us all living together in one house, eating together and having fun together. I see you having my kids one day, and all four of us raising them as our own. I picture the four of us growing old together".

"Hmm" I hummed, finishing the last of my pasta as well. "So in this little foursome are you and the other men…involved? Dario is obviously into women but if this is some sort of cover for Enzo and you to be relationship, I deserve to know".

It had occurred to me that the 'all married to the same girl rouse' could be to give them an excuse for a gay sexual relationship. The Mafia was still very much in the stone age when it comes to any sort of deviation from 'the norm'. That wasn't to say there were no LGBTQ+ mafia members, there were, but they usually had false relationships and fake marriages. I had wondered if that was what this whole 'three husbands' thing was about.

Salem snorted, "nope, we're all very much in this relationship to be with you, Vannah. Do I have a problem seeing another guy's cock? No. Do I want the cock anywhere near me? Also no".

"So, what, you just plan to pass me from bedroom to bedroom whenever you guys want?" I tried to keep my voice even, but my annoyance was obvious.

"We could do that" he said slowly, "or we could all just share you".

I frowned, "I don't understand".

His eyes turned wicked, "you've got three holes, don't you Little V?" A wink had me gasping in shock. He leant forward and lowered his voice, "although both Enzo and Dario will have to fight me for your asshole. Because you can bet I'm going to be the first one to fuck that tight hole".

I blushed brightly, just as another knock came on the patio doors. The waiter returned and cleared the plates, as I sat their silently burning like a tomato. Salem was obviously amused but there was seriousness in his eyes. I spoke again when we were alone. "Is that seriously what the three of you planned? To all have sex with me…at the same time?"

He shrugged, "if you are into it. Or, you can just go between our beds. At the end of the day it will be your choice, we'll never force you to do anything you don't want to".

"You seemed determined to force me into a four way marriage".

He raised an eyebrow, before snorting a laugh. "Touché, Little V, touché".

The waiter returned and brought our Osso Bucco. It went silent as we both began to eat; I sighed heavily in disappointment. Osso Bucco was my favourite dish but rarely anyone got it right. The Pavanettos had made several classic errors, which were very common in America, and I was disappointed.

"Problem?" Salem asked, "I think it's delicious".

"It's fine but when you've had true Osso Bucco, then you know this is just a little lacking in technique. The broth should have been dredged with flour to keep it thin and unmuted, and it is too tomato heavy. Only the flesh of the tomatoes should be used. Plus, I can taste the beef stock".

"What's wrong with beef stock? Veal is a baby cow,

right?"

"Either make a stock with the bones or you use chicken, it gives it a better depth of flavour and doesn't overpower the veal".

Salem smirked, "you're a serious food snob".

"I don't deny it. I have high standards and, yeah maybe, that can make me seem like a bit of a stuck up bitch. But, I'm just passionate about good Italian food".

"I love getting to know you" he grinned, giving me an evil look. I just rolled my eyes at his suggestive tone and ate a little more of the saffron risotto. I ate a fair amount, while Salem almost inhaled everything, before the waiter returned and took the plates. He left us alone with our wine and the scenery.

I held the glass of rosé in my hand, as I stared out at the gardens. I could see Salem's eyes on me but I didn't turn to him. "I know you're scared, Giovannah, but all we want to do is make you happy. Dario, Enzo and I will *do* anything, *be* anything, *give* you anything to make you happy. Just tell us what you want and we'll give it to you".

I held up his wedding ring, "I want to keep this and I want both Dario's and Enzo's as well. You don't get to decide you're my husbands without consulting me, I didn't sign up for that".

Salem was silent for a long while, before speaking

carefully. "What if you decide you want to be our wife?"

"Then I'll give you your rings back".

CHAPTER ELEVEN

Vannah

I was full of determination when we arrived back at Conti Manor. I had only had sex with two people throughout my entire life and both of those people had been chosen by my father. It was about time I started choosing my sexual partners for myself. I wasn't going to sit back and let three mafia bozos decide who did and didn't get to be married to me. That was my decision and my decision only.

I had Salem's wedding ring tucked securely in my purse, but I needed the other two in order to gain full control. But, I doubted the other two – especially

Dario – would hand theirs over as easily as Salem had. So, I had to prepare myself for a fight.

When I walked into the house, I was relieved to see several boxes in the entrance way that the home security had brought in. Salem helped me carry them upstairs to my bedroom – I expected sexual comments and flirting when he entered my bedroom, but surprisingly he was quiet.

We placed the boxes in my closet, next to my still packed luggage. I was glad to have all my stuff and I was looking forward to unpacking it all and trying to make the new house feel a little more comfortable. Salem watched me from the closet doorway as I checked I had all the boxes I had asked Gio to send. "You're quiet" I commented, as I unpacked and put my shoes and purses away.

"I want my ring back" he commented.

I rolled my eyes, "too bad. You'll get it back when I think you deserve it".

Salem straightened up and grinned at me. Moving into the closet, he backed me up against the half empty shoe rack. He pressed a hand to either side of me, closing me in as he smiled down at me like a maniac. "What?" I demanded.

"You said when".

"What the hell are you talking about?" I pushed against him but it did nothing but make him press closer against me. His body was hard against mine, making butterflies flutter in my stomach nervously. Salem leant down, his mouth next to my ear.

"You, my beautiful little wife, just said you'd give me my ring back *when* I deserved it. Not *if* I deserved. That means you already know that we're going to be together at some point". He pressed his lips against my neck, his soft lips dragging across the skin. A shiver went through my entire body. "You're mine, Little V, and you know it".

I wet my lips, taking a moment to push my lust away, before speaking. "I'm not yours, Salem. I cannot be owned by you or anyone in this house".

He gave a dark chuckle, "wrong again, wife. We already own you and we will always own you. You are ours to kiss, to love, to fuck, to ruin. You are ours and we will never let you go".

The words did unspeakable things to my body and completely ruined my underwear. Damn these sexy men. "Get off me and get the hell out of my room, Salem" I hissed.

He pressed against me tighter, his arousal obvious from the large erection pressing against my stomach. "I'll make you a deal, Little V".

"What?"

"I'll let you go and leave you in peace…but first I want to give you an orgasm". His eyes were brimming with mischief. "You don't have to do anything for me, just stand there and let me show you how good a husband I can truly be". For good measure I gave him a push, but the man made from stone didn't even budge. He laughed, "I can stay like this for a long time". He rubbed his erection against me.

"Pervert" I growled.

"A pervert for you, yes". He cupped my cheek and forced my eyes to meet his. I loathed how good looking I found him. Dario was suave and sophisticated, but Salem was rough and messy and made me think of the dirty sort of sex I had never experienced but always fantasied about. He was like forbidden chocolate...all I wanted was a taste, even though I knew it would just make me want more.

"I hate you".

Salem smirked, "no you don't". His breath fanned over my face and wetness pooled in my underwear. "Come on, Little V, just say yes and let me show you".

"Fuck" I breathed out.

"If you want, but I think that you might regret it afterwards. So, let me just make you feel good". Still trapped against the show rack, caged by his body, I hated how much I wanted him. My heart was throbbing and my entire body was on fire – these men were going to kill me one day.

And honestly? I wasn't sure I actually wanted to say no anymore. I was twenty six and had spent years dreaming about someone whisking me off my feet and giving me orgasm after orgasm. Dario had started that, maybe Salem could add to it.

"Okay" I whispered, as I stared into eyes.

He gave me a wicked smile, eyes glistening. "Sorry, Little V, I'll need you to speak up just a little bit".

"Asshole" I spat at him, making his smile widen. "I agree with your terms, Matusalemme. Give me an orgasm and then get the hell out of my room".

"Yes Ma'am". Grasping my chin, Salem squeezed it tight, before kissing me deeply. His kiss was teasing and playful – constantly changing in pressures, a tongue that dipped in and out, as his teeth nibbled at my lips. The kiss was as flirty as the man himself. Typical of him really.

Despite my objections, I eased into the kiss and my arms wrapped around his neck. He was so much taller than me, that I went onto my tip toes and tried to get closer. "So tiny" Salem chuckled against my lips. He trailed his kisses over my jaw line and to my neck. I let out a small moan as his teeth nipped at my neck.

Salem's large hands slid down my body, skimming my hard nipples, before reaching around and clasping my ass. I groaned as it pushed me further into his erection. He chuckled, before his hands returned to the front of me. Slowly his hands settled onto my thighs and moved up and under my dress. I shivered as his fingers brushed the edge of my panties.

His thumb ran over my underwear and I shivered. "Damn, so wet already, Little V. You can play it all tough, but you want me as much as I want you". He pushed my dress up and his head went straight between my legs. Teeth scratched my thighs and I shivered in anticipation. Salem chuckled softly, "your pussy smells amazing".

His head dived between my legs, licking me over my underwear. His teeth gripped my panties and dragged them down. They pooled around my ankles and I stepped out of them. Salem took them and tucked them into his pant pocket. He smiled up at me, "something to catch my cum with later".

"Ick, you're a pig" I rolled my eyes.

Salem just laughed, before sealing his mouth over my cunt. I groaned as his tongue licked up and down my slit, before slipping inside me. My knees instantly went weak as he moved up to my clit. The second he touched my clit I gasped in shock as his cold metal tongue stud grazed me.

I had minimal experience with receiving oral sex. Dario had been great, but Salem was mind-blowing. His tongue moved like a wave, licking and rolling and sucking on the softest and most sensitive parts of me. And then a sharp touch of cold from his piercing. It was like nothing I had ever experienced before.

And just when I thought it couldn't feel any better, he slipped two fingers inside me. "Fuck" I hissed, as he sucked on my clit and his fingers fucked my cunt. I wasn't sure anything had felt that good before. I came so hard I almost saw stars, my knees weakened and my legs shook. My arousal gushed all over Salem's face, which he happily lapped up.

He leant back on his calves and smirked up at me. "Fuck, you are perfect. Look perfect, smell perfect and taste perfect". He licked his lips sinfully, just to get his point across.

Trying to pull on some bravery, I cleared my throat. "You've given me an orgasm, you can get out now".

His hands went dramatically over his heart, "so cold, Little V, so cold". He stood up, towering over me once more, before leaning down and kissing me. He then lowered his voice to a whisper, "I am never going to forget this day, Vannah, never".

And then, he was finally gone.

CHAPTER TWELVE

Enzo

I pulled a gun out of my holster and levelled it at the punk bastard nicknamed Viper. He was no Viper, he was worm. The bastard just smirked at me – he would never smirk at Salem. Everyone knew that Salem was the twisted on, the sadistic one, the one to fear. Little did they know, I had no trouble putting bullets in people heads either…I just did it with less flare and less torture.

"I will ask only once more, shithead" I growled – bored of this game before it had even started. I may have not enjoyed killing like Salem did, but I was good at it. I would rather be at home with

Giovannah and leave this sort of work for Salem. But, I couldn't call myself an enforcer and leave all the enforcing to someone else.

Viper scoffed at me, "whatever man. I told you, I don't know nothing about no missing hookers". His accent was grating – nothing became nufink and hookers became hookhahs. I didn't know where the hell that accent was from, but he deserved to die just from the assault it caused on my ears.

"Uh-huh. Well those dancers didn't just up and vanish into thin air now did they?" I glanced around the dodgy alley – I could have dropped the fool instantly and no one would have ever thought again about the degenerate pimp. "You work your girls on Fremont, you have your beady little eyes all around and you have your scummy little fingers in every pie outside of Conti territory".

He growled, "well you bastards keep kicking me out of the nicer places".

I pushed the gun into his forehead and he gave a small yip in shock. "You should be grateful we give you any place at all, you little worm". I scowled at him – fuck the game, I was sick of dealing with scum. "You have one more chance. Three dancers working at Purple Velvet took a break outside at three pm today…they never came back in. You have your girls working around Purple Velvet, trying to poach our guests if they leave because they can't afford to pay for our girls". He began to splutter again. "Shut it, we know you do. So, once more, what happened to our girls?"

"I don't know man, I swear I don't know" he stammered. "But I can ask around, maybe some of the girls know something. Whores talk see, even the classy ones that work in your whore houses talk". He was rambling and it was giving me a damn headache.

"Twenty four hours". I pushed him away and he fell to the ground. I smirked down at him – yes, definitely a worm rather than a snake. I pulled a business card from my pocket, Davide's information on it, not mine, and flicked it at him. It spun wide and landed on the ground beside him. "You speak to this guy and you tell him everything you know. If I hear you've not contacted him by the twenty four hour mark?" I paused, shrugging as I slipped my gun back into my holster. "Well...I hope your whores throw a good funeral for you".

I turned my back to him, showing him how little I thought of the two bit thug, before heading back to the main strip. I found my car easily and was glad to be back inside and driving towards home.

The three days that Dario and Salem had been in New York, everything was quiet. But that had changed once more. Three of our strippers, and part time escorts, had disappeared midway through their working day. And since they left their money and cell phones, we assumed they didn't just leave for a new life. Not to mention the death of a random of cartel thug in Conti territory.

It had been a busy day and all I wanted to do was go home, slide into bed beside my new wife and get some good sleep. I sighed heavily as I arrived home – I doubted that fantasy would go past my mind. Not with the way that Giovannah had freaked out about finding out about being married to all three of us.

I got out the car, absentmindedly twirling my new black wedding ring, and headed into the house. Salem and Dario were talking in low voices in the lounge, I could hear Giovannah banging around upstairs. "Hey" Dario nodded, as he noticed me. "Find the girls?"

"Nope, no trace at all. Davide still has everyone looking around but it's as if they vanished into thin air" I sighed. Slipping off my jacket, I hung it on the back of a chair and stripped my gun and holster off. The gun thumped onto the island loudly. "Davide or John Paul will call if anything changes".

"Damn, I gotta bad feeling about this" Salem muttered.

"Might be best if you spend some time Downtown tomorrow" I commented, as I headed to the fridge to grab three beers.

Salem snorted, as I handed him one bottle. "Why so you can stay here with Vannah?"

I narrowed my eyes at him. He was right, of course,

but I wouldn't let the cocky fucker know that. "No, asshole, you're the sadistic motherfucker out of us three. Street thugs are nervous of me, they're piss-their-pants terrified of you".

He smirked, chuffed with himself, "hell yeah they are".

A large bang sounded above our heads, we all glanced towards the ceiling. "Is she alright up there?"

"She's just finishing unpacking all her stuff" Dario replied, "I offered to help her but she just locked the door and told me to go away".

I cringed, "is she still pissed about the whole 'three husband' situation?"

"Oh I think she is *cumming* around" Salem teased, putting his fingers in a V shape and licking in between them. It took me a second to realise he was making a crude oral joke.

Dario snorted, "you have no idea how good she tastes".

"Oh I have a very good idea". He ran his tongue over his lips, "a very very good idea".

"Wait? What?" I gasped, "you had sex with Giovannah?" Dark jealously ran through me; ugly and borderline psychotic.

"Not sex, but I did get to taste her". He licked his lips suggestively again. My hands curled into fists as my rage built. It wasn't fair. It wasn't damn fair.

That should have been me and not Salem. It was bad enough I had to share the woman I loved with two men – despite how much I cared for them – but to be the last to have her? That wasn't fair. It wasn't fucking fair.

The conversation didn't progress further, as we heard Giovannah leave her room and make her way down the stairs. A few minutes later she appeared in the kitchen door. She looked over us all sceptically. Before walking forward and holding her hand out. The three of us exchanged odd looks.

"Did you want something, my love?" Dario asked.

"Wedding rings, now, both of us". She looked between Dario and I. "You want to be my husband? You have to prove to me that you're worthy of it". She stayed with her hand out impatiently, her left foot tapping.

Salem gave a dark chuckle, I glared at him. I was angry Giovannah hadn't asked him for his ring. He must have realised as he held his hand up – it was bare. "She got my ring earlier".

"Vannah, love, maybe we can talk this out and--"

"No" she cut Dario off. "My entire life people have been making decisions for me. I was hoping I was going to come here and I might finally be able to think for myself. Then, the three of you hatched this little 'secret husbands' plot. It made me realise that if I want to make decisions, I have to start standing up for myself". She gave us all a long look. "And this is where I am starting. I will keep my ring on, and if you want to think of me as your wife then that is fine, but I get to choose when, or if, you get to be my husband".

"If?" I growled. My temper, my ugly anger, was rising again. I didn't want to show that side of myself to Giovannah, so I took a long deep breath and forced the fury down deep inside me. "I am your husband, Giovannah, you will not take that away from me".

She turned to look me straight in the eye and put her hands on her hips. "You want to be my husband, Enzo? Then prove to me that you're worthy. Make me want to be your wife so much that I ask you to be my husband".

I calmed my fear with a momentary pause. I could do that – out of the three of us, I knew Giovannah the best. I had studied her, followed her, watched her for almost a year. I knew her likes, her dislikes, her loves and her hates. Dario and Salem both loved her, but I was obsessed with her. All I had to do was make sure that I showed Giovannah how well I truly knew her.

I slowly took my ring off, sliding it down my finger before holding it out to her. There was a hush in the room, before she stepped forward and took it from me. "Thank you" she smiled, giving me a bashful look. She turned to Dario, who cussed under his breath, before taking his ring off too.

Giovannah took both rings, and Salem's from her pocket, and threaded them onto a delicate gold chain. She then put the necklace on – the three black rings hung delicately in the hollow of her throat.

CHAPTER THIRTEEN

Vannah

I woke up the next morning to a quiet house. Being the first awake, gave me a proper chance to explore the large mansion. I then went through the yard and garden. I had a big green thumb and was disappointed with the outside of Conti Manor. Obviously someone came occasionally to cut the grass, but apart from that it was nothing but a large green area with hedges that hid the perimeter gates.

My mind was twirling as I began picturing what I wanted to do with the landscaping. Putting my hands to good work, I whipped up breakfast as a plan formed in my head. My mental picture was coming together, as the men woke and emerged in the kitchen.

"Morning, my love, do I smell coffee?" Dario smiled, swagging into the room. He wore a dark blue suit, perfectly tailored, and diamond earrings sparkled from his lobes. Salem followed behind his friend, dressed the stark opposite – leather jacket, motorcycle boots and a psychopathic grin. And, if they fell on the ends of a spectrum, Enzo was dead in the middle – all black, no bling and no fuss. They were all so damn gorgeous I wanted to drool.

I put a cafetière on the table between them. Enzo gave me a soft smile, before gently pushing the coffee press down as I put small jugs of cream and sugar on the table. I then put the pastries I had made down, along with jams and butters. "Oh croissants" Salem grinned.

"That's a cornetto" I replied, giving him a deadpanned look. "Are you sure you're Italian?"

"Matusalemme Galluci is one hundred percent Italian, baby" he winked at me. I ignored him, that seemed to be the best course of action when dealing with Salem.

Instead, I sat beside Enzo – who gave me a soft smile – before moving some of the sweet pastries onto my plate. The others also dug in. Despite the fact I put sugar and cream out, every one drank the coffee black and from espresso cups. Maybe they were a little more Italian than I teased.

"These are beautifully light, my love" Dario commented, munching on his pastry.

"Our girls a food snob" Salem laughed, "I took her for lunch yesterday and I was surprised to see such a vicious side to her".

I rolled my eyes at his dramatics, "I'm not vicious. I just think if you're going to cook Italian food, you should at least use the traditional methods".

"You should have taken her to Pavanettos place" Dario commented to Salem.

"I did".

Dario blinked back at me, "you didn't like the Pavanetto's cooking?"

I shrugged, "there was room for improvement".

Salem snorted, "she's being nice now. She was visibly disgusted when she was trying to eat the Osso Bucco".

I rolled my eyes again, "you're being dramatic". I finished off my breakfast, before loading the plates and cooking utensils in the dishwasher. I had assumed that Conti Manor had staff, and they did, but only external security staff. Which meant we did all the cooking and cleaning ourselves, which I actually preferred. Plus, I was glad there wouldn't be the risk of someone finding out about the three husband situation.

After cleaning, I turned to Dario who was finishing his coffee and browsing the news on his iPad. "We signed the marriage certificate before we met" I commented, he glanced up at me with a raised eyebrow.

"Yeah?"

"I didn't sign a prenup".

Dario's eyebrow crept even higher, "I don't need a prenup. What's mine is yours, my love. Why? Are you planning to spend all my money?"

"Not all of it. But, I'd like to do some landscaping and maybe get some house accessories" I admitted.

"You don't like the way we've decorated?" Enzo asked – sounding almost offended.

"Oh no, I do, the colour schemes are great. But a house needs little personal touches".

Salem smirked, "you mean girly knickknacks and pointless pretty crap".

I levelled my gaze at him, "I mean things to make the house more inviting and homey".

Dario pulled a black platinum card from his wallet and slid it over the table to me. "We will all be busy with work today, but I'll get Johnny to play driver".

"Do I have a spending limit?"

There was a long moment, where Dario looked at me as if trying to work something out. Finally he put his coffee down and gave me a serious look. "You are not a prisoner or a pet or a child, Giovannah. You don't get spending limits, or curfews, or rules. As long as you're not out buying ten Lamborghinis on a whim, you can spend what you like".

I wet my lips, considering for a moment. "So if I wanted to buy a new purse, that would be fine? I wouldn't need your permission?"

"You're an adult, my love, you don't need to ask permission". Dario got up and put his dirty plate away, before walking around and pressing a gentle kiss to my forehead. "You said yesterday you want to make decisions for yourself, so make decisions". He glanced at his phone and nodded to the others. "Davide messaged, let's get going".

Salem grabbed my head and gave me an aggressive kiss, before leaving the room with Dario. Enzo waited back a moment. "I did a little landscaping work back in high school, so if you want help with the yard, just let me know and I can make sure I hang around tomorrow".

I gave him a soft smile, "that's very sweet, Enzo, thank you". He gave me a bashful smile before also leaving. Out of my three husbands, I had yet to work out Enzo.

Dario was easy to read, he was dominant and controlling but took care of the people he considered important. Salem was a classic flirt, with a dangerous edge, but I had a feeling that both were covers for whatever was buried underneath. But

Enzo? He was still somewhat of an enigma too me. He was cold, almost permanently pissed off, but there was a sweetness there that felt almost innocent.

Once I was alone, I dressed for the day. As I was planning to spend a few hours in a garden centre, I went for jeans and sneakers rather than a classic dress. Johnny, the head of the security, met me in the garage. He was a very quiet, non-descript guy, who simply held the door to the car open and drove silently.

As we drove, I texted my brother and fielded sexual texts from Salem. I had blocked his number, yet somehow it was unblocked again. He obviously knew computers or the bastard kept stealing my phone without me realising. I ignored those texts, but he would still be smug over the fact he could see I had read them.

Johnny waited outside the garden store – leaning against the driver's door with a travel mug of coffee – and gave me instructions to let him know when I was done, so he could help me load all the plants and furniture into the car. He'd driven a large SUV simply for the trunk space.

Giovanni called me as I was looking at garden furniture. I took a seat on a rocking porch chair and answered. "Hello, brother of mine".

"Hello Mrs Conti" he chuckled, "how is Vegas?" We caught up for a few minutes, which was nice.

Despite being twins, Gio and I got on a lot better when we had a little distance from each other. We both loved and hated each other in the way only siblings could. But, he was still my lifeline to home.

"What happened with the shooting?" I asked, rocking on the porch swing.

"Nothing, I'm afraid. No chatter on the streets, no whispers among the family and no leads on who tried to take a shot at you" Gio replied, sighing heavily in annoyance. "I don't know what the hell, or who the hell, tried to hurt you and it's driving me crazy".

"Do you or Dad have any--" I glanced around my public setting "--unsavoury business associates that are angry with any business".

"Not ones who would go after women". He sounded so much like my father when he said things like that I cringed a little. The Mafia was not an equal opportunist work environment and a lot of the men's views on women were still stuck in the fifties. I enjoyed keeping house, but I also believed that women should choose if they wanted to do that. I wasn't sure my father, or brother, would agree with that. They would consider targeting me, a mere woman, as equally barbaric as targeting a child – both helpless and innocent.

"How is Dario treating you?" Gio questioned, changing the subject.

"Good". I wasn't going to explain the whole 'three

husbands' deal to anyone. Gio would turn up in Vegas, branding Dario and the others as perverted sinners. And, as much as I was still uncomfortable about the situation, I felt protective over the three men.

Gio and I said our goodbyes and I finished shopping. I paid for the items, cringing at the ridiculously large price, before calling Johnny to come help take them to the car. He didn't answer. I rang three more times and he didn't answer again. In the end, I got three sales assistants to help me carry everything.

Johnny wasn't at the car, but the keys were in the ignition and his coffee was perched on the hood. I glanced around, pouting in confusion, as all the things were loaded into the trunk of the car. Once that was done, and Johnny was still not around, I tipped them and they headed back into the store.

As I stepped up to the driver's side door, I noticed a bright red splodge on the floor. I knew instantly it was blood. I looked around, seeing other smaller droplets – nothing you would notice at a glance, but obvious if you were looking for them. I knelt down, frowning in confusion.

As I knelt I noticed a hand under the car. "Fuck" I swore, before bending down to look underneath the car. And there was Johnny.

Well, Johnny's headless body.

CHAPTER FOURTEEN

Dario

How could I get through another day without feeling her tight cunt spasm around me as she came? It was the single greatest experience I had ever had. Only second to having her squirt into my mouth when I went down on her. Vannah was my greatest possession and my most intense obsession.
"Focus" Enzo growled at me, looking at me over the top of his coffee cup. We were sat at the bar in Conti Capital, drinking cappuccinos, and waiting for information on my three missing escorts. We'd been working like dogs all morning, my best friends and

Davide, and the coffee was well needed.

"He can't help he's love drunk" Davide teased.

Salem snorted, "he's pussy drunk". He leant forward and lowered his voice to a whisper, "and no one can blame him for that". I kicked him under the table, hoping that Davide hadn't heard anything. Before I could comment back, my phone rang. I smirked at the name. "Oh that must be the new Mrs Conti now by the smile on your face".

I didn't argue, just answered the call. "Hey beautiful".

"Dario" Vannah whispered, her voice didn't sound right. My face instantly fell and both Salem and Enzo sat up straighter.

"Vannah, what's wrong?" I urged.

"Is she hurt?" Salem demanded, at the same time that Enzo asked "where is she?"

"Johnny is dead, someone killed him…they chopped his head off". Her voice caught, a barely contained sob sounded. My heart nearly pounded out of my chest as my adrenaline flooded my body.

"Are you safe?"

"I'm inside the garden store, there are people everywhere" she replied. I sighed in relief, but was already getting out of my seat and grabbing my suit jacket from the back of my chair. Salem and Enzo were right there with me. Davide, confused, tripped after us as we sped outside.

"Stay inside, with the crowds of people. We're on our

way to get you" I reassured her.

"Okay".

"Is there a coffee shop?"

"Yes, a little one near the checkouts".

"Perfect, go and take a seat. Order a drink and just wait for us to get there. Doesn't matter what happens, or if anyone tries to talk to you, you stay in that damn café. The crowds of people will keep you safe".

I could hear her feet moving, her breathing hitched slightly as she tried to reign in her fear. I got the address from her, as we reached the car. As we'd all been doing different investigations that morning, all of us – bar Davide – had our own cars. I told my friends the address, before we all jumped in our individual cars. Enzo was the first to speed out the parking lot.

Davide rode with me, as Vannah explained what happened – from arriving, to talking to her twin brother, to finding Johnny's body. She was giving me too much information, her mind whirling as she went through her shock. I gave soft reassurance, as my foot pushed the accelerator flat down. I needed to get to her. I should never have left her without one of us with her.

I kept her talking as we rushed to the store. Enzo got there just seconds before we did. I told Davide to find the body, as we both rushed into the store. We found Vannah easily and the moment my eyes landed on her, the knot of tension in my chest disappeared. She was safe, she was alive.

She rushed towards us; her eyes red rimmed. She blinked up at us, as if confused who to go to. Enzo didn't give her choice; he simply folded his large arms around her. Vannah paused for less than half a second, before wrapping herself around him and the waterworks broke through.

"Hush, Giovannah, don't worry I won't let anything happen to you" Enzo whispered. He gently kissed the top of her head. I was surprised – Enzo was a completely different person when he was with Vannah. Usually the idea of anyone touching him, let alone him touching them, was enough to send him into an angry meltdown.

Enzo carefully walked Vannah outside, whispering to her softly, as I followed them. A little part of me was actually glad that Enzo had scooped Vannah up, because I struggled with crying girls. And as much as I loved Vannah, and hate seeing her upset, I wasn't sure that I would have been able to comfort her as well as Enzo was doing.

Back in the parking lot, Salem and Davide joined us – both looking serious. Davide frowned at seeing Enzo's arms around his boss's wife. I should have intervened, but I was more concerned about getting Vannah out of the open.

I cupped the back of Vannah's head, enough for her to pull her face away from Enzo's chest and turn to look at me. "Enzo is going to take you home, my love. Get some rest and don't worry about anything".

She sniffed and nodded at me. I leant forward and kissed her gently; I was glad she didn't push me away. Enzo held onto her the entire time. I gave my best friend a nod, and he led our wife away and to his car. "Wait, Dario" Vannah turned to me, sniffing. "All my stuff is in the car".

"I'll bring it home with me later" I assured her. She nodded, sniffed as her eyes filled with tears once more, before being led away. Once she was gone, and safely in Enzo's car, I turned to Davide. "Tell me" I demanded, as we walked over to one of my large SUV's.

"From what I can see, Johnny was outside of the car but then got back inside, were he was killed. Backseats are soaked in blood, so he was probably shot and decapitated there. Then his body was stuffed under the car. It was quick, effective and almost...professional".

I cringed at the information. "Decapitation? Poor fucker".

"Yeah and the head is missing. Sadistic fucker who did this obviously took it with him" Salem added in.

"Poor Johnny, I liked him".

"The ground is a little wet around the car, like someone threw a bottle of water to wash away the blood" Davide continued, "like I said, boss, this is controlled". His phone beeped and he glanced down at it. "I called Frank, his nephew works for a scrap yard. He's going to get a tow truck from him, so we can try and move the car and the body at the same time. Around here--" he eyed the numerous civilians coming and going "--no way we can move that body without a big ass truck to block the view".

I nodded, "good call". I looked around the garden store, rubbing my temples. "None of this shit makes sense to me. I feel like someone is setting tiny little nuisance fires, nothing that will really harm us, but enough that we're running around pointlessly putting out each fire".

"Maybe they're not all connected" Salem shrugged, "maybe this was all about Vannah. Someone tried to shoot her at the wedding and now this...maybe the missing escorts are one thing, the cartel murder is another *and* someone is trying to get to Vannah. Three annoying shit storms at the same time".

"But who the fuck would want to hurt Vannah?" I frowned.

"We'll have to ask her".

I shook my head, if anyone was gunning for Vannah then Enzo would have known. Our obsessive chosen brother would have known if someone else had been stalking Vannah...as well as him. "Maybe it's all just a coincidence" I shrugged, not believing my words for a second.

"Guys, I hate to make this worse but..." Davide interrupted. Salem and I both turned to where

Davide was watching a cop car pull into the lot. I cussed, as the two uniformed officers got out and one pointed towards my SUV.

"This is definitely no coincidence" Salem growled, breathing heavily out of his nostrils like a raging bull. "Whoever did this knew we'd come rescue Vannah, so they threw us to the pigs".

Cold anger settled into my stomach. "I don't know who the hell thinks they can fuck with us, but when I find them, I'm going to destroy them".

CHAPTER FIFTEEN

Vannah

"Hush, Giovannah, I won't let anyone hurt you" Enzo whispered to me. He gently led me to a small two-door black Aston Martin, softly soothing me. In that moment he was everything I needed and more. Gentle and caring while being solid and safe. I felt like I was in a giant's palm; cocooned in safety as he carried me away from the danger.

Inside the car, Enzo pulled his gun from the holster under his jacket and placed it on his lap. "We're going to be fine, Giovannah" he reassured me, before driving out of the parking lot. I was quiet for a long moment, as we drove back towards the house. "Do you want to talk about it?"

I did, so I babbled and babbled – going over my day again and again. Enzo was quiet, listening carefully, as I described finding Johnny's body over and over until I was out of adjectives to explain 'decapitated'. I was in shock, even I could register that, but I just needed to get everything out to someone.

I went silent as we rolled up to the Conti gates. I cringed when a guard came to Enzo's door, as usually that was Johnny's job. "Cal, we gotta problem" Enzo sighed. He turned to me, before leaning over and pressing a gentle kiss to the crown of my head. "Give me two minutes". He stepped out the car.

Enzo spoke to the guard, Cal, as a different guard ran a bomb scanner over the car. I had to say, I was impressed with the Conti security. I hadn't had any of that when I was back in New York, but then, we lived on a street where every house was owned by my father – so I guess living on a street of Mafia families was probably security enough.

I watched as Cal ran a hand down his face in grief, before saying something else to Enzo. He then began to radio people, as Enzo climbed back into the car. It was silent between us as we drove through the gates and onto the Manor's drive.

My energy drained as Enzo pulled into the ten car garage and parked. I didn't make a move to get out of the car, just stared blankly out the window. I turned to Enzo when he put his hand on my thigh. He was blurry through my unshed tears. "I hate this part".

"What do you mean?"

"I hate this part of being a Mafia family" I admitted. "I don't know if you know, but I had an older sister but she died over ten years ago. She always wanted to be involved in the business. She wanted to know how to shoot and how to fight, she would beg my father to let her work in the Family. He refused, he always said that a woman's place was at home. Patrizia used to get so angry at me because I didn't back her up".

I went quiet for a moment, wiping my eyes. Enzo silently let me speak. "She used to say I was brainwashed and not a feminist. I tried to tell her it wasn't that I didn't think a woman should work for the Family, it was that *I* didn't want to work for the Family. I don't like blood, I don't like violence. Maybe I live in a fantasy world, ignoring the things that everyone around me does, but it doesn't matter to me. I like being in the dark about these things... I can't handle knowing how dark and dangerous the world is".

"Giovannah" Enzo whispered, taking my face in his hands and gently cupping it. "You don't have to handle these things. The three of us – Dario, Salem and I – are more than happy to keep you out of it. In fact, I much prefer the idea of you having a danger-free life while we take all the risks".

I gave him a watery smile, "you don't think that makes me a pathetic coward?"

"Of course not. I think it's brave and strong that you know your limits and have your boundaries". He pressed a sweet kiss to my forehead – the action melting a little of the ice in my heart and the tension in my stomach. "Let's go inside and I'll make you some tea".

Back inside the house, I headed into the 'den' and settled into an armchair and put the TV on. A few minutes later, Enzo came in carrying a tray. A beautiful ornate tea pot, and two matching cups and saucers, sat precariously on it. The tea pot was white porcelain with delicate painted blue flowers on it.

"That's a beautiful teapot" I commented.

Enzo looked almost embarrassed as he looked away from me, pouring us both cups of tea. "I'm glad you like it...I painted it".

"Wait? Really?"

He gave a small nod, handing me the cup before taking his to the couch next to me. With the cup and saucer in my hands, I studied the beautiful detail. "Did you use a kiln? It's beautifully done".

Enzo shifted uncomfortably in embarrassment. "My aunt owns a pottery studio, where she makes and sells her art as well as teach some classes. I lived above the studio for a while, when I was a teenager, and she taught me. I'm not very good at the pottery part, my bowls are always wonky, but I liked the painting part of it".

"Do you still do it?"

He shrugged, "sometimes. My aunt was always good to me, but we don't exactly have a perfect relationship. It's better for both of us if we just see each other every few months or so".

I snorted a laugh, "sounds like me and Gio. We're twins, and I love him to death, but too much time in each other's company and we'd end up fighting and bickering like we did when we were children".

"I can't imagine you fighting" Enzo smirked, looking happy to get away from the conversation of his pottery painting hobby.

"There is no technique to it, just a lot of swinging arms and kicking legs. I can get a good groin aim if I need to though" I admitted, making him laugh. We both fell into silence, drinking our tea and watching the TV. "Thank you" I said, as I finished my tea.

"It's just tea, Giovannah".

"I meant for being everything I needed today". I put the teacup down and moved over to the couch beside him. I kissed his cheek, "thank you, Vincenzo". I cuddled closer to him and rested my head on his shoulder. Enzo was frozen for a moment, as if not sure what to do, before he put his arm around me and hugged me close into his side.

I fell asleep curled up against Enzo, realising that despite our lack of time together that he might become the one who won my heart first. Thinking that had me dreaming of the first conversation we had had over a year ago.

I glanced over at Aldo, who despite our brutal argument, was already fast asleep. Sniffing, as the tears I had been holding in began to surface, I got out of the bed and grabbed the robe from the back of the door. I opened the bedroom door, glancing down the villa's corridor to make sure no one was around, before sneaking out.

In the kitchen, I rifled through my purse and found my secret stash of cigarettes. I took them outside; the beautiful gardens of the villa were shroud in darkness. I perched on a small wall of the patio and put a cigarette between my lips. I flicked my lighter but it did nothing. I tried a few more times, but nothing happened. I shouldn't have been surprised, I rarely smoked so the lighter fluid had probably dried up months ago.

"Here" a male voice called out, making me jump in shock. I turned to see an overlarge figure stepping out of the shadows. I was scared a moment, before the lights through the French doors lit up his face. The man from the Conti Family...Vincenzo. He held out a lighter for me.

I was nervous as I reached out and took it from him. I used it to light my cigarette before handing it back to him. His fingers brushed mine as he took it. He had done nothing to make me fear him, but he was large and a stranger and I wore nothing but skimpy pyjamas and a robe.

He pulled a hand rolled cigarette from his pocket and lit in. We both smoked in silence for a few minutes – the smell of his cigarette told me he cut his tobacco with weed. I almost asked for a drag, hoping it would take the edge of the awful night I was having. But, I didn't know him well enough to share a cigarette with him.

"You okay?" Vincenzo finally asked, voice gruff and powerful. I looked up at him in confusion. "You look like you've been crying. If there is something wrong you can tell me...I don't know anyone here, I have no opinions and no loyalties. If you want to talk to me you can".

That was the most I had ever heard Vincenzo talk since we'd met. We'd sat next to each other on the flight over and he'd not spoken a single word to me. He had seemed bored the entire week we had been there. So hearing him talk so much took me back slightly.

I released a long breath of smoke. I had drank a lot of wine earlier, enough to take me past tipsy but not quite drunk. Enough to have me airing my dirty laundry to a stranger though. "I've been having some...problems" I began, not giving a fuck I was spilling my marriage secrets to a stranger. "I went to a doctor yesterday who took some blood work from me, he called me earlier to tell me what was wrong with me". I took a final drag of my cigarette and flicked it away.

I sniffed as tears filled my eyes once more and my hands shook. Vincenzo stayed silent, but pulled a cigarette from his pocket. He held it out to me, "it'll take the edge off". I considered it for a moment, before taking it. He lit it for me and I smoked it for a few minutes in silence. The small amount of weed settled into my body.

"You're sick?" he prompted, after a few minutes of silence.

"Chlamydia". I spat the word out in anger, making Vincenzo visibly gape at me. "I'm twenty four and my fifty two year old husband cheated on me and has given me chlamydia". A few angry tears trailed down my face, I angrily pushed them away as I finished the laced cigarette. I sniffed, realising I had just admitted to a complete stranger that I had an STD.

I stood up and awkwardly cleared my throat, "I should go back inside. Please keep this between us, Aldo would be angry if anyone found out". I gave Vincenzo a kind smile, before walking back towards the villa.

"Giovannah" he called out to me, as I reached the patio doors. I turned back to him – his huge body illuminated by the moonlight. "I'm sorry about your husband. He should be worshipping the ground you walk on and thanking God every day that he gets to call you his wife". His eyes bore into mine, "if you were my wife, I would give you the world and you should never settle for less than that".

His words were hollow in my chest. Because I would never get that.

"Goodnight, Vincenzo".

He nodded at me, "goodnight Giovannah".

I woke up, still curled up in Enzo's arm and smiled. Perhaps being married to these three men would be exactly what I needed. The three of them each brought something different to my life. Dario gave me protection and strength. Salem gave me fun and cheekiness. Enzo gave me grounding and support.

For the first time since I had found out about the little 'foursome' marriage, I was optimistic about my future.

CHAPTER SIXTEEN

Dario

The police turning up at the garden store, and going straight to my car, had definitely not been a coincidence. Apparently they had an anonymous call about a dead body under the car. Since the car was registered to me, I had sent Salem and Davide away to try and find the fucker who had killed my head of security, while I dealt with the fallout.

After finding the body, the cops had escorted me straight to their cop shop. The only reason I didn't kick up a fuss, was because the chief of police was in my pocket and I knew Vannah was home safe with

Enzo.

So I sat there, in a dingy interrogation room with a wobbly chair and a sticky table, in a three thousand dollar suit and tapped my fingers impatiently. As good as it was having dirty cops on your side, they still couldn't just let me walk out instantly without raising eyebrows. I had to play the game, until either they 'found' evidence to absolve me or someone else confessed to the crime. Ironically, I hadn't had a hand in this death.

The door finally opened, after me sitting there for an hour, and a detective walked in. He introduced himself as Detective Pinto and sat opposite me. "So, Mr Conti, we've looked at the CCTV at the garden store and we'll be letting you go shortly".

I blinked in shock, "oh well that's easy. I expected to be here a lot longer than that".

Pinto gave a low laugh, "I bet you were. The murder of Johnathon Leison was caught on the store's cameras. It also caught you arriving almost forty five minutes later".

That surprised me. We had assumed this guy was professional – but being caught so clearly on camera was a grade A amateur. "Did you catch the guy then?" I asked, my interest piqued.

"No, we can't see his face or any distinguishing features. He keeps his back to the camera as he used a gun to get Mr Leison into the car, before five minutes later pulling his body out and pushing it under the car. It's hard to see, as there were cars parked either side. But we can say for sure it wasn't you".

I must have looked as shocked as I felt, because Pinto opened up the file in his hands and showed me a dodgy picture of the man. It was zoomed in, so therefore blurry, but it was obviously he was fairly heavyset – not fat, just bulky and a little shorter than me. He wore nothing but black and his hair was hidden under a beanie.

"Who was the woman who discovered the body?" Pinto asked, slipping the question in there like a snake. I kept my face impassive as I looked at him. Pinto was a good cop, a clean cop, and I had no doubt he knew who I was. He probably assumed – like me – that Johnny had been killed in a Mafia related rivalry. But, he wasn't going to let it go at that.

"Woman?" I raised an eyebrow.

"The brunette who spent a little while searching, I assume for Mr Leison, before finding his body under the car. By the way she ran back into the store, hand over her mouth, I assume it wasn't a discovery she expected".

I shrugged, "I don't think anyone expects to find a decapitated body under a car".

His eyes narrowed as he leant back in his chair. "The woman, Mr Conti, is a witness. We need her statement, that is all".

I blew out air out my nostrils like a bull. "My wife, Giovannah" I finally admitted. When going up against cops, I had to pick my battles and hiding Vannah would just make Pinto suspicious and I didn't need to give him any ammunition to further this investigation. I was sure the Chief would have the case 'shelved' soon enough, but I still didn't want to drag this out any more than it was needed to.

"My wife is very traumatised by this" I explained, giving Pinto my 'don't fuck with me' look. "If you want to talk with her then you can come to our house, at an arranged time, to take her statement. I'm not bringing her here".

Pinto's jaw ground together, but he gave a jerky nod. He knew who I was and he wasn't going to push me. He was a smart man and he knew that a lot of his colleagues were in my pocket as were most of the politicians in Nevada. Some boats you just can't rock, no matter how righteous you were.

"My lawyer will contact you tomorrow to set up a time for you to speak with Giovannah" I said, standing up and buttoning my jacket. I offered him my hand to shake, he looked at it for a moment before reluctantly shaking it. "We want to help you as much as we can, so that you can catch this psychopath".

"I'm sure you do, Mr Conti" Pinto replied. His words said one thing, his face called me a bold faced liar. I gave him a smile, before exiting the interrogation room and back into the main precinct. I saw the police chief, Darrel Morn, standing in the doorway to his office – there was a nervous edge to his face. I nodded at him slowly, and the nervousness disappeared into relief, before nodding back. He would live to serve another day...for now.

Salem picked me up outside, driving a different SUV. The trunk and backseats were full of garden things that Vannah had brought earlier. I explained the situation to Salem as we drove home. He was quiet, which worried me. "What's wrong, brother? You're never this quiet".

He cringed, "someone on the street called Davide earlier. Apparently a bunch of junkies found the bodies of three women inside a trap house in North, off Judson Avenue, thinks it might be our missing escorts".

"Fuck" I sighed heavily, leaning my head back. "What the fuck is going on? No one has messed with our business for years, yet four of our own dead within two days and the body of a cartel gangbanger left in our territory. What the fuck...what the actual fuck is happening?"

"I wish I knew boss, I wish I fucking knew". Salem pulled the car to a stop at the gates and Cal stepped up to the window. "Hey Cal".

"Boss, Boss" he nodded at both of us. "Helluva thing about Johnny, damn shame".

"Shit way to go" Salem agreed.

"I spoke with Enzo earlier, I've commissioned a new background check on all contract employees to make sure no one's financial levels have suddenly changed in the past few months. I've also reset all codes, cameras and gates around the estate. Enzo also asked me to look into potentially getting a full time bodyguard for Mrs Conti while she's out of the estate".

I was impressed with Enzo – but, then, he would do anything to keep Vannah safe. For Salem and I, Vannah's safety was our top priority. For Enzo, it was his biggest obsession. I doubted he'd leave her side until he knew who had killed Johnny and tried to shoot her in New York.

"Make dossiers of the bodyguards you're considering and get them to me as soon as possible" I informed him.

"I will get the prospects over to you pronto, Boss".

"Also" Salem cut in, "try and find as many unavailable options as possible".

Cal frowned, "I don't understand what you mean, Boss".

"Giovannah is a very beautiful woman, as I'm sure everyone around here has noticed" Salem began. A little blush hinted at Cal's cheek – showing that *he* had definitely noticed. "So it would be better for all of us, if this bodyguard were gay or female or, if nothing else, married with kids at home".

"Ah, I see" Cal nodded, "I'll make sure to get as many 'unavailable' bodyguard options as possible, Boss".

Salem gave him a two fingered salute. "Keep up the good work, Cal, and you could find yourself as Head of Security now that Johnny is gone". He drove the car through the gates and up the long drive.

"Good call on the gay bodyguard" I muttered, as we parked and climbed out the car.

Salem shrugged, "what can I say? I'm at my quota for the amount of people I'm willing to share my wife with".

CHAPTER SEVENTEEN

Vannah

I woke up confused and unsure where I was. It took me a few blinks to clear my eyes, before I noticed the dark décor of a bedroom. The awful day's events came flooding back to me in real time, leaving me shivering and sad. It had been a hard day. I glanced around the bedroom, not recognising it. It was clean, obsessively so, with no personal affects at all.

I took a guess that due to the unpersonal room, and the fact I had been placed in the bed fully dressed, that I was in Enzo's bedroom. Dario's bedroom I knew and Salem would have undressed me or at least got me down to my underwear.

Slipping off the bed, I headed towards the adjoining bathroom where the door was slightly ajar and water was running. Glancing into the room, I saw Enzo in the shower. His back was to me, his overlarge form standing under the running shower. His skin was pale and glistening under the lights and water.

I should have backed out the moment I saw his naked form. But, for whatever reason, I pushed the door open silently and stepped further in. As I did, I noticed the medicine cabinet above the sink was open – it was stuffed full with so many medications and a whole row of needles. Enzo obviously had some sort of serious health conditions.

I turned to face the shower again, just as he turned around under the water spray. His face was blank for a moment, before his eyes found me. They widened in shock, as I took in the front of his nude body. His chest was perfect, sculpted and huge, but my eyes were drawn to his groin.

Enzo's had a massive, pink, scar that went from just under his belly button all the way down his penis. His penis, albeit big, was heavily scarred and his left testicle was missing and his right looked disformed. Enzo's upper and inner thighs were also covered in long healed white scars.

"Shit" Enzo cussed in shock, grabbing his genitals and covering them with his hands. My eyes went back up to his face, which went from a picture of surprise to a picture of fury in a moment. "What the fuck? Who said you could come in here?" he yelled, "get the fuck out! Get out". He threw open the shower door and grabbed a towel to cover himself.

"I'm sorry, I'm so sorry" I babbled, backing out. Enzo kicked the door and it slammed in my face. I heard him cuss again, before there was a loud crash from inside the bathroom. I cringed, as I moved away from the door. I rushed towards the bedroom door, before stopping.

Despite the shitty day, I had set out to make my own decisions and take control of my life. And, yeah, Enzo was angry with me – but he also had been kind and caring to me, in a way no one had ever been before. He was a good person and if I had ever had a choice of husband, I imagined I would have picked someone like Enzo.

The way he had comforted me the year before in Amalfi, while we had been complete strangers, meant a lot to me. Plus, the way he had made me feel safe and protected today. He was also the only one, out of my three husbands, who hadn't kept the marriages a secret. He'd been upfront from that first morning.

And I had seen that medicine, and his scars, he had not had a good life. He'd suffered trauma and I'd been spying on him – he deserved to be angry. Heck, if I had caught him watching me in the shower I would have freaked out. I moved away from the bedroom door and walked back over to the bed.

I sat on the bed for about fifteen minutes, before the bathroom door opened and Enzo came out with a towel around his waist. He froze, surprised, at seeing me sat crossed legged on the bed. "I'm sorry, I invaded your privacy and that is not okay".

Enzo was quiet for a few moments, before moving and sitting down on the edge of the bed. He looked away from me, staring at the window. I didn't dare move as I couldn't read how he was feeling. Luckily, he broke the silence before I needed to work it out.

"My father was abusive to my mother and he would rape her through their entire marriage. He was a monster and he completely messed up my mother mentally. After his death she become extremely catholic...as in obsessively so". He paused, staring out the window. "She was mentally broken, so she put her everything into the bible to the extreme where she got rid of our TV and any music in the house because she thought it encouraged sin".

"That must have been hard to grow up in" I commented, saying something after he was quiet for a few minutes.

"It was. When I was thirteen, Salem gave me a secret gift for my birthday". He gave a snort, but it was with sadness rather than humour. "I had told him that I had never seen a naked girl before, so he brought me a lovely magazine intitled 'Busty Babes'. Let's just say the only difference with Salem now, and then, is the height not maturity". He shook his head at his friend.

When Enzo went quiet again, his entire body static, I moved to the edge of the bed next to him. I took his hand in mine and he turned to look at me. "It's okay, if you don't want to tell me you don't need to".

"No...I want to" he nodded, giving me a small sad smile. "A few days later, my mother came home from church early and caught me...discovering my body for the first time with the magazine. She went crazy, full psycho, telling me I was a sinner and I was going to become a rapist like my father. To her all sexual acts, even just a thirteen year old boy jerking off, made me unsavable to her god. She got an axe and attacked me".

"Shit, Enzo". I squeezed his hand. I couldn't believe any woman, and mother, could do that to their own son, no matter how mentally ill they were.

"Even though my father was dead, he had still been a Conti man and I knew where his guns were stashed. I fought her off enough to get a gun and shoot her... but the damage had mostly been done. She took off the majority of my genitals in her attack, not to mention all the other damage she caused". He gestured to the scar down the left side of his face. "My neighbour heard my screaming and called the cops, the EMT's were able to save me seconds before I bled to death. But, my mother died".

He turned back to face me; his eyes were blank but

there was a tightness to his face. "I had a lot of surgery back then. My penis was reattached, and one of my testicles was salvageable, but there was a lot of nerve damage. Long term, it caused hypogonadism, which just means I lack testosterone production naturally".

"That's what all the medications are for?"

"Yeah, testosterone injections weekly and a daily tablet for the pain".

I blinked in shock, "you still get pain?"

He gave a sad laugh, "yep, it's been almost eighteen years and I'm still in pain every day of my life. I *was* going to tell you, and show you, but you just surprised me because I hadn't prepared for it to be today. No one has ever seen my cock...you're the first one, so I freaked out a little".

"So you make all the women have sex with you in the pitch black?" I asked, giving a small chuckle. Enzo just silently stared at me, not saying anything. It was then it clicked for me. "Oh...*oh*". He was a virgin.

"The lack of testosterone meant I have never wanted to have sex" he shrugged, "I'd see some women and I'd think 'huh they're attractive' but it never went past that. I was never able to get an erection, so the doctors assumed that the nerve damage was so extreme that I would never be able to have one".

"Well sex is only a very small part of life, Enzo".

"I tried everything; pills, porn, having whores play

with each other in front of me. But, nothing worked and so I gave up. And then…and then I sat next to you on the plane to Amalfi". His eyes bore into me seriously, his fingers tightening around mine. "I saw you and that was it. The first time I had ever had an erection since before the attack".

Enzo's large hand cupped my cheek, as a few tears slipped over my cheeks. "Why are you crying, Giovannah?"

"Because I hate how much pain you've been through".

He gave me a smile, "but don't you get it? You're the reason I've been through so much pain, everything has happened to bring you and I together. My body only reacts to you because we were made for each other".

"Yet you're happy to share me with Salem and Dario?" I didn't understand – after everything he had been through, he should have been grabbing me tight with both hands. If he truly believed that we were soulmates.

"Salem and Dario are more family than my own blood. Sharing with them seems natural. Plus, there are things I can't give you. I don't have the ability to father children and my sex drive is nowhere as high as they have, plus other things. I would never be able to be everything you deserve, but together the three of us can give you anything you want".

I unclasped our hands to wipe my cheeks of my

tears. "And do you feel like you're ready to have sex with me? To actually experience that?"

Enzo took my hand again, and put it over his towelled lap. I felt the beginning of an erection underneath. "Salem once paid four women to have sex right in front of me. My cock didn't even twitch. Yet, you sit beside me and I'm hard. I want you more than I have ever wanted anything, Giovannah, but I want you to want me too". He reached up and touched the three wedding rings on my necklace.

I gave him a wicked smile, "how about we start with baby steps?"

His eyebrow arched, "what did you have in mind?"

"I'll show you".

CHAPTER EIGHTEEN

Vannah

I got up onto my knees on the bed and cupped Enzo's large jaw, the beginnings of stubble tickled my fingers. I brought our lips together, a gentle kiss to start with. Enzo didn't move for a moment, before one of his giant hands cupped my head and deepened the kiss. Our lips battled together, passion and lust flowing between us.

As we kissed, my hands ran down Enzo's hard chest and stomach. He was obviously a little ticklish, as goosebumps pimpled his skin and his stomach muscles contracted as my nails teased a few areas. I giggled against his lips, making him smile as he kissed me harder. My fingers reached the edge of the towel, wrapped around his hips, and his breath caught.

I broke the kiss and looked into his brown eyes. "Can I try something?" I asked, my voice heavy with lust.

"I trust you completely, Giovannah". He kissed me again, before I pulled away. I knelt down in front of him, as he looked down at me from the bed. His eyes were shining with excitement and little nerves. Which, given the fact he was a thirty-one year old virgin who had suffered unbelievable trauma, it wasn't a surprise.

With gentle hands, I pushed the towel away and left him exposed. Enzo sucked in a breath, as my eyes got a clear look at all the crude scars and uneven skin grafts. Leaning forward, I pressed a gentle kiss to both his thighs. He bit his lip as he watched me. I then turned my attention to his cock, which was hard and straining.

Carefully, I ran my hand up and down his length – making him groan and gasp in shock, as I gently pleasured him. After a few moments, I raised onto my calves and bent over his lap. I wasn't sure if Enzo would get any pain from oral, so I very gently took him in my mouth. "Oh fuck, oh shit, oh Giovannah" he breathed out, hands moving to my head to hold me gently.

I began slowly, sliding my tongue up and down as I sucked on his hard cock. His length was large, and my mouth was open so wide that saliva dripped down my chin as I sucked. "Oh wow, don't stop" Enzo breathed out.

His hands were on my head, but they were gentle and it was so nice I almost wept. When I had been with Aldo, he would grip my hair hard and force me to take all of his length to the point I was gagging. I hated giving him head, but he had always told me it was 'part of my wifely duties'. But, with Enzo it was different.

I realised that was what it was supposed to be about. I may have not been receiving the sexual activity, but I still should have enjoyed giving it. I loved how Enzo was holding me gently, cussing and writhing with pleasure, as salty pre-cum leaked from his tip. I was enjoying giving Enzo pleasure and I hoped that would never change.

I suctioned my cheeks more, moving faster as I felt his cock pulse in my mouth. "Holy shit, Vannah, I think I'm going to cum". His hands brushed my hair from my face so he got a better sight of his cock sliding in and out of my lips.

Suddenly, he came. His seed spurted into my mouth, salty and hot, as I swallowed everything he gave me happily. When he was done, groaning as he relaxed, I cleaned him up with my tongue, before sitting back. Enzo looked down at me with awe, as I grinned up at him.

"Was that okay?" I asked. Enzo made a noise of

disbelief, before pulling me to my feet and kissing me again. When we broke the kiss, I rested my forehead against his. "I never did say thank you for last year".

He frowned, "what did I do?"

"You were the first person who made me realise my feelings were valid" I admitted. "Aldo had cheated on me before, a year or so into the marriage. I was so upset and so angry. I spoke to my dad, and my brother, about how I was going to divorce him and how much he had hurt me. And they just told me that 'that's what men do' and that as long as I had the house and the car and the surname, then I should be happy".

"That's bullshit".

"I know. But, I was barely twenty and without my family I wouldn't have had anyone else. I had no choice but to stay with him. When I told you about him giving me chlamydia, your words made me realise that I was a person and not just a housewife. I was Mrs Bianchi for so long, I forgot about being Giovannah".

Enzo wrapped his arms around me, "you're everything to me, Giovannah".

✝

The following day, I barely saw my husbands. Dario and Salem left at the crack of dawn, while Enzo stayed in the home office on conference calls for Dario all day. I was beginning to understand the dynamic a bit. Salem was the main enforcer, who kept the criminal operation running, while Enzo mainly kept the legal part of The Conti Group on track. Dario wore the crown, which meant going wherever he was needed at the time.

I spent the majority of the day in the yard, planting and soiling the flowers and seeds I had gotten the day before. It was a warm day, so I was glad for the lemonade in the fridge that Enzo brought out to me at one point. A few of the security guards even helped me put together a porch swing I had brought, which was kind of them.

By the time afternoon rolled around, I was freshly showered and making use of the large kitchen. "Hey" Enzo greeted, coming into the kitchen, "something smells nice".

I smiled, "I'm making Osso Bucco".

"Salem's favourite".

"I know" I laughed warmly, "I was mean about the Pavanetto's one, so I thought I better make him a truly traditional one to show him what I meant".

Walking over to me, Enzo pressed a sweet kiss on the top of my head. "Yard looks good from my window".

"I have more plans and more to do, but it's fine for a start".

"I have one more business call to make and then I can help you if you need it" he offered.

"I'm fine. I like to cook, it's therapeutic to me".

Four hours later, I was dishing up the food as my three husbands sat at the table. Dario helped me carry the plates to the table. "Shit, Little V, this smells amazing" Salem grinned, "did you make Osso Bucco because you know it's my favourite?"

I gave him a small smile, as I sat down opposite him, "maybe". Silence fell around the room, as the three men ate like they'd been starved their entire lives. By the grunts and happy noises, I assumed they liked my cooking. That was confirmed when all three went back for a second helping.

"Holy fuck, I think that's the best thing I have ever eaten" Salem announced, leaning back in his chair and unbuttoning his pants. "You really know what you're talking about, baby".

Finishing the last of my own food, I smiled to myself. As Dario, Salem and Enzo all discussed how good my food was, I realised that I had been wrong. I could do this. I could be married to all of them. Whatever we had between us, the four of us worked together.

Like Enzo had explained to me, each man brought something different and together it filled everything in my life that I wanted or needed.

The four of us could create a perfectly balanced marriage.

I was still going to make them work for their wedding rings back, because I deserved some control, but I was actually excited for them to truly be my husbands.

CHAPTER NINETEEN

Salem

Two weeks with Vannah living with us went by in a blast. Dario, Enzo and I had worked like dogs the entire time – but it was nice to always come home to a mind blowing amazing dinner cooked by our wife. I could get used to having a little domestic goddess at home, if I only I had the sex part of the marriage too.

I knew it would only be a matter of time. She was comfortable around us now, enough to give us goodbye kisses each and allow us little touches and hugs. If we weren't so damn busy, we could spend more time pushing things to the next level. We'd get there soon enough. My brain understood this, but my penis was desperate for her.

As I was thinking of ways to spend a little alone time with Vannah, my cell phone rang. I was driving, so I used my hands free. "Yeah?" I answered.

"Mr Galluci, it is Chief Morn" the police chief replied. I rolled my eyes but didn't hang up.

"I hope this isn't about the dead man under Mr Conti's car. Mrs Conti gave some yahoo her statement last week" I stated. A twitchy little detective had come by the house a few days after Johnny's death to get Giovannah's statement – our girl had been vague but detailed, which was perfect but drove the detective crazy.

"Oh no Mr Galluci" Morn babbled quickly. He knew what happened to people who pissed me off, so he wouldn't dare. He'd seen the bodies – fuck, when I first became enforcer I left bodies all over the city to make sure everyone knew what I did when people pissed me off. "I'm calling because the ME just finished the autopsy of those three women found off Judson".

The three missing escorts. We hadn't wanted to involve the police, but they had been fucked up so badly we couldn't be sure it was them. We had lots of people in our pockets, but didn't have the ability to identify mutilated corpses. "Tell me everything you know".

"We confirmed through dental records the remains

belonged to; Denise Smithson, Maria Lopez and Caroline Nowitzki" he began. "All three girl's COD was blood loss. The sick son of a bitch who killed them, simply beat them and cut them so much they all just succumbed to their injuries. None of them had been sexually assaulted, although Caroline Nowitzki was mutilated repeatedly in her genitals. They were also found with a high level of barbiturates in their systems".

"So they were drugged, kidnapped and then mutilated when they were brought to a second location". I was speaking out loud, trying to work things through, but Morn answered anyway.

"Seems like it, whoever did this is a sadistic son of a bitch. Not to mention, angry. The bodies had so much overkill, even after they were dead this psycho keep stabbing and beating the bodies. That much rage seems personal to me".

"Sure, but personal to who is the question here" I sighed heavily. "Thank you for all your help, Chief, if you could send all this over to me in an email that would be great".

"Of course, Mr Galluci, I will do that right now".

"Any identification on our Hispanic friend yet?" Hours before the escorts went missing, a young Hispanic male with the Luis Morales Cartel tattoo on his skin was found dead. He'd been shot, execution style, in the alley behind Conti Gold. We'd destroyed the body immediately, but we'd still had Morn take fingerprints and pictures of his body first so we could identify him. We didn't need the cartel finding out one of their own has been murdered in Conti territory – that was just asking for a gang war.

"Nothing yet. But don't worry, if he's even been picked up for jay walking before, we'll find him" he promised, before saying his goodbye.

I completed the rest of the drive, contemplating that information. If the same person who killed Johnny, also killed the three escorts, then I was confused at their end goal. If they were looking for chaos for chaos reasons, then I was going to be sure not to give it to them. I didn't care what they did in our territory, I sure as I hell wouldn't let them derail the Conti hold on Vegas.

I finally got to my destination, a warehouse in Boulder City, just as my phone rang again. I considered ignoring it, until I saw it was Vannah. She'd not called me before and I instantly got a tight gut of worry. I answered quickly, "Vannah? Are you alright?"

"I got your flowers" she replied coyly. My heart rate slowed back down as I relaxed. I shouldn't have worried; Enzo was still working from home with her until we found an appropriate bodyguard.

"Oh, did you like them?" In a bid to get my wedding ring *on*, and Vannah's clothes *off*, I had sent her a large bouquet of red, yellow, white and black flowers this morning.

"They're beautiful, Salem, but I can't say the same for the adjoining card". Her voice told me that she was not amused – but I also knew that Vannah secretly enjoyed my flirting. To offset the beautiful roses, the card had a little poem I had written to her.

Red because I want you lying in my bed.
Yellow because I'm your perfect fellow.
White because your pussy is such a delight.
Black because I can't wait to get you in the sack.

"You didn't like my poem?" I smirked.

"I'm sure Byron is spinning in his grave" she snorted. I could picture her shaking her head, as her lips pulled at the corners in barely hidden amusement. "But despite the poem, which by the way sounds like it was written by a horny twelve year old, the flowers are beautiful".

"Good, I was thinking about maybe taking you out tonight".

"Like a date?"

"Not 'like' a date, an actual date. I'd like to take my beautiful wife out and show her a good time. What do you think? Will you be ready for eight o'clock?"

There was a long pause from Vannah, before she sighed heavily. "What's the dress code?"

"Slutty".

"No idiot, I mean formal or unformal. Heels or walking boots".

"Sexy but we'll be doing a bit of walking outside, so a jacket and sneakers are probably best" I admitted.

"Fine" she sighed, as if I was asking a big task of her. I grinned to myself; damn I loved my girl. "If this is a first date, I expect you to be a true gentleman".

"Oh, Little V, I am nothing if not a true gentleman".

"Uh-huh. Goodbye Salem". She hung up without another word, as I struggled to wipe the grin off my face. But, I took a moment to push the happiness away, before pulling on my mask of darkness. Taking my gun from my holster, I stepped out the car.

Inside the warehouse, workers shuffled around as they busied themselves with shipping stolen good to different places. I walked all the way through the lower floor, without making eye contact with anyone, before finding the manager's office out back. I didn't knock, just pushed my way inside.

Aiden McGregor's face turned in annoyance, as he looked up at who stormed into his office without knocking. His expression cooled instantly when he saw who it was. "Mr Galluci" he jumped to his feet, "we weren't expecting a visit today".

"I'm just going around the city, reminding people" I smirked, pushing the office door closed behind me.

Aiden eyed the gun in my hands, but tried to stay

cool. "Remind them of what exactly?"

I shrugged, "just reminding them". I gave him my perfect 'I'm a crazy motherfucker' smile, before perching on the corner of his desk. "See the Conti's have always had a good relationship with everyone around here, because everyone has their own thing. We deal in sex and money. Bianchi filter drugs through us. The Russians deal in weapons. The Irish deal in stolen goods. And the Eastern Europeans stay the fuck out the way".

"Right" Aiden said slowly, "I can promise that we're staying in our lane, if that's what you're getting at". The older Irish man glanced around the room, wondering at what scale of sanity I was at.

"Let's hope you are. Because a few rumours are flying around out there at the moment, Aiden, and I would hate for some of them to be true".

He gulped, "rumours?"

I changed the subject – let him sweat the idea of rumours about his loyalty. "Luis Morales, and his cartel, have their eyes on our territory. And, that's fine, they can look but as long as they don't touch we'll have no problems. But, when some people in the Conti employment start turning up dead, I can't help but think that Morales is trying to piss me off".

He shook his head thoroughly as I watched him. The Irish were a small gang, most of their money coming from illegally shipped cigarettes and alcohol, but you could never trust any ex-IRA fuckers to be loyal.

So, sometimes they needed to be reminded just how easily little gangs could be squished. "I know nothing about no cartel".

"Good, let's keep it that way, Aiden". I leant over and gave him a condescending pat on his cheek. "Now if you know anything about my dead people, it would be your time to start talking now". I shifted the gun in my hand just a little, to remind him it was there.

"I swear, Mr Galluci, I hadn't heard anything. But I can ask around, get some of my men to put their ears to the floor and see what they can find out". His voice was bordering on desperation. Oh yeah, Aiden McGregor knew what I did to people that displeased me. His brother had displeased me once. Aiden was an only child presently.

"Good" I stood up and put my gun into my holster. "I'll swing by on Friday and I expect you to have something good to tell me". I gave him a crazy grin, "if you don't have anything useful…well maybe we can some fun". Aiden had a full body shiver in fear.

Ah, I wasn't sure what I loved more. My Giovannah or my ability to make grown men piss their pants. Both got me equally hard.

CHAPTER TWENTY

Vannah

Dario and Enzo were home before Salem, but he had made them aware of his evening plans – so they talked about heading out to one of the casinos for an evening of work and gambling. As they discussed business, I readied for my 'date' with Salem. His flowers had been beautiful and even his stupid poem had made me smile.

I had decided that jeans, and flat boots, were the way to go. But, considering Salem's 'sexy' brief, I had paired it with a red low cut shirt. As I finished my makeup, I heard the garage open and a few minutes later I heard Salem's voice as he spoke to Dario and Enzo. I did my signature red lip before heading downstairs to meet him.

Salem gave a wolf whistle when I walked into the lounge. "Damn look at my girl". He wrapped his hands around my waist and tugged me flush against his body, as his eyes dipped into my cleavage.

"Our girl" Dario corrected, standing up and pushing Salem away from me. He gave his friend a cool look, "and since you're about to get her for the night, I'm stealing her for ten minutes". He grabbed me around the waist and picked me up easily. I yelped in shock as he perched me on the back of the couch.

"Dario" I warned him, as he stood in between my legs with his arms still around me.

"What? I'm not allowed to give my wife a goodbye kiss?"

"Does a goodbye kiss really need for you to be wrapped around me?" I shot back, making Enzo chuckle from the other side of the room.

"Hell yeah it does" Dario smirked, before capturing my lips. I melted into his kiss, it was hot and passionate, and I was completely whisked away in lust. Not being able to help myself, my arms went around his neck as he brought our bodies flushed together. He felt like sin but tasted like heaven.

When Dario's hand came up and cupped the side of my breast, Salem finally spoke up. "Alright, alright". He pushed Dario's head away, making him stumble when he lost his balance. Once more Enzo just laughed. "You got her on the wedding night, time to share".

"I can share, but I just needed to remind Vannah who kisses the best" Dario smirked, before giving me a cocky smile and wink. He leant down and whispered, not so quietly, in my ear. "If Salem can't get you wet tonight, just remember how much I can make you cum and maybe that will help".

"Dickhead" Salem commented, kicking him like he was a child. "I have no problem making our girl's eyes roll into her head".

I sighed heavily and looked over my shoulder at a smirking Enzo. "You're the only one not being an asshole. You want to take me out instead?"

He boomed a laugh, as Salem gave a noise of outrage. Enzo walked over to me and pressed a kiss to my forehead. "I don't need to fight over you, Giovannah. As I'm the only one who has had you on your knees".

"Wait? What?" Dario demanded, eyes wide at Enzo.

"When the fuck did this happen?" Salem asked.

Enzo just smirked, "have fun, Giovannah. Come on D, we need to get going". He gave Dario a pat on the shoulder and walked out the room and towards the garage. I giggled at his shocked face, before he shook his head and followed his friend out.

Salem gave me a small smile the moment we were alone. "Giovannah Conti, you're secretly a bad girl". He wrapped his arms around my waist and pulled me to him. "Are you ready for the best night of your life?"

I rolled my eyes, "let's just get this over with".

"That's the spirit, baby". He smacked a kiss on my lips, before leading me to the garage. We climbed into a black sports car and he drove us out the estate. Silently, we wound through the streets.

"Are we going to be safe tonight?" I questioned, hating that I sounded cowardly. I hadn't been out of the estate since Johnny had been killed, so I was nervous.

"Don't worry, Little V, you'll always be safe with me" Salem replied seriously. "Plus I'm looking at getting you a full time bodyguard and I have all the prospects auditioning tonight". He gave me a look that was full of mischief and I rolled my eyes again.

We drove for about forty five minutes before I got excited, as we parked outside a brightly lit fairground. I grinned like a child at Salem, "seriously? A fairground?"

"Well you said you wanted us to prove we were the husbands you would want. And, according to most romcoms, I needed to woo you with a magical first date. So according to all these movies, the best choices were a fairground in which I would kiss you at the top of the ferris wheel or a hot air balloon. So the obvious choice was the ferris wheel kiss".

"I'll make you a deal" I smiled, as I climbed out the

car.

"Oh yeah?"

"You win me three stuffed toys and I'll kiss you on top of the ferris wheel".

Salem chuckled softly, "three huh?"

"What can I say? I'm growing fond of the number". I shrugged, giving him a teasing smile, as he rounded the car and took my hand. "And I expect three different teddy bears. One for each of my... gemstones". I held up my ring hand so the three gems caught the distant light.

Salem leant down so that his lips were a brush away from mine. "Deal".

✝

Two hours later, I was full up on cotton candy and junk food. I had two stuffed toys under my left arm as I watched Salem prepare to dunk mini basketballs for my third. I giggled as the ball bounced off the rim. "This is rigged. It's fucking rigged" Salem yelled, pointing angrily. I laughed more, as he got angry and tried again. "Bastard".

"Salem" I laughed, "there are children around".

"Stupid fucking rigged fucking bastard game" he

swore. I saw a few people giving us dirty looks as I just continued to cry with laughter. He cussed so much; I was surprised women weren't clutching their pearls in horror. Salem threw the basketball and missed once more. "Fuck it". He pulled cash from his pocket and held it out to the man running the game. "Just give me a toy and I'll pay for it".

"Um no" I cut in, pushing his hand down before the man could accept the money. "The deal was that you had to *win* the toys. You can't pay for them".

Salem growled at me, "I already won you two, is that not enough?"

"Maybe I could say the same about men in my life? I've already got Dario and Enzo...do I really need Salem as well? Surely two is enough".

"Damn" Salem groaned under his breath, before looking around. "Fuck this game, let's find another one". Taking my hand, he dragged me through the crowds of people and passed games booths. He stopped at a shooting one. "Finally". He pointed at the air-rifle like a child, "gimme".

He got the bullseye in one shot and gave a childish 'whoop' of happiness. I rolled my eyes at him, but couldn't help mirroring his giant grin. Salem was so happy in his own skin that it was infectious. Salem knew exactly who he was; he could be childish at a fairground, be a dangerous murderer and an outrageous flirt. Those were all just part of him and he had made peace with all of them.

He had two more shots so he took them, just to prove he could, before he let me pick the stuffed toy I wanted. I looked over the cheap toys as if they were thousand dollar purses – because I felt like they were. They felt more important than any piece of jewellery I owed, excluding the wedding rings around my neck.

"The wolf" I decided, pointing to a smaller white wonky-faced wolf toy.

"You sure? Three bullseyes mean one of the large toys" the man behind the booth said, pointing to the stuff toys that were almost the same size as me.

I laughed, "I'll take the small one thanks". He shrugged and passed me the small wolf, before Salem and I moved away.

"Are you happy now?" Salem smiled, "you got your three stuffed animals".

"Don't you want to know which one you are?"

He raised an eyebrow, "these animals are supposed to represent us?"

"Of course". I held up the three toys – a black bear, a purple pony and a white wolf. "The black bear is Enzo. Large, dependable but a little grouchy". I explained, making Salem chuckled softly. "The wolf is Dario. Cunning, loyal and possessive over his family".

"Hold on? That makes me the purple pony?" Salem exclaimed, pretending to be outraged. I laughed warmly, as he put his arm around my waist to pull me closer. "I feel like I've drawn the short straw here".

"Don't you want to know why I picked the purple pony?"

"Fine, rip me to pieces".

"You're a horse, or a pony as that was all they had, because you're strong and noble. You're loyal to your friends but you have complete freedom in who you are. That's why I picked the purple one. Because you're fun and flirty, not caring what people think of you. I have no doubt you could dye your hair purple and somehow people would still be scared of you".

Salem whisked me into a passionate kiss. "Alright, I'll take that. I agree with everything you just said, but I'm not a pony I'm a stallion".

I raised an eyebrow at him, "oh really?"

"Oh yeah. I'm stallion because I can't wait to put a baby in my mare". With that he grabbed me by the waist, causing me to yelp in shock, before carrying me through the fairground and to the ferris wheel – where I kissed him at the top, just like I promised I would.

CHAPTER TWENTY ONE

Vannah

A hand curled around my neck, as I reached the car. I gasped in shock, as Salem spun me to face him – a wicked look in his eyes. "It's the end of a date. Do I not get a kiss?" he smirked, backing me up against the car.

"You had a kiss on the top of the ferris wheel" I mused, but didn't pull away from him.

"That was a kiss on the lips". He put his lips by my ear, "I want a kiss someplace else". To make his point clear, he pressed his groin against my stomach – the beginning of an erection pressing against me. "I want a kiss that's nice and slow and warm".

"I thought you were a true gentleman, Mr Galluci?"

"Oh baby, I am nothing but that. I won your deal, so how about I make one this time. You give me a mind *blowing* kiss and I'll return the favour". Salem trailed kisses over my neck, making a shiver rack through my spine. Instantly my underwear became wet and my heart sped. These men were truly irresistible.

"Hmm". I pressed tightly against him, getting his eyes to shine in lust. "I guess I could consider the deal. But, just a kiss?"

Hands clasped onto my hips, "I'd give you whatever the hell you want, Little V. A kiss? Absolutely. More than a kiss? No doubt. Heck, you want me to knock you up right now? Baby, I've waiting to do that for four years".

I was quiet for a long moment, trying to work out how serious he was. But his eyes were open and honest. "You really mean that don't you?" I whispered.

"The first time I saw you, it was at your grandfather's funeral. You were playing with two kids and it was like a lightning bolt hit me. Because I realised that that was exactly what I wanted. I wanted you, and you to be like that with kids of my own. And then someone came out and took the kids, their mother obviously. And that look on your face? That look of pure desire to be a mother". Salem rested his forehead against mine. "I had to physically stop myself from going out there and putting a baby in your stomach".

"It was probably my niece and nephew".

"Not a day goes by, since then, that I don't dream of a future with you. I think the reason that Dario, Enzo and I have such a strong bond, is that we all had shitty parents. I mean, my parents are nothing on Enzo's mother, but they are still not worth much. All I want is a family, to be a proper father, and I want to do that all with you".

Tears brimmed in my eyes as I looked up at him. "I want that too". His thumb brushed a tear away, and he pressed a kiss to my forehead. I sniffed and wiped my eyes, as I stepped away from Salem. "Can we go home now?"

"What about that kiss?"

I laughed through my last few tears. "You get me home and I'll give you more than a kiss".

"Deal". He winked at me playfully before we got into the car and headed back to Conti Manor.

We spoke a little on the way home, but mainly we drove in a comfortable silence. "I didn't see the bodyguards tonight" I finally commented, as we got through the estate gates.

"That was the point, for them to blend. I saw them, they were there. I think I know which I will have as your personal guard, while I'll hire the others as general security" Salem explained.

"Why am I being targeted?" I asked, as he parked the car.

Salem sighed heavily, "we think a cartel is behind this, they've been trying to move their drugs into Vegas for a while but we've been keeping them out. The Bianchi's have been bringing in their products for us to distribute, so maybe because you're both Dario's wife and a Bianchi they want to separate the two groups so they can bring their drugs in".

"That makes sense, I guess".

Salem took my hand and walked me into the house. I called out for Dario and Enzo, but they were still out. "Looks like we've got the place to ourselves" he smirked, pushing me up against the banister. I giggled as he kissed me, his lips igniting the lust from earlier and making my knees feel weak and my stomach flipped in excitement.

I let Salem lead me upstairs and to his bedroom. His room was busy, with lots of pictures and trinkets, and was brightly coloured. Oh the purple pony was perfect for Salem. My husband led me to the bed, sitting me down on the edge. He gave me a sweet smile, rare for the flirty bastard. "We really don't need to have sex, Vannah. You're in charge here, you make the decisions around here. We had an amazing date, I'm happy to have just spent the evening with you".

I smiled up at him. "I want you Salem, I want to have sex with you". I pulled him down onto the bed next to me and our lips quickly found each other. His large, callous, hands cupped the back of my head as we kissed. My body pressed flush to his side, as the heat of his body drew me in.

Being with him, with Salem, was different. There were no marriage papers, or ethical bonds, that dictated that I was to sleep with him. Having sex with Salem was to be my own choice, simply because I wanted too and not because I felt like I needed to or had to. I had wanted to have sex with Dario, on our wedding night, but that was because I was excited to get to know him and start a life together. Sex with Salem was simply because I wanted to have sex with Salem.

Our kisses turned from loving into lustful quickly. Salem's hand moved down and cupped my breasts over my shirt and squeezed. I giggled as I arched my back to give him more to cup, feeling giddy like I was drunk. "You're so…different" I commented between kisses.

Salem pulled back, raising an eyebrow comically. "Different how?"

"I've only ever been with two guys. Aldo and Dario and they're both so typical in who they are. Suave, sophisticated and charming".

Salem snorted, "that old fart was not any of those things".

I rolled my eyes, "you know what I mean. They're both typical mafia men, whereas you're so different from what I'm used to. Tattooed, brash and covered in leather".

He threw back his head in a hearty laugh. "Giovannah Conti, am I the equivalent of your high school bad boy?"

"Well, we're a mafia family, so that doesn't really work. But, if Dario and Enzo are bad boys, then what does that make you?"

His teeth nibbled at my ear, "darling, I'm your own personal psychopath".

His fingers tweak my nipples, as he kissed me deeply again. My hands ran up and down his chest, feeling his built up muscles, as our groins began to rub together through our clothes. Pulling back, Salem pulled my shirt off, before reaching around and unclasping my bra. He threw both across his room, uncaring. His eyes scanned over my naked top half. "Fuck me" he breathed out, shaking his head and smirking proudly. "Now that is a sight".

Grabbing me, he pulled me back down to him. I straddled his waist, as we began to make out once more. I could feel his erection stirring in his jeans under me – which just spurred me on to deepen the kiss. His hands ran over the span of my back, warming me better than any fire ever could.

I shivered, as his tongue teased mine and I moaned as his hands slipped up to my chest. As soon as I moaned, I felt his erection spring straight up in jeans, and I felt desire circling my stomach I knew that we were past the 'talking' and 'joking' part of the night. The only words we would be trading were dirty talk from that moment on.

Salem trailed his kisses down my neck and to my chest. I sucked in a deep breath, as he took one of my nipples into his mouth, making me squeal. He laughed as he teased my breast, so I ground my hips against his erection in reply. He groaned around my nipple as I did so.

My hands slipped to his back and pushed his shirt up. I felt his scorching skin underneath my fingertips – alighting the desire between my legs. Salem pulled away for barely a second, to remove his shirt, and grin at me. "Fuck" was all he said and all he needed to say.

His chest was beautiful; sculpted and large, with deep contours highlighting his six pack. All the skin covered in colourful tattoos that were pure works of art. I ran my hands over the muscles as I bent down and brought our lips back together.

Salem moved his lips over my flaming skin, paying attention to my neck and collar bones, before reaching his goal of my chest once more. I moaned again, as his tongue tickled my nipple, and my hands slipped down to grasp his belt. I hastily unfastened it.

"God I want you so bad" Salem moaned against my skin, I rubbed against his erection through his boxers as I pushed his jeans down.

"You got me. Take me" I breathed out, chest heavily rising as I looked over him with satisfaction. He spun us quickly, laying me back against his pillows, before standing up he quickly kicked his jeans off from around his ankles. I raised my hips and pulled my own jeans off. His eyes cast over my almost naked body with scorching heat.

I knelt on the bed in front of him, bringing our lips together again, as my hand slipped into his boxers. Salem made me feel confident, because *I* chose sex and *I* chose him. He groaned in delight as I pleasured him with my hand – as his hands ran over my body once more. Lust spurred us on fast, but our bodies were in no rush to speed through.

Salem ran his hand between my legs, his fingers running over my sensitive clit through the material of my underwear. Desire shot through my body as I soaked through my underwear in excitement. I knew he felt it, because his cock gave a small jump in my hand.

He pushed me back onto the bed, my hand leaving his boxers as he climbed over me. Salem started the kisses once more, beginning on my neck before trailing them down my body, paying special attention to my chest and stomach. The cold metal of his tongue stud sending shivers over my skin. I squirmed desperately as he reached my navel, and his index fingers slipped into the waist band of my panties. I was desperate for them to go.

Slowly he peeled my panties off, admiring the view of my completely nude figure as he did so. Once they were off he threw them over his shoulder, as he grabbed my legs and pulled them apart even further. He ran his kisses up my legs and to my inner thigh. I moaned as he bit onto the flesh – turning me on even more than I thought possible. The memories of the last time he'd gone down on me, in my own closet, made me even wetter. He gave unbelievable head and I wanted it again.

When his lips finally touched my delicate spot, I threw my head back and moaned. I could feel Salem smirking as he went down on me. My hands slipped into his hair, as I held him against my cunt, as my legs wrapped around him. I moaned and struggled to breathe as he put his dexterous tongue to work.

"Oh god, Salem, don't ever get rid of that piercing". My head flopped backwards, as I felt my climax beginning. "No" I complained, when he pulled away from me – seconds before my orgasm hit. Salem laughed warmly, as he looked up at me with wicked eyes.

"I'm not going to let you cum until I'm inside of you" he purred, looking at me like I was his prey. "You're going to cum, and then I'm going to cum and we're going to make a fucking baby". He moved up the bed, and I grabbed him tightly, as we brought our lips back together. I could taste myself on the tip of his tongue for a moment, before it was taken over by the overwhelming taste of *him* that exploded in my mouth.

"Salem, please, I need you" I whispered to him. I didn't care I sounded desperate, I didn't care it didn't make me seem 'cool' or 'composed'. I didn't need to hide with Salem, there were no barriers and no expectations. I kissed him with everything I had.

Our lips carried on battling, before he ran the tip of his cock over my core a few times, causing me to moan. "I've been dreaming about this for so many years". Salem's lips brushed my neck, his facial hair tickling the sensitive area, as he pulled my skin between his teeth. I breathed out, as I buckled my hips into his as I tried to get some much needed friction from him.

"You ready for me, Little V?"

"Yeah. Salem, I need you now, please" I begged him – I didn't even care how I needy I must have seemed to him. All I knew was that I needed him or might just have died.

"Anything for you" he told me sweetly. Salem kissed me deeply, as he pushed himself into me. I moaned deeply, as he filled me. "Fuck, you feel amazing" he complimented me. I looked into his eyes and for a moment neither of us moved. "So tight and so wet for me. Oh my wife, you're so perfect".

"Salem" I sighed, shivers running over my entire body. We paused for a moment, both of us breathing in each other. Carefully, I reached up and cupped his cheek, feeling his short beard against my fingers.

"Thank you for the best date of my life. I will always cherish that memory, my purple pony".

"I will always cherish you too, Vannah. The love of my life, the wife of my dreams, the mother of my future children". His forehead rested against mine. I didn't respond to the 'love' comment, but I also wasn't shocked. Salem was someone who said everything he felt without care who heard. I wasn't there myself, but the idea of someone loving me, and truly choosing me, was enough to start me on that track.

Salem gave me a small smile, before kissing me deeply. His tongue piercing slid across my tongue, forcing a small moan from me. Salem deepened the kiss, before he began thrusting. Moving in and out of me with firm, definitive, hip gyrations that had me begging for more. I brought my hips up to meet him, and soon we were working together in quick, passionate, thrusts.

After a while, when my orgasm was building, Salem pulled out of me and spun me around onto my front. He bit down on my shoulder as he slid back into from behind, before we picked up our pace once more. "Salem I'm almost there" I breathed out, hands gripping onto the sheets.

"No" he complained, pulling out of me and turning back to face him. "I want you to look at me when you cum". We kissed again, and once more he slid into me. We quickly got back into our rhythm, him leading with me trying as hard as I could to not fall over the edge. But my vision was spotting and my abdominal muscles were beginning to spasm.

"I'm coming" I told him, as I looked into his beautiful brown eyes.

"Come for me, Vannah, let me hear you come for me". And for him, I did.

CHAPTER TWENTY TWO

Vannah

For the next five days, Dario was livid with envy. It didn't help that Salem kept rubbing my stomach, making comments on how we'd had so much sex he wouldn't be surprised if I gave birth to a whole football team of his babies in nine months. Enzo wasn't jealous that Salem and I had had sex – and that I had also spent the past five days in his bed – but he was just full of wishful thinking that I would make my way to his bed soon, while still making sure I was happy and healthy. Dario...not so much.

My 'legal husband' walked around with a permanent scowl of annoyance. Every touch, or kiss, or look between Salem and I just pushed his foul mood further and further. He was perfectly nice to me, kissing me hello and goodbye and always complimenting my cooking, but his eyes looked at Salem with murder. Pure green eyed jealousy – Salem assured me he'd get over it when I decided to spend another night in Dario's bed again. He was just sexually frustrated and addicted to a girl he'd only had once, almost a month ago.

Opening the floodgates of my desire, with Salem, actually made me want to take a step further with both Enzo and Dario. Salem wasn't jealous of sharing my time, heck if anything he was excited for me to be with the other men as well as him. I was still hesitant with the idea, but I found myself wanting it, wanting them. I felt greedy with my men – because, they were, *my* men. But, Dario's childish pouting made me decide to punish him just a little more. Just in case he forgot who was in charge.

Since I had married Dario, things had been a little crazy – both with the marriage, and with that first week of murders and beheadings. But, whatever that craziness was, it seemed to have calmed down. No mention of cartel problems, no more attempted shootings at me and no more missing escorts. Whatever had been happening seemed to have quietened down. So, Dario informed me that Friday we were spending the evening at Conti Deco. Apparently most Friday nights were spent at one of his casinos, the three of them – and now including me – used the night as a chance to catch up and relax after busy weekdays.

So, at seven thirty on Friday, I was dressed up and waiting for Enzo to finish on his phone call. Enzo was still working at home mostly, despite my new full time bodyguard Aliza. I had spent the week in the garden, covered in soil and loving it, but it was nice to dress up again. I had been doing some online shopping with Dario's card – or, well, the card he put in my name that went to his bank account. I might have gone a little crazy.

When Salem had told me that Conti Deco was themed on the nineteen twenties, I had decided that I was going to honour the dress code. I had brought myself a silver dress, with hanging bead details, and a back so low that it rested just above the curve of my rear – from the front it was classic flapper, but at the back it was a bit slapper. I'd even brought myself a love-heart shaped clutch bag, which was also covered in hanging diamante beads.

"Holy shit" Enzo muttered, as I met him at the front door. He looked me up and down appreciatively. Feeling cheeky, and flirty, I gave him a twirl. He cussed under his breath as he looked at the backless dress. "You might just kill Dario tonight" he laughed darkly.

Getting up on my tiptoes – despite having heels on – I gave Enzo a small kiss on the lips. "You know I haven't chosen Salem over you and Dario, right?"

His arms went around me, his large hands spreading

over my bare back. "I know that, Giovannah, and Dario does to. But, Dario is used to getting his own way, and what he wants is you". He gave me a sweet passionate kiss. "There is no timeline with us, things move as they move. You know I want you and I hope you'll want me back at some point. But, honestly, I'd be happy just being your friend for the rest of my life".

My heart melted a little. Enzo had such a sweet side to him that it always surprised me, because his intimidating appearance was so juxtaposed. But, I liked that about him. I knew that Enzo would only ever show *me* that side of him – that made me feel so special that it scared me.

I gave him a small smile, "you keep saying stuff like that and you'll be the first to get your ring back". I reached up and touched the three wedding rings around my neck. Salem had been hinting that since we had been having sex, that he should get his back. But, as much as I liked him, I wasn't in love with him. These rings deserved to be worn by men that I was in love with.

Cal, the new head of our security, drove us to Conti Capital in a stretch town car with bulletproof glass. The oldest casino that Dario – or well, Dario and myself I guessed – owed was a little off the strip, so we swung by to pick him and Salem up first.

The door to the back of the car opened, before my other two husbands climbed into the car. Salem looked me up and down, eyes shining bright with lust as he looked me over. "Holy shit" he grinned like a cheshire cat. "You look unbelievable". He moved to sit next to me, but Dario pushed him out the way to slide in between us.

"We're going into public" Dario muttered, turning and giving his friend a death look. Salem just grinned in reply, like a naughty school boy. "She's my wife in public".

"Sure, but she's mainly my wife in private" he taunted back.

Before the car could even pull away from the curb, Dario opened the door once more and pushed Salem straight back out again. Salem fell backwards out the door, letting a cuss in shock as his leather clad ass hit the sidewalk. Enzo pushed the drivers speaker button instantly, "hold here for a little while, Cal. These two dickheads need to Mike Tyson each other for a few minutes".

"Sure thing" Cal chirped back, as Dario followed Salem out the car. Salem jumped to his feet, his lips growling in anger. His arm pulled back, before he swung a punch straight at Dario's stomach. He wheezed at the impact, before punching him back.

Enzo leant over, pulled the door shut once more, just as the two idiots tackled each other to the ground. "They're fighting" I commented, frowning in both annoyance and upset. Annoyance because this arrangement was supposed to work because they weren't jealous of each other, and upset because I didn't like the idea of coming between two men who were practically brothers.

"The three of us fight all the time. We're men, we don't talk about our feelings, we punch them out instead". He pulled me over his lap.

"That's an awful stereotype, Enzo" I rolled my eyes, "men are just as able to talk about their feelings. You just think being meatheads is easier". As I said that, there was a bang against the side of the car, before Dario swore at Salem in Italian. "They're going to hurt each other".

"Nah, they never aim for the face or the gonads" he shrugged. Another bang sounded on the side of the car, as Enzo just got his phone from his pocket and began to scroll through the New York Times as if he didn't have a care in the world. A third, and final, crash against the car sounded before it went quiet.

A few minutes later, the door opened and Dario and Salem climbed back in together. They were both red faced and breathing hard, but neither were sporting blood or visible wounds. Enzo put his phone away and pressed the intercom. "All good, Cal, continue on to Deco as planned".

"Sure thing boss" Cal chirped back, before the car pulled away from the sidewalk.

I frowned at my two idiot husbands, "was that really necessary?"

"Absolutely" Salem grinned, "asshole needed to remember that you chose who you fuck and when".

Dario rolled his eyes, "I remembered. Didn't mean you weren't being a douchebag though".

"Why don't you both just shut up and focus on how hot our wife looks tonight?" Enzo shot out, speaking before either of them could start up another fight. Grabbing my waist, he spun me around and had me straddle him. Both Dario and Salem let out a soft 'whoosh' of air at seeing that my dress was backless.

"Damn baby" Salem whistled.

"You're trying to kill me" Dario moaned, reaching over and running a finger down my spine. A shiver of desire shot through me at his touch. He was like fire and I was like ice – one touch had me melting.

The three of them together were like an inferno, it was no wonder I had melted around them so fast.

CHAPTER TWENTY THREE

Dario

Eyes followed her everywhere she went. As they should, she looked like a movie star. She walked gracefully and seemed to float across the ground in her heels. And the best part of it all, was that she was on my arm. My arm, my wife, my Vannah.

Vannah was so beautiful, and sexy, that if I didn't get to be inside her again soon I might have to physically drug myself to stay away from her. My entire body was tight with tension and need. I had desired many women before, but I had never needed someone like I did with Vannah.

We started the night in the restaurant, the four of

us in a booth eating steak and drinking champagne while chatting happily about our week. My brothers and I listened silently, all of us in awe of our wife, as Vannah told us about her yard projects. Honestly, we didn't even care what she talked about, it was just blissful to have the girl we'd all been obsessed with for years with us and happy.

I knew I needed to apologise to Vannah, as I had been a moody bastard for the past week or so. She'd been having sex with Salem, which didn't bother me, but I'd been taking my sexual frustration out on Salem – which made Vannah uncomfortable. I never wanted to make her uncomfortable.

"I got you a gift" I said, as we finished eating and poured the last of the champagne.

"For me?" Vannah grinned.

"Well he doesn't have interest in fucking us, Little V" Salem snorted, winking at her. I rolled my eyes at him, before pulling the Cartier box from my pocket and slid it across the table to her.

Her beautiful brown eyes glistened in excitement as she took the velvet box. "You didn't need to get me anything, Dario". Even as she spoke, her hands were opening the box. She gasped as she looked at the bracelet inside. I had considered a necklace, but with our wedding rings still around her neck, I decided to get jewellery for a different part of her anatomy.

"It's beautiful" she grinned. I took the bracelet from the box and fastened it around her wrist. It was a delicate gold chain with small sapphire jewels hanging on it.

"So you're my sapphire, huh?" she mused, a finger running over her black wedding ring. I just smiled softly. But yeah, I was the sapphire, Salem was the emerald and Enzo was the citrine. We all had our own gemstone but our favourite was ruby, always ruby.

Vannah leant across the table and kissed me. The kiss was quick and contained, but there was still heat there. Her eyes glistened and I relaxed – she'd allow me back into her bed soon, maybe even tonight if the lust in her eyes said anything.

Just as we finished the last of our drinks, a familiar man in a suit came over to the table. "Mr Conti" James nodded, as he approached the table. "I wasn't aware you were here tonight. Do you need your office set up?"

"No work tonight, James" I replied. I gestured to Vannah across the table. "James, have you met my wife yet?"

James turned to Vannah; his eyes widened slightly as he took in her undeniable beauty. "No, I haven't yet". He held his hand out. "Mrs Conti, it is a pleasure to meet you".

"Giovannah" she replied, shaking his hand.

"James is the manager here" I explained, before turning back to him. "Please get a private room set up for us with a blackjack table and a dealer".

"Of course, I'll do that now" James smiled. He said goodbye, before clicking his fingers and sending a waitress over with another bottle of top shelf champagne. We drank another glass; I could see that Vannah was getting a little tipsy – as did Enzo who topped up her water as well. Before we finish the new bottle, James returned and told us a private room was ready.

We stood up again, and my already frustrated cock twitched as Vannah stood up – giving me her back. Her dress was extremely tight, and the back stopped less than an inch above her ass. If I wanted to, I could slip my finger under the seam and into her ass cheeks. It took all my restraint, to place my hand on her naked lower back. By the smiles of amusement that Enzo and Salem had – they also enjoyed the view and struggled with the same internal thoughts that I did.

James led us to a private room and I was glad. Too many men were looking at my wife. Like yes, she was unbelievably sexy, but the outright staring was too much. They were lucky I didn't punch their eyes back into their sockets. Salem obviously agreed, as his hands clenched into fists and he glared at any man, who stared too long, with murderous intent.

I curled Vannah closer into my side. She smiled up at me; lust still in her eyes which just fed my own. She rested her hand on my chest as we walked together, weaving through our casino. *Our* casino, *our* life together. "I'm sorry about the fighting earlier, Mrs Conti" I whispered into her ear.

"You have nothing to worry about, Mr Conti" she replied, resting her head on my shoulder as we walked into the private room. I nodded James out, as Enzo and Salem followed us in. The private room had its own mini bar, two sofas and a poker table with a dealer already setting up a game of blackjack.

The four of us sat and played a few games, before I could see Vannah's attention dwindling. When the game finished, I tipped the dealer and told him he could leave us alone now. He thanked us, before leaving us in the room alone. "Are we done for the evening?" Vannah asked.

"Nope" I grinned, grabbing Vannah's waist and lifting her onto the table. She yelped in shock, as Salem threw back his head and laughed. Enzo smirked, shaking his head at our playfulness. I pushed Vannah's legs apart and stood between them. My hands skimmed her beautiful soft thighs as we pressed together. "Our night is just beginning, my wife".

Cupping her cheek, I kissed her deeply. She tasted like ecstasy with an afterbite of champagne. My tongue swirled against hers; causing a moan to slip out from her and vibrate against my lips. I pressed closer to her, my cock straining in my pants just at the sounds of her pleasure. I needed to be inside her wet cunt again, I needed to feel her squeeze and drain my cock as she came apart. I needed my wife again.

I pushed the dress up Vannah's thighs, as I kissed her. She pulled back, dark eyes heavy with lust, as she looked at me. She glanced over at Enzo and Salem, before looking back at me. "We should...we should wait until we get home" she muttered.

Salem laughed warmly from across the room. "No point being shy now, Little V".

I turned her face back towards me, "why don't we give those cocky bastards a little show?"

Her face flamed scarlet, "I don't know...". Her eyes shifted around the room, looking between Enzo and Salem. As she considered, I buried my face into her neck and slowly began to nibble at the exposed skin. She may have been questioning exhibitionism, but her body instantly pressed into mine, her nipples hard enough to cut glass, as my tongue ran over his neck.

Enzo, seeing Vannah's nervousness, headed over to the bar and poured a shot of tequila. I continued kissing her neck, my hands pushing her dress up, as he brought the shot over. "For dutch courage, Giovannah" he told her. Vannah's eyes watched Enzo closely for a moment, before she opened her mouth slightly. Enzo tipped the shot in and she swallowed with a gulp.

Enzo wasn't trying to get Vannah drunk, heck he'd

been making sure she'd been drinking water along with alcohol all night. No, he was reassuring her that he was fine with the idea and giving her a drink for her nerves at the same time. I didn't know how much had happened between Enzo and Vannah, neither of them discussed it with us, but I knew they hadn't had sex yet. I assumed that Enzo had told Vannah enough about his attack that she understood his limits.

If he was happy to watch, and maybe join in, then that was enough for her. She smiled up at him, as he leant down and gently kissed her – I stayed close, still nibbling at her neck. Enzo pulled away and went to the bar to pour himself a drink. Vannah turned back to me, more engaged in the growing lust. She didn't ask Salem if he was comfortable with this – both of us knew the horn dog would be setting up a tripod and camera if he could.

Vannah kissed me deeply, as I ran my hands up her body and over her breasts. She moaned softly, as my fingers caressed her taunt nipples, before I moved onto her shoulder. I pushed the straps of her dress down – because it was backless, the entire thing fell down and pooled at her waist.

I looked over her naked chest with a grin. "Perfect" I commented.

Salem gave a dark laugh from the corner of the room, "isn't she just". We ignored him, as I captured her lips again, my hands taking her breasts and massaging them firmly. Vannah's hands ran up and down my body, before rubbing against the erection in my pants. It was my turn to groan at her touch.

I pulled her dress the rest of the way off. Both my brothers, and I, groaned at seeing that Vannah hadn't been wearing any panties. "Such a tease" Salem laughed, as I pushed her legs further apart.

Vannah pouted, as her fingers undid my belt and pants. "The dress was too tight for underwear" she shrugged. She was playing innocent, but I could see the playful glint in her eyes – she may have let me instigate, but she had had every intention of getting fucked by one of us tonight. I had a feeling we were beginning to corrupt her.

I kissed her again, as my hand cupped her pussy. She moaned, as I slid a finger inside of her – she was wet and tight and inviting. I pushed another finger inside, as my thumb rested on the top of her clit. Her entire body twitched, as I began to fuck her with my fingers and tease her clit with my thumb.

Her hands quickly undid my pants, and boxers, pushing them down around my thighs and gripping my erection. "Fuck" I cussed, as one of her hands began to slide up and down my cock, her other hand massaging my balls. As she pleasured me with her hands, I did the same to her.

I could feel her tight cunt squeezing around my fingers, as I pushed harder against her clit. "Dario" she moaned. Her perfect tits bounced as her hips began rocking against me, riding my hand as she continued to jerk me off. If she wasn't careful, I'd cum before I could get inside her. Which I wasn't going to let happen.

Vannah's moans began to build, as her entire body began to shake. "Oh yeah" Salem laughed, "she's almost there". At his words, Vannah came apart on my hand. Her head fell back as she moaned, wetness gushing out of her and covering my hand, her stomach twitching as she rode her orgasm out.

"Damn" Enzo muttered.

"I know. I've never seen anything so perfect in my life" Salem agreed. He was right, there was nothing like seeing and feeling Vannah cum for you. I pushed her hand off my cock, as I pulled my fingers from her soaking cunt. With my hand, covered in her juices, I ran over my own cock – coating myself in her wetness.

Vannah's brown eyes reopened and she looked at me. I didn't say anything, just captured her lips with mine as I lined up my erection with her entrance. With one hard definitive thrust, I entered her – keeping her on the edge of the table as her legs wrapped around me. "Fuck, baby, you're so wet" I whispered, as my hands gripped her hips.

My fingers dug into her skin as I fucked her – thrusting in and out fast, as her hands gripped my arms. The table squeaked as our hips met with heavy slapping, both of us moaning and groaning as we let out bodies take over.

"Does she always sound like that?" Enzo asked, voice low and gritty.

"Oh yeah" Salem agreed – his own voice heavy with lust. "It's like a siren call, listening to Vannah cum. The most beautiful melody in the world".

"If she was a siren in the water, I'd happily drown to listen to that" Enzo agreed.

Vannah looked over at them, her eyes heavy with lust as I slid in and out of her dripping cunt. "Oh yeah, baby, we're talking about you" Salem laughed. She met his eyes, and her walls squeezed my dick tighter. It was turning her on, having us all together. I was sure it wouldn't be long before someone else joined in.

I pulled out further, until my tip was back at her entrance, before slamming into her. She yelled, her head falling back as I repeated the action. Then, I pulled out all the way and she whined at no longer being full. Grabbing her waist, I pulled her to her feet and spun her around. Vannah gasped as I bent her over the poker table and entered her from behind.

"Shit" I cussed, as my fingers dug into her ass cheeks. I pounded into her, my entire body like a live wire and she was the electricity powering me. Knowing I was close, I slid my hand under her and rubbed her clit.

"Oh my god, Dario" Vannah cried, "I'm so close". I

rubbed her clit faster as I fucked her with everything I had. Her moans turned to cries, as her legs shook violently.

"And here comes that beautiful siren song again" Salem mused, voice teasing, seconds before Vannah orgasmed. Her wetness gushed from her again, warm against my cock, as her entire body flopped against the table. Her cunt squeezed me tightly, an iron grip that had my orgasm building.

I pulled out of her instantly, running a hand over my wet erection, and spilling all over her back. My cum painted her creamy white skin, as I recited her name like a prayer. From the moment I had seen her in that backless dress, I knew the night was destined to end with her back covered in my cum.

I looked over my shoulder at my non-blood brothers. Both of them had erections straining their pants as their lust filled eyes focused on Vannah. I smirked as I turned back to her. Wearing that dress had really been a mistake by her, because it had ignited an almost primal pack instinct in us all.

Vannah was already sweaty, shaking and showered in cum. And the night was only just beginning.

CHAPTER TWENTY FOUR

Vannah

My heart felt like it was going to beat out of my chest. Exhibitionism was never something I had ever given much thought to. If my sex life could be described any way, it would have probably been vanilla. I'd never had sex outside of the bedroom, except for maybe once or twice on a couch, I'd never worn a costume, or used a sex toy or done anything 'risqué' before. But these three men, my three husbands, were pushing all of my boundaries.

Sex with Dario on a table, in a semi-public place, while Enzo and Salem watched was the wildest thing I had ever done. But the moment it was over, and Dario had cleared his cum from my back, I looked into everyone's eyes. And I knew that things were going to get a lot wilder.

I perched on the blackjack table, chest shaking with my deep breaths, naked and sweating. Dario gave me a long kiss, smiling warmly, as he stepped back and put his penis back into his suit pants. He was so beautiful, and powerful, that it was no wonder I have given into an almost primal need – despite being where we were.

His hand cupped my cheek affectionately, "my perfect beautiful wife".

A different hand touched my bare shoulder, making me jump in shock. Salem gave a dark chuckle, as he rounded the table to face me. Dario moved out of the way, smirking to himself, as Salem moved in front of me. His fingers ran over my jawline. "Dario's right, you are the most perfect beautiful wife. You made such beautiful sounds for Dario, will you make them for Enzo and I now?"

My heart skipped a beat as I glanced at Enzo, who was edging closer with a tumbler of scotch. Both men had obvious erections through their pants. My entire body was still tingling with the two orgasm that Dario had given me, but I couldn't deny that desire surged with the idea of more.

"Both of you?" I whispered, swallowing deeply. "At the same time?" Salem held his hand out to me to take. Nervously, I took it and he helped me off the table – I still had my heels on and they clicked as I stood again. He kissed the back of my hand before leading me across the room and to the couch in the corner.

Salem sat down and pulled me to straddling his lap. The leather of his pants, rubbed against my bare skin. Enzo sat down beside us, but he simply watched me as Salem moved forward to kiss my neck. Goosebumps pimpled my skin in desire.

"Do you want both of us together?" Enzo asked, his face was blank but there was desire swirling in his eyes. He wanted it, wanted me, but he didn't want to push me too far or too fast.

"I do" I said carefully. "But...maybe not". I blushed, squirming in Salem's lap. "Not in my...you know".

Salem smirked, "are you talking about your tight little asshole, Little V?"

"Yes" I admitted, my face and neck hot with embarrassment. "I've never...I've never done that before".

He cupped my chin, pulling me in for a deep but loving kiss. I sighed against him, the familiarity of his kiss, reminding me that there was no judgement among the four of us. I could give into my desires, into my wants, and they didn't judge or remark or scold. They understood and they reciprocated.

Salem's hand ran down my back, slipping between

my ass cheeks and running over my puckered hole. I squealed against his lips, making all three men chuckle. I pulled back and narrowed my eyes at Salem, even though I wasn't actually annoyed. "I said not there".

He winked at me, "I was just making sure we were both talking about the same place". His finger moved away from my asshole. "Don't worry, Little V, that hole is mine but not tonight, not here. That is something we need time and patience for".

Without warning, Salem lifted me up and off his lap. He dropped me onto Enzo, so I was straddling him, as Dario came over to the couch with a glass of scotch. I looked up at Enzo, who chuckled at my surprise. His eyes were full of lust, as they had been the time I had gotten on my knees for him.

He kissed me deeply, our tongues crashing as I wrapped my arms around his neck. All three men had such different kisses; Dario's were hard and rushed, Salem's were teasing with constant pressure changing but Enzo's were stilted. Enzo kissed like he didn't know what to do, which I guess made sense with his lack of experience. But, somehow Enzo's kiss was the best. It was clumsy and stilted, but with such eagerness and charm that it made me feel like nothing in the world, except kissing me, mattered. I loved that.

He pulled back, eyes looking my naked body up and down. "I've never made a girl cum before. Will you let me try?" he asked sweetly. He had lowered his voice, a tinge of redness on his cheeks. We both knew that Salem and Dario could hear, but it was a private moment for the two of us.

"Of course, Vincenzo". I kissed him again, as his hands came up and settled onto my waist. They paused there for a moment, before slowly sliding up my torso before each hand cupped a breast. I moaned as his fingers teased my nipples.

After a few minutes of kissing, he moved me back to Salem's lap and spreading my legs. He knelt between my open legs, as Salem held me still on him. Leaning forward, Salem dragged his lips over my shoulders and neck, as Enzo looked up at me. Slowly, he lowered his mouth to my wet pussy.

A shiver went through my entire body as his tongue ran my labia. Enzo used his fingers to open me up, exposing me to his view. "She's soaking wet, right?" Dario laughed, sat beside us and chuckling darkly. "Soaking wet and desperate for cum".

His words forced a shiver through me, as Enzo's tongue dipped into my most sensitive area. A long moan came from my mouth, as he dipped into my cunt and lapped at my wetness. Before these men, I could count on one hand the amount of times that I had received oral, but they had no problems giving me head – if anything, they all enjoyed it. And despite it being Enzo's first time, he sure as hell was a quick learner.

His tongue dipped in and out of my cunt, tasting me and getting a feel of my tightness. "Make sure you focus here" Salem commented, reaching around me and pressing a finger to my clit. I moaned loudly. "Tease it and be gentle with it. This little clit will have our girl drowning you with her cum".

Enzo groaned in excitement, as his tongue moved up and slipped over my clit as Salem moved his finger away. I whimpered, my previous orgasms making me ever more sensitive than normal. "Does Enzo lick your pussy good, baby?" Salem whispered into my ear. I simply moaned in reply.

"Salem asked you a question, Giovannah" Dario mused, watching us as he sipped his scotch. Despite the fact we'd only just had sex, the lust in his eyes was obvious – even if his erection hadn't bounced back as quickly. Enzo sucked onto my clit.

"Yes" I screamed, unsure if I was answering Salem or encouraging Enzo. "Fuck, Enzo, don't stop, I'm so close". My words spurred him on, as his tongue worked my clit faster and harder.

"Oh yeah, she likes that" Salem laughed, before reaching around me once more. Suddenly I felt him slip two fingers inside me, as Enzo continued to tongue fuck my clit. I yelled in pleasure, feeling the orgasm wave build, as they both worked together. My nails dug into Salem's leather pants as I neared. "Oh she's almost there, Enzo. Our girl is about to cum all over your face".

And his words sent me off the cliff. I yelled as wetness squirted Enzo, as my back arched against Salem as my entire body shook with the force of my third orgasm. These men were on the track to kill me with pleasure.

Enzo moved away from me, as I caught my breath again. I looked down at him, as he used his jacket sleeve to wipe his glistening chin. His eyes shone lustfully at me. "First time's a charm" I smiled, as he moved up and kissed me briefly.

Salem helped me onto the couch, as he stood up and unbuckled his pants. I watched as he pushed the leather pants down, before positioning me so I was on all fours on the couch. He moved behind me, pushing his cock inside me instantly. He filled me, just as Dario had, and made my shaky legs feel even more like jelly.

His fingers dug into my hips as he began to fuck me from behind, the sound of his balls slapping against me. His hands ran up and down my back, running over my skin as we both groaned and moaned. "You going to let Enzo fuck your mouth, Little V?" he asked.

I nodded, unable to form words, as I looked up at Enzo. His eyes checked mine for a moment, before he eagerly slid his suit pants down to his ankles and moved onto the couch. He raised onto his knees in front of me, as I willingly opened my mouth.

"Damn she's so fucking eager" Salem groaned,

pausing his pounding as I took Enzo's hard cock into my mouth. My saliva coated him, as my tongue felt all the bumps and scars on his ridge, as my lips pursed around him. I quickly began to suck.

Once he could see I was working Enzo's cock, Salem went back to pounding me hard from behind. I moaned, the sound muffled by cock, as my body rejoiced of the feeling of being filled at both ends. Enzo gathered up my hair with one hand, so he could see me better but he didn't force me to gag or take more of him – just watched me work his cock with gleeful lust.

It didn't take long before I was a quivering mess, another orgasm on the horizon. Dario, who was watching as he drank, was the first to notice my nearing pleasure. "She's close" he chuckled. He put down his glass before walking over to the couch, once he walked passed me I couldn't see him because my eyes were firmly on Enzo. But I quickly worked out what he was doing, when I felt a cold finger reach under me and rub my clit.

It took me seconds until I was screaming and spasming my way through another orgasm. "Shit" Enzo cussed, as he gripped my head and began to cum down my throat. I swallowed his salty taste, as his cock pumped against my lips, seconds before Salem dug his fingers into my hips and came inside me.

Two minutes later, the three of us were a sweaty

mess laying on the couch together. My body over Salem, but my head resting on Enzo's thigh. "Fuck baby, you did so well tonight" Dario mused, bring me over a small glass of ice. I thanked him as I took a chip and sucked on it.

Salem nodded his head towards Enzo, "give my boy a few minutes and then it's his turn to fill this pussy up with his cum".

"No" I shook my head, moving to sit up.

"You can go one more round, baby, don't worry" Dario smiled.

But I shook my head again, turning to Enzo. "I don't think we should have sex yet". The lust and joy that had been in Enzo's eyes early, instantly shuttered out. His beautiful kind eyes instantly became like ice.

"I see". He moved my head from his thigh and stood up. I pouted in shock, not understanding why that would offend him so much. I'd already given him a blowjob, it wasn't like I left him out.

"Enzo" Dario said carefully, frowning at his friend. Enzo ignored him and he pulled his pants up and quickly fasten them.

"I have some things I need to do" Enzo blurted, heading for the door. "Enjoy the rest of the night without me". And he practically ran out the door, with me naked and unable to chase.

CHAPTER TWENTY FIVE

Enzo

The problem with crossing boundaries, is the momentarily awkwardness afterwards. I had pushed her too far; I should never had expected Vannah to be happy having sex with such a scarred and fucked up man when she had two perfectly unflawed men to choose from. I was stupid to think I could ever have her too.

The rage that boiled into my blood was sickening. My heart felt like it was going to burst out of my chest and that bubble of adrenaline began flying through my bloodstream – more potent than any alcohol I had ever had. A sharp shot of pure undulated fury.

"Enzo?" Vannah called after me, as I pushed through the doors. The overwhelming wall of noise from the slot machines and gamblers was an assault to all my senses, matching the rage and fuelling it further. "Enzo?" She called again, but didn't follow as she was still naked. I kept walking. "Vincenzo!" The door shut behind me, silencing her hollers.

She couldn't see me like so angry. She couldn't see me when I was more emotion than man. She already didn't want the physical, if she saw me like that she wouldn't want the emotional either.

I left her behind, left all of them behind, as I rushed through Conti Gold. The sparkles and the glitter made me feel sick, another thing to overwhelm me when I was already on the edge. Why not? Just throw everything at me.

I stormed through the assault of lights and noises, pushing past people that yelled in shock as I barrelled towards the small side exit. I needed air more than anything. "Mr Rossi?" someone called to me in worry. I saw James, the manager, heading over to me. I waved him away, and seeing the look on my face he stopped his beeline towards me.

Within the Conti mafia, I was considered a no-go for most people. Meaning they had all heard the stories and rumours of me and kept their distance – which was fine, if anything I actually preferred it. Perhaps it was because they didn't know what to expect.

With Salem they knew they were getting an out-and-out psycho, but with me they saw the bubbling of craziness under the surface but didn't know when I would erupt.

I escaped the casino and into the small alleyway beside the restaurant's kitchen. There were a few workers having a smoke break, but one look at my face and they went straight back inside. Which was good, because I was in the mood to kill someone. And they didn't deserve that because they were innocent, just like my beautiful Giovannah.

She was softness and light while I was heaviness and dark. She wasn't my love, not like I wanted her to be. No matter how much I wanted to believe it, she wasn't made for me. True, I was made for her but she wasn't made for me. The universe was laughing at me once more – giving me one more thing I desperately wanted but couldn't have. A mother, good health and my wife. Simple things I'd never get.

I roared, turning and punching the wall. A loose brick crumpled and dust fell, the rest of the wall didn't move just cut my knuckles – mainly scuffing of the top layer of skin but no blood thankfully. I considered continuing to wail on the wall, but it wouldn't make me feel better. Walls didn't bleed.

Leaving the casino behind, I stormed out onto the street – growling in frustration at all the damn tourists around. Fucking Vegas. I gave a cathartic yell of annoyance, making the crowd around me jump. After that people gave me a wide birth as I stormed down the sidewalk.

I walked for about ten minutes, before coming upon Jenks. It was a dive bar just off the strip – the bright lights were still visible but the bar was nothing but dinginess. I stormed into the parking lot, getting the attention of a few people around. Despite how much I preferred to be in the background, my height and bulk would always make me noticeable. But, then, when I was spoiling for a fight, I hoped for it.

I turned to the toughest looking bastard and brought all that rage to the surface. "Hey asshole, what the fuck do you think you're looking at?"

The first punch was like a euphoric release. And that, how extremely fucked up I was, was a clear indication that I would never get Giovannah Conti to love me.

†

Salem handed me a glass of ice and nodded to my soon-to-be black eye. I took it from him, taking one cube of ice and putting it against my eye with a cringe. Salem just shook his head at me as he downed a glass of scotch. "You're a fucking idiot, you know that?" he complained.

"Is Giovannah okay?" I asked.

"She's pretty upset. She doesn't understand what she did to make you run away" he replied, leaning back into the booth. Salem turned up just as I finished beating the crap out of five drunken assholes in the parking lot. He'd simply leant against the wall, waiting until I was finished, before dragging me inside Jenks Bar for a drink.

"Needed space. Didn't want her to see that" I muttered, nodding my head back to the parking lot.

Salem sighed heavily, "I get it, man, but she doesn't. Vannah isn't like us, she's sensitive and you upset her. You gotta explain shit to her or you're just going to make her think she is the root of your problems".

I cringed, "it's not like that".

"I know that, but she doesn't" he shrugged, as I dropped the ice cube back into the glass and drank my own scotch with one gulp. He stood up from the booth, giving me a look of annoyance before jerking his head to the door. "Let's go. You're going to grovel and you're going to make sure Vannah knows she did nothing wrong".

I sighed heavily but reluctantly followed him, taking an ice cube with me for my eye as I walked. Salem was quiet as we walked back towards the strip – he understood me, as did Dario, but I had a feeling they both would prefer for me to not be so reactive to Giovannah. But, I couldn't help it. My anger, my uncontrollable rage, was a side effect of my medicine and nothing could stop it. I didn't want to have upset Vannah, but it was better than having her witness or – god forbid – receive that fury.

As we neared Conti Deco, Salem nodded me to look. We both saw Giovannah and Dario exiting the doors. Cal had just pulled up in front, opening the back door of the town car for them. "Hey" Salem called out, making them both stop and look over at us.

Giovannah turned and took a few steps towards us, just as the sound of a car backfiring sounded. She paused, confused, before a large explosion sounded. "No" I whispered, before a wall of fire filled the street – blowing Giovannah, Dario and Cal away like leaves in a storm.

Salem and I both stepped forward, before the ripple of the explosion hit us and we both were knocked to the ground in shock.

CHAPTER TWENTY SIX

Vannah

I had lost of my necklace. I pressed my hand to my neck, as I tried to remember where it had gone. "My necklace" I muttered, "my necklace is gone". My head was pounding, my entire body hurt and I couldn't hear anything. I couldn't remember what happened, but that wasn't as important as my necklace.

I pushed myself up until I was sitting, but there was so much smoke around me that I couldn't see much. I could feel warmth, despite the fact I was outside, and I could smell something coppery...blood maybe?

I tried to move but the pain was so strong I screamed and the world went black. When I opened my eyes again, I was in a different place – less smoky, less warm. I looked around, seeing exposed bricks of buildings on either side of me. My eyes took a second to focus, as I noticed a figure standing over me.

When I finally got a clear view, I smiled. "Patty" I whispered, my body getting cold. "Patty, my necklace is missing. Will you help me find it?" I asked. She said something to me, but I couldn't hear her.

My sister, Patty, was the complete opposite to me. Tall, bulky and scruffy. Her dark hair was short like a boy's and her body was that of a female wrestler – thick thighs, melon breasts and wide hips. Her large brown eyes looked down at me. "Patty, what are you doing here?"

She knelt down beside me, pushing a hair out of my face. She held a golden chain in her hand, it caught the distance flashing lights. Three rings hung on the chain – my necklace. My eyes blurred again, obscuring her image, before Patty leant forward and put her lips beside my ear. "You're even pretty when you're bleeding, Vannah". She gave a small chuckle, "but this necklace is mine now".

"Patty, my necklace please give it back". I reached out to her, but she wasn't there anymore. I blinked, trying to clear my vision, but I was alone again. I began to cry – not sure if it was from the pain in my body or the pain in my heart for losing my sister twice. Maybe it was because I couldn't find my necklace.

Time was different. I blinked and suddenly everything was bright. I closed my eyes, but fingers pried them open and shone a powerful light straight into them again. There was an annoying whine I could hear – a high pitched shrill. The light moved away and suddenly I was looking at two men dressed in green.

"Can you tell me your name?" one of them asked. I could hear him, but it sounded like I was underwater.

"Vannah" I replied, swallowing deeply. My throat hurt, but not as much as my head. "Giovannah Conti".

"Conti, huh?" the man said, trying to give me a soft smile as the other man began to inspect my body. "You have something to do with Conti Deco?" He nodded to the brick wall to my left.

"My husband owns it". I wet my lips; they were so dry. "I lost my necklace, I think my sister took it?"

He gave me a soft smile, "let's focus on you first. A necklace isn't important right now. Why don't you tell me where it hurts".

"Head and…I don't know. Everywhere". I sniffed as I began to cry, not being able to focus on anything but the pain. "Everywhere hurts".

"Hey, hey, now don't cry" he said, taking a tissue and wiping my cheeks.

"The left wrist is very swollen, but I'm not sure if it's broken or just sprained" the other man in green replied. "I think I can feel one or two broken ribs, but no signs of a lung penetration. I'm mostly worried about that pretty extensive head wound".

"Definitely a concussion at the minimum" the other agreed, "let's get her onto a stretcher".

As the fog in my brain cleared, I worked out the men were EMT responders but I couldn't remember exactly why I was injured. I remembered having a crazy threesome, and sex with Dario, before Enzo stormed out. But after that it was all blank, but something bad had definitely happened after Salem had left.

The EMT's carefully loaded me onto a stretcher, before carrying me out of the alleyway. As the lights and noise flashed around me, I heard a loud yell of my name. "Vannah! Vannah!"

"That sounds like someone is looking for you" the EMT said.

"Yes" I replied. My throat was so dry and painful that I couldn't tell him it was Salem. "Please" I whispered. They loaded me into an ambulance, before one EMT nodded at the other. Salem was still shouting my name, almost manically, before suddenly going quiet.

"Vannah?" his voice said, suddenly close. My head was strapped in, so I didn't see him until he was hovering directly over me. "Oh god, Little V, look at you".

"What's your relationship to Mrs Conti?" the EMT asked. Salem blinked, not sure how to answer. He couldn't say he was my husband, because legally he wasn't, but he also didn't want to get kicked out the ambulance.

He could have lied, said he was my brother or something, but Salem was a self-proclaimed psycho. "Doesn't matter, I stay with her at all times". He turned back to me and ran a finger down my cheek.

"Sir, family only can--"

Salem pulled his gun from the holster under his jacket and levelled it at the EMT. He paled and his eyes widened. "I stay with her at all times. Got it?"

The EMT swallowed deeply, "got it".

Salem grunted, before putting the gun back and staring at me. "What happened? Where are Enzo and Dario?" I asked.

"There was a car bomb" he explained, as the EMTs closed up the ambulance and began to drive. Salem moved to sit above my head, as the EMT worked on me. "Enzo was fine but I don't know about Dario. I found you first".

I began to cry again, "I lost my necklace. Patty she stole it".

Salem frowned, "who is Patty?"

"She stole it! Why would she steal it?" I cried.

"She has a concussion and she's in shock" the EMT explained, giving Salem a nervous look. "Patients in shock often get hyper focus on one specific thing. They often don't make sense, it's nothing to worry about".

"No, but Salem" I sobbed, "my necklace, the rings, my necklace". Realisation dawned in his eyes – knowing I was talking about their three wedding rings which I wore around my neck. "I lost them... Patty she stole it. She stole my necklace". Both the EMT and Salem tried to calm me as I became hysterical.

"Hey, Little V, it's alright". Salem kissed my forehead, "we can get more rings made. It's just jewellery, the most important thing is that you're safe". His words didn't calm me, so the EMT put a weak sedative into the IV bag that was connected to me. That was enough to stop my hysterics, but I still couldn't believe that Patty had stolen my necklace.

Salem's phone suddenly rang. He fished it out his pocket and answered quickly. He talked to someone swiftly, but I was too focused on the necklace to care. When he ended the call, he moved to catch my eye again. "Vannah, baby, that was Enzo. He's with Dario and they're in another ambulance going to the hospital, alright?"

"Will you tell them I'm sorry about the necklace?" I whispered, the sedatives making me extremely tired. "Tell them I couldn't stop Patty stealing it".

"Of course I will, Little V". Salem gave me a small smile, but there was worry in his eyes. His concern was the last thing I saw before I succumbed to the darkness once more.

CHAPTER TWENTY SEVEN

Salem

Using a damp cloth, I cleaned the blood from my beautiful wife's face and neck. Vannah, despite being literally blown away, was still supermodel hot. She would always get my dick hard, and if the situation was different – her covered in blood because she had killed someone – I would be in heaven, but I felt the opposite of turned on. Looking at her, pale and bloody, filled me with pure terror.

I was beginning to truly understand Enzo's obsession over her safety. She was so delicate and it would be so easy for someone to take her away from us. I could never allow her to get hurt like this again.

A knock came on the hospital door, I turned to see Enzo. There was a dark layer of ash on his face, but his scowl was obvious. He rushed into the room, eyes zoning in on Vannah's injuries. "Fuck" he whispered; eyes full of horror.

"She's going to be fine" I reassured him. "Doctors said that head wounds always bleed heavily so it looks worse than it is. She's got a concussion and she's confused but the doctors said she'll be fine".

Enzo didn't relax, his hands clenching into fists. "Someone bombed her. They fucking blew up our wife and I wasn't there because I was off being a fucking child".

"You couldn't have stopped what happened. The car bomb wasn't in our car, it was in another one in front of ours. Nothing we could have done to stop that".

"I could have been in front of her. I could have taken the worst of the blast". Enzo gently stroked her ashy covered hair. "I can't lose her, Salem, I can't".

I put my hand on his shoulder, "none of us can, brother. We get it too". We both went quiet as a nurse came in and checked on Vannah's vitals, before leaving again. "How's Dario?" I questioned, once we were alone again.

"Banged up and bruised, but better than Vannah. They're just stitching him up at the moment" Enzo explained, "he's more pissed at not knowing about Vannah than anything else".

Enzo went quiet, staying at her side and softly caressing her hair. I watched for a moment before leaving to go and find Dario. I knew Enzo wouldn't leave her alone, not after this, so I didn't worry too much about her.

Dario was sat on the hospital bed, legs over the side, growling like a wolf as a doctor stitched up some wounds on his arms and chest. His eyes lit up when he saw me. "Vannah" was all he said.

"She's going to be fine" I told him, holding my hands up when he made a move to stand. The doctor muttered at him, but didn't say anything directly – either she knew who he was, or he too had threatened staff with a gun. "They've sedated her because she was very confused and in a lot of pain. She's got a concussion and they think some broken ribs. When she's awake they want to do an MRI and some x-rays to make sure nothing else is wrong".

"How the fuck did that happen, Salem?" he asked, shaking his head. He looked as beaten down as Enzo had. While those two felt defeated, I simply felt furious – rage that I could keep well contained but I was ready to unleash. Ideally on a whole fucking cartel.

"I have no idea, D. The bomb wasn't in our car, Cal always checks, it was in one parked in front. It was obviously detonated remotely, someone obviously waited until you were near and set the bomb off". We both went quiet, not wanting to say any more than that while in the company of non-family members.

Once the doctor had finished stitching his wounds, Dario announced he was checking himself out. The doctor harped and complained, worried about internal injuries, but he just waved away her concerns. After signing the discharge papers, we both went back to Vannah's bedside.

"Doctor came about ten minutes ago and checked her over" Enzo explained, once we had closed the door to the private room. "They're scheduling an MRI for the morning, they want her to rest overnight. He also said she might have a broken wrist or a really bad sprain, but they can't tell without an x-ray".

"Did she say anything earlier? When she was conscious, I mean" Dario asked, sitting down next to her bedside.

"No, she was just confused. She was crying a lot because she lost the necklace with our weddings rings on" I sighed, pulling up another chair and collapsing into it. "She was hysterical, sobbing that someone named Patty had stolen it".

"Patty" Dario frowned, "is that someone we know? We should look into it".

"Patty was her sister" Enzo commented, with a heavy sigh. "She was obviously confused and seeing things. Patrizia has been dead for over ten years".

"Shit" Dario leant back, his only lead drying up.

"Guess we'll just have to buy some more wedding rings, damn those things were expensive".

I snorted, "don't tell Vannah that, she's already scared to spend your money. She'll be devastated if we tell her how much money was lost with those three rings".

The three of us were quiet for a moment, but my anger was getting the best of me and I couldn't sit still. Sighing heavily, I walked over to Vannah and pressed a gentle kiss to her forehead. I turned towards my best friends, "don't take your eyes off her".

"Where are you going?" Enzo questioned.

"See how much we caught on CCTV and if we can get an idea who almost killed our wife" I growled, almost spitting the words in fury. "And then I am going to after the Morales Cartel myself. They're going to rue the day they ever targeted my wife".

"No" Dario sighed, leaning back in his chair. "I've already put steps in place to take down the Morales Cartel and they're in motion now. If you can find the fucker who placed the car bomb, then go ahead and have some fun, but do not get the attention of Morales. When I give the go ahead, Luis Morales's empire is going to crumble around him curtesy of the DEA suddenly finding out every detail about them from a personal source".

"Uncle Marco" Enzo nodded, "that's why you send him away. To become an FBI snitch".

Dario gave a slow nod, "I gave him all the possible information he needed and then sent him running to an FBI agent desperate for a promotion".

"He deserves more than that. Morales, he deserves to suffer for daring to touch a single hair on our girl's head" I snapped.

"Agreed" Dario nodded, "but first he'll be arrested. I will then have him transferred to Clark County, where I hear the three of us are suddenly going to be wanted for outstanding warrants".

"Oh yeah?" I smirked, "wants this warrant for?"

"A robbery charged. They'll send us to Clark County, same week as Morales arrives, just for the charges to be dropped when it is proven it wasn't us".

"You've planned this all out" I commented. I should have known; Dario was a crafty fucker. Me? Give me a gun and a person to shot, and I didn't need to think. But Dario was a planner, a fixer, a creator. He didn't want to just have Morales killed – he wanted to destroy his cartel, tarnish his name and *then* kill him. Perfect.

"Where will Vannah be when we're in jail?" Enzo asked.

"Back visiting family in New York" he explained, "I'll tell Emanuele that we've got to clear a bit of heat and it'll be safer for Vannah to stay there for a week or two".

I stared at Vannah – the woman who was soon going

to be the mother of my children – and curled my lip in fury. "We're going to teach Luis Morales exactly what happens when you touch Mrs Conti-Galluci-Rossi".

Enzo gave me a dangerous grin, "I want him begging for his life".

"Begging and crying" I agreed.

Dario shared our grins, "let it be a lesson to all those who try and touch our wife. The Conti's don't give mercy".

CHAPTER TWENTY EIGHT

Vannah

The day after the car bomb, I was cleared to return home with my husbands. My left wrist was sprained, so I was given a sling, and I had two broken ribs – but I had been lucky, as had Dario. Too lucky, really. It felt like these people, the Morales Cartel my husbands had told me, were toying with us. A cat and mouse game.

Cal, our head of security and driver that night, was staying longer in hospital. He would be fine, but the burns he had sustained needed more treatment to stop infections. Dario covered all the bills, and upgraded him to a private hospital, but his injuries were just a reminded how much worse it could have been.

Enzo drove me home, as I sat in the passenger's side and awkwardly touched my bare neck. He followed my hand movement, "they were just rings, Vannah. Nothing compared to your life".

"I wouldn't have lost them if I had let you all keep them" I replied, shifting position as it hurt to breathe too deeply.

"You were right to take them off us. We were assholes who decided we were married to you before we even asked" he shrugged, focusing on the road ahead. "A piece of jewellery doesn't define us, just like the marriage contract between Dario and you doesn't mean you're more married to him than Salem or I".

"I guess". I swallowed a lump of guilt, "but I still lost them".

"You were blown up, Vannah, don't be silly. You didn't lose them, they were lost during a near death attack". He reached over and took my good hand in his. "Dario's already called the jeweller and ordered three wedding rings, exactly the same. So don't stress out".

I silently looked down at my large ruby engagement ring, and black three stone wedding band, and began to twist them. "You really scared me" I told Enzo suddenly.

He raised an eyebrow, "me? I wasn't the one blown fifty feet in the air by a bomb".

"Before that. When you ran out on me. What happened? I thought we were all having a good time". As much as I had enjoyed our little orgy, I couldn't help but cringe when I thought about it. We'd all crossed lines that we couldn't uncross. Nothing would go back to how it was before – I definitely felt different as a person because of it.

"You said you didn't want to have sex with me, it hurt my feelings" Enzo explained, knuckles white on the steering wheel as he didn't dare turn to look at me, instead studied the road like he was mad at it. "IED" he suddenly blurted out, saying the word like it hurt him.

"That's a bomb, right? Is that what the bomb type was".

"No...I mean it might have been, I don't know. I was talking about me. Yes an IED is a bomb, but it's also an illness I have. Intermittent Explosive Disorder, it started after the attack and all the physical and mental trauma, plus my testosterone medication, I'm basically just a ball of rage waiting to explode. When I can't control it, I become a monster. I don't want to ever be around you when I'm like that, because I can't guarantee I won't hurt you".

I considered that for a long moment as we neared the Conti manor. "I still don't understand what triggered it. I thought we were having fun?"

"You rejected me, Giovannah, it hurt my feelings and I became irrational". Still, he didn't dare look in my eyes, as he rolled up to the gates and the guards began inspecting the vehicle. "It was stupid, and I acted like a child, but I can't help it".

"What, so every time I don't feel like having sex with you, you're going to storm out on me? What happened to 'you're in charge of things, Vannah' that you all preached when I first came here?"

Enzo cringed, but didn't say anything as the guards opened the gates and waved us through. I understood that he was trying to explain things to me, but I couldn't help being a little pissed off. "I have the prerogative to say no, Vincenzo, everybody has that right".

"Shit, Giovannah, of course you do" he sighed, pulling into the large car garage. He stopped the car and turned to face me, finally meeting my eyes. "I wasn't upset that you didn't want to have sex with me. I was hurt because you happily had sex with both Dario and Salem but not me...you picked them over me and it hurt".

"I didn't pick them over you, Enzo, that wasn't what happened". I reached over and took his hands in mine. "I lost my virginity to Aldo on our wedding night and it was awful. Aldo was pretty drunk so he was struggling to stay hard, but instead of just saying 'shit I'm too drunk, we'll do this tomorrow', he got embarrassed and started blaming me. He told me it was because I was too tight, I wasn't wet enough, that I wasn't putting enough effort in to keep him aroused".

Enzo's lip curled in disgust, "you should have never been married off to that old, fat, bastard".

"I'm telling you this because I don't know anyone who had a good experience losing their virginity. Mine was worse than most, but for everyone it's awkward and its trial and error. That is not something that should happen in front of other people".

His dark eyebrows burrowed together as he worked through what I was telling him. "You were protecting me?" he asked slowly – either he wasn't sure he believed me, or he didn't understand.

"Yes, Enzo, of course. You just watched me have sex with Dario and Salem, both who know how my body works and what pleases me. If you hadn't managed to get the same reaction to me, you would have felt like you did something wrong and it would have ruined your confidence. We need time together, just us, to understand each other's bodies before anything else happens".

"Oh". He went quiet for a long while, his eyes full of confusion and almost panic. I had quickly worked out that Enzo had a lot of problems and even as his wife, I couldn't solve those for him. I leant forward and pressed a gentle kiss to his cheek, before unclipping my belt and opening the door with my good arm.

Seeing me struggling to push the door, Enzo

snapped out of his deep thoughts. He got out the car, then helped me out, as I whimpered at the pain in my chest from the broken ribs. It was like being stabbed with a hot poker. "It's almost time for you to take your next lot of pain meds" he said, as he helped me into the house. It was quiet, Salem and Dario were obviously off working.

Enzo helped me upstairs and to my bedroom. I looked at my clean bed and cringed, as Enzo began pulling the covers back and getting some of my pyjamas from my drawers. "I'm dirty, I haven't showered so I'm still covered in ash and smell like smoke".

Carefully, Enzo helped me shower before he brushed my hair and helped me get into my pyjamas. "Will you lay with me?" I asked, after taking my medications and climbing into bed.

"Sure". Enzo cautiously climbed into the bed, careful not to jolt me too much. Luckily, the medication was fast acting and I was already beginning to feel the pain easing. His large body took up most of the bed, so I simply rested my head on his chest and arranged my bad wrist gently on a pillow.

"Can I ask you about you sister?" Enzo asked, after a few minutes of quiet cuddling.

"Patrizia?"

"You were confused with you concussion and you kept telling us that Patty had stolen your necklace".

I cringed, "I was just muddled. When I was eight my father brought me a beautiful necklace for my first communion, Patty was jealous and she stole it. I didn't understand a lot of the family dynamics back then, so I kept asking everyone why she would steal my necklace. I guess when I realised my chain with the wedding rings on was missing, and I could see a figure of someone finding me, so I confused that memory".

"I thought I knew everything about you, but until you mentioned it a few weeks ago, I didn't know you had a sister".

I grimaced, "Patty was illegitimate. My father got his high school girlfriend pregnant, who was not Family and was not catholic, so it caused a big scandal. My grandfather paid the girl's family off and gave the baby, Patty, to his maid to raise. My father saw Patty occasionally, but was warned that no one was to know she was his daughter, born out of wedlock".

"This was back in Italy?"

"Yes, when my father moved over to the States and took over the Bianchi branch here, he brought Patty and the maid over with him. He put them in the house next door to ours". I was quiet for a long moment, "Patty was eight years older than me, so we weren't close. She was mean, especially to my mom, so we argued a lot. But, as I grew up, I realised that she saw me as a representative for everything she wanted".

"The legitimate daughter".

"Exactly, she'd always been my father's secret. While, he was would take me to dances and be at my communion and buy me most things I wanted, she was a secret. To Patty I got the life she thought she deserved. Ironically, I was jealous of her. She got freedom and didn't have to live up to crazy expectations".

"Grass is always greener".

I snorted, "exactly. But, like I said, Patty is dead. I obviously confused the missing necklace to the one she stole when I was a kid".

"You sure she's dead?" Enzo asked, "Salem said you were pretty adamant she had been there".

I shivered at the memory, "I'm sure...I watched her die".

CHAPTER TWENTY NINE

Dario

A knock came on my office door and Isabella, my assistant, came inside. "Mr Conti, I have the Fire Chief here to see you about the incident at Deco last week" she informed me.

"Thank you, Isabella, send him in" I informed her. She exited again, as I locked my computer and pushed a few discriminatory documents into my top draw. Chief Horowitz knew who I was and what I did, as he was on my take, but it was still best not to leave information that could be used against me around prying eyes.

Horowitz came in, dressed in his uniform, his beady eyes twitchy as he greeted me. "Have a seat" I said, gesturing across my desk. He did, obviously uncomfortable. "So, Chief, I hear you have some information about the bombing at my casino last week".

"Yes, sir" he nodded, "we've ruled it as a vehicle fire due to a leak from a defective fuel tank. The car was stolen and we haven't be able to locate whoever parked it outside of Conti Deco".

I leant back in my chair and sighed. "Alright, and the real findings?"

Horowitz cringed, "homemade device made up mainly of C4 in the trunk, but only a small one, mind you. I think it was more of a warning than an assassination attempt, sir".

I frowned, considering that. It had crossed my mind a few times in the past week. Vannah and I were close enough to be blown to pieces, but we both only suffered superficial wounds. Oh, it was enough to put me on a war path – no one harmed a hair on my wife's head and survived. But, odd that the cartel didn't just blast us to hell.

"The C4, can you tell where it came from?" I asked.

Horowitz shook his head, "not exactly, sir, however the bomb expert did say that bomb makers all have a specific signature on how they make their bombs. Like a unique fingerprint of bombs. The maker of this bomb has been matched to five other car explosions within the US and Mexico. Mostly in Texas and Monclova".

My lip curled in disgust, "cartel territory".

"So it would seem, sir" Horowitz replied.

I got as much information out of the Fire Chief as possible, before Isabella showed him out. The confirmation that the bomb was tied to the Morales Cartel was enough for me to finally put the last piece into play.

I picked up my office phone and called Marco. "Sir" he answered – not using my first name as he knew I was pissed at him and he wanted to get off my shit list.

"Hello dearest uncle" I mused, "I hope you are ready to get things started. I wouldn't like for you to disappoint me once more". I could practically hear him sweating through the phone as I spoke.

"Absolutely not, sir. I've got everything ready, you just tell me when".

I grinned, "when".

✝

I met Enzo at Conti Gold where we spent a few hours dealing with the legal side of The Conti Group.

If we were planning to be AWOL for a few days, in order to 'deal' with Morales, then we needed to get everything set to run smoothly in our absence. Billion dollar companies didn't run themselves.

Once we were done, we headed home. "I don't like the idea of leaving Giovannah on her own, D" Enzo muttered, as I weaved through the traffic.

"It's only for a week and she'll be safe with the Bianchis".

Enzo snorted like a boar. "They married her off to a fat, lazy, bastard when she was a teenager. I don't trust them to wipe their own assess". His words were like the growl of a rapid animal. His worry for Vannah was always over the top, but since the bomb he was downright certifiable.

"Her brother will keep her safe. Plus, by then the actual threat, Morales and cartel, will be too busy trying to keep their hides out of a cell to go after her".

Enzo frowned, "I don't fucking like it".

I rolled my eyes at his behaviour. But, I could understand where he was coming from. Vannah was our reason to live, when she wasn't in sight, my stomach was a knot of anxiety. I frequently teased Enzo that he was obsessed with Vannah, but fuck, I had been infatuated by her for seven years.

When we got home, we parked and headed into the house through the garage door. As we stepped into the corridor, I paused, hearing a familiar sound. I smirked, as I turned to Enzo who smiled when he realised what I also heard. We followed the sounds until we came to the main lounge.

Vannah was sat in one of the arm chairs, dress up around her stomach, as Salem knelt between her legs. My best friend worked his tongue in Vannah's cunt, as she moaned and squirmed. "Oh fuck" she moaned; eyes closed as her head threw back in passion. I bit my lip to be quiet, as my dick swelled in my pants.

One of Vannah's hands reached down and gripped Salem's head, as her hips unconsciously raised up to meet his skilful mouth. "Oh god, Salem, I'm so close don't stop" she panted. Her left breast was poking out the dress, no doubt from a previous fondling, and her nipple was hard and calling to me.

I glanced at Enzo, whose eyes were fixated on Vannah as he rubbed himself over his pants. I stepped forward, desire circling my stomach, before pausing when I saw the healing bruises on Vannah's arm. I cringed. As much as I was desperate to get my cock in her tight cunt, Salem had the right idea with focusing on Vannah's pleasure before she was fully healed.

Vannah gasped, as Salem continued to eat her out, before her eyes opened and she saw us. "Fuck!" she screamed in shock. She stared at us, like a deer in headlights, before screaming as her orgasm slammed into her. I heard the gush of her wetness, as her back arched and her eyes shut again. "Oh fuck" she quivered, her legs shaking around Salem's head.

After a moment, Salem sat back on his heels and chuckled as he licked the juices off his chin and face. Vannah opened her eyes once more, blushing brightly as she looked over Salem and to us. It didn't escape her notice that both Enzo and I were rubbing our cocks over our pants.

Salem turned, face still glistening, to see what she was staring at. We shared a silent look of amusement – Salem and I fantasied about sharing Vannah together for years. In the past year, Enzo was also in those fantasies, but we'd never played those out as Salem and I had.

In the years that Salem and I wanted Vannah, but she was married to Aldo, we'd often shared escorts. We'd paid the girls to dress up like Vannah, occasionally even making them wear a mask, as the two of us fucked her – dreaming of the day we would get to do it to the girl of our actual dreams. Having now had Vannah, no other girl would ever compare.

"Does she still taste like heaven, brother?" I mused.

Salem obnoxiously licked his lips, "if she tastes like heaven, then I guess I better get my sinning ass to church". Both Enzo and I laughed as we walked closer. Vannah, still embarrassed, rearranged her dress to cover her – although she was still sat in a wet patch of her own making.

"What you blushing for, wife?" I smiled, as I reached the arm chair and looked down at her. She swallowed deeply, as Salem moved out the way and I reached down and slipped my hand up her dress. She let out a long breath as my fingers slipped inside her drenched cunt. "Come on, Vannah, there is nothing to be embarrassed about".

Salem chuckled, "especially not after our fun in the casino last week".

At his words, Vannah's eyes hardened and she pushed my hand away from her. I grunted in surprise, not expecting her to push me away. Tears gathered in her eyes, as she jumped up and ran out the room. The three of us watched her disappear upstairs in shock.

I raised an eyebrow at Salem, "did something happen today?"

"No" he shrugged, "she was quiet, a little sad, but I thought she was just in pain".

"Should we go talk to her?" Enzo asked, frowning in confusion.

I shook my head, "let's give her a few minutes. She might just be a little overwhelmed, we've been pushing her out of her comfort zone a lot lately, not to mention she's probably still scared after the bombing".

Salem nodded, "why don't I order us some food and

after dinner we'll try and talk to her".

"Nothing Italian, even Pizza she gets picky over" Enzo added. The three of us shared a look of amusement – Vannah's food snobbery was a little hidden gem none of us had known before she moved into the house. She was very sweet and demure, caring about others and their feelings. The only time our little Vannah got truly feisty was when it came to Italian cooking.

Salem walked over and grabbed his car keys, "good call, I'll go pick up sushi

CHAPTER THIRTY

Vannah

I felt like such a fool. If it wasn't bad enough that just seeing Enzo and Dario watching Salem give me oral, had had an earth shattering orgasm crashing into me, but I actually wanted them to join in. It was too much. *I* was doing too much.

I showered and dressed in my most frumpy unsexy pyjamas I owned. A fluffy pink long set with little frogs on it. They were an old pair and very unflattering – Aldo used to get angry when I wore them as he knew they were my 'sex is not happening' pyjamas. Usually I wore them when I was on my period, but then I wore them because I didn't want a repeat of the night at the casino. My wrist was healed enough that I didn't put the sling on, but took a few painkillers just in case.

A knock came on the door as I was braiding my wet hair. A second later Enzo poked his head inside. "Hey, Salem picked up sushi. You want to come downstairs and join us?" he asked. I bit the inside of my cheek, trying to calm the ocean of anxiety in my stomach. "Hey" Enzo said gently, walking further into the room.

He hugged me to his chest, his massive body dwarfing mine and making me feel safe. It was different with Enzo than it was with the others – I felt like he understood me more. Perhaps it was because we were both scarred by our childhood trauma; him physically, me emotionally.

"Is this about the attack or something else?" he asked gently, stroking my hair.

I glanced up at him, "can we go outside and smoke? Like back in Italy?"

"Of course". He gave my head a sweet kiss, before taking my hand and leading me out the room. He stopped briefly by his room, coming back with a joint and a lighter, before we headed to the back garden. I sat down on the porch swing, as Enzo went inside to tell the others to give us a few moments alone.

Enzo came back and sat beside me. As he lit the joint, I turned to face him, tucking my feet onto the swing and drawing my knees up under my chin. He took the first drag, before handing it over to me. He coughed slightly, "Salem rolled that one so it's strong as fuck".

We silently smoked for a few moments, before I finally spoke up. "Do you remember what we talked about last time?" I wet my lips nervously.

"In Italy? Yeah, you told me about Aldo cheating on you".

"Aldo and I had a bad marriage and often I would dream about someone whisking me off my feet and taking me away. I wanted nothing more than to feel loved and protected and like I was someone's priority. But in all these fantasies I had...I never...I never gave sex much thought".

Enzo shook his head, "I don't understand what you're trying to tell me, Giovannah". He took my hand in his, as I finished the last of the joint. "I want to understand so I can help you".

"Aldo once told me the reason he kept cheating on me, was because there were certain sexual things that only whores do. He told me he liked anal sex, but a wife doesn't do that with her husband, that is only for dirty whores. He told me that he liked to have more than one girl in the bedroom, but again that is only dirty whores, not wives".

"You know he was a fucking idiot, right?" Enzo frowned, giving me a 'this is obvious information' look.

"I know, he was a hypocrite more than anything. He had these rules for what a good wife does and doesn't do" I rolled my eyes, "but he still expected me to give him a blow job at least twice a week, yet he thought giving a woman oral was disgusting".

"Which makes him certifiably insane, because nothing in the world tastes better than your pussy, Giovannah". Enzo spoke so precisely, and so evenly, it was like he was stating the most basic fact rather than giving me a dirty compliment. Salem spoke smut to me all the time, but hearing Enzo say those words had my underwear suddenly becoming wet.

"I had always fantasied about a classic knight in white shining armour turning up to whisk me off my feet, and yeah in the fantasies there would be sex…but I didn't think it would be much different than being with Aldo. Just, you know, with both parties satisfied".

Enzo gave a slow nod, as he worked through what I was talking about. "You're just feeling a little overwhelmed".

I blushed, "a little, but it's more than I am worried I want this too much. I'm going to embarrass myself and I worry that maybe Salem and Dario might be… a little more likely to hurt me. *Emotionally*".

Enzo raised an eyebrow, "I'm a thirty one year old virgin who has no dating experience. You're going to have to spell this out for me, Giovannah".

"I'm going to fall in love with the three of you and

I'm going to be so used to having three men who worship my body every chance they get. I'm worried that before long that will change and I will go back to being just the housewife, while they find 'whores' to do the things that wives don't".

Enzo was quiet for a very long time. Too long. Long enough that I began to squirm. Finally, he sighed and cupped my hands with his. "You don't feel like I'm going to do this to you?"

I shrugged, "you're a virgin and before I came here I had only ever been with Aldo, which isn't much sexual experience. I worry I won't be enough to satisfy them, but I feel like you and I don't have as high expectations".

"Ah" he chuckled, "I get it now. This is a self-esteem issue, which is why you came to me. The unofficial king of low self-esteem. You are more than enough for them, Vannah, you're just in new territory and that can be scary. You've gone from boring, beige, sex to having three men who want you at the same time. It's like going from the kiddie pool straight to the middle of the ocean".

I glanced down at out joined hands, "I'm just not sure I'm going to be enough to keep them both entertained for long".

Enzo leant forward and kissed me gently and slowly. Before taking my hand and pulling me to my feet. "I know how to sort this out" he promised. He led me back inside the house, where Dario and Salem were in the main lounge arguing about what they wanted to watch.

The four of us sat down and ate, before Salem suggested we watch a movie. They could see I was upset and he was trying to distract me. Once more Dario and Salem began to banter and bitch about what movie to choose.

"Guys" Enzo interrupted them, "I'm going to head out for a few hours. In the meantime, I think you guys need to show Vannah the boxes under your beds".

They both turned to Enzo in shock. "What the fuck, Enzo?" Dario growled.

"Dude!" Salem threw his hands up in annoyance.

I looked between the three of them in confusion, "boxes under your beds? I don't understand. What are in the boxes?" They stayed quiet, as I continued to whip my head between them. Dario and Salem were not happy with Enzo.

Enzo gave them an emotionless, straight, look. "Vannah is worried she's not enough for you two. She's concerned you'll get bored of her and look for other girls more 'experienced' than her".

"Enzo" I yelled, my turn to be outraged at him. "I told you that in confidence".

"And keeping it between us will just end up causing problems". He stroked my cheek affectionately. "You need to see some truths in order to move forward".

Salem looked at me with guarded eyes. "You really think you're not enough for us? You think we'd *ever* cheat on you?"

"Vannah, you can't be serious?" Dario frowned. He walked over and cupped my face with both his large palms. "You are my wife, there will never be anyone else for me".

I pulled away from him and turned back to Enzo, "did you ever tell them about the chlamydia?"

Both Dario and Salem made noises of confusion, as Enzo shook his head. "That was a secret between us. You asked me not to tell anyone, so I never told anyone". He quickly kissed me again, before giving me a sad smile. "I'll be back later".

He disappeared towards the garage, as both Dario and Salem turned to me in confusion. "I think we need to talk" I sighed heavily, rubbing a hand over my face.

Salem nodded, "I'll go get scotch. I feel like we all need some dutch courage". We all agreed with that.

CHAPTER THIRTY ONE

Vannah

I sat on the couch, having had two glasses of scotch, as Dario and Salem placed two identical shoe boxes on the coffee table. "What's inside?"

Dario shook his head, "you first. I think you'll probably want a little space after you see inside those boxes". At his words Salem cringed, looking like he agreed. It made me very nervous as to what was inside those mysterious boxes. "Vannah" Dario prompted when I went quiet.

"Last summer, when Enzo and I were in Amalfi, I went to the doctors because I had been getting some problems. I found out that Aldo had given me chlamydia after cheating on me. He'd cheated on me before, but it pushed me over the edge into truly hating my life that time, because I had just had a miscarriage".

Salem dived to his feet, "*he* cheated on *you*! That old bastard, who didn't deserve to breathe the same air as you, let alone be married to you, he cheated on you? If that bastard wasn't dead, I'd cut his diseased dick off".

"Salem, calm" Dario snapped, giving his friend a look. His lips pulled back in a look of pure disgust, before he sat down and gritted his teeth. "Go on, Vannah".

"I'm clean now" I promised first. "Anyway, Aldo told me the reason he *had* to cheat on me, was because there are things that wives do for their husbands and then there are things only whores do. There was a list of things, but the general gist was anal, threesomes, choking and stuff. Basically, anything that wasn't missionary, or maybe doggy style sex".

"That's what you meant" Dario sighed, leaning back in his chair. "On our wedding night. I went down on you and you said I didn't need to and that we could just have 'normal' sex".

I blushed, "Aldo only ever did that to me twice and he told me he hated it both times. He complained I was messy and it took too long".

Salem snorted, "amateur".

"The point I'm making is that I couldn't even make a fifty year old man happy, how could I possibly keep all three of you guys sexually satisfied?"

"We don't want anyone else, Little V" Salem assured me, "you are more than enough for all of us. We have zero desire for any other women". My face must have been sceptical because he sighed and looked at Dario. "Fuck, Enzo, was right we have to show her the boxes".

Dario ran a hand over his face, "Vannah, baby, you need to know something before we show you these, alright? We've been obsessed with you for a very long time. Seven years for me, five years for Salem".

"We didn't think we'd ever actually get to have to for ourselves. So, we collected a few things over the years to...curb our appetites, if you will".

I frowned, "you mean sexually?"

"Yeah" Dario groaned, looking embarrassed. "These are our...masturbation boxes, if you want to call it that". He waved for me to look inside them. I paused for a moment, a weird feeling bubbling in my stomach, before I knelt down in front of the coffee table. "They both have the same contents" he continued, when I paused. "We're fairly fond of sharing, if you hadn't worked that out yet".

I opened up both of the boxes, and slowly shifted through the items with baited breath. First was a stack of pictures of me, mostly just ones from my Instagram, but some were of me in a yellow bikini looking unaware. Enzo had obviously taken those and shared them, as they had been taken in Italy the previous summer.

There was a small book of pictures of naked women, each with my face photoshopped onto them – they were so good, for a moment even I thought they were real. I knew Salem was good with computers so he must have made those. There was also a USB stick and a small tablet to go with it. There was also a brown wig and a red lipstick at the bottom of the box.

"What's on the USB?" I asked them. They didn't reply, just shared a look, and shifted uncomfortably. I plugged it into the USB in and started up the tablet. There were two files. One labelled 'VannahSOLO' and the other named 'VDS'.

I clicked on the first one, VDS, and a video started playing. It took me a few seconds to understand what I was seeing. It was a sex tape, of Salem and Dario having a threesome with a woman. She was wearing the brown wig from the box. I turned the volume up, curious, as they began to kiss and caress her. Confused I skipped further ahead – stopping at a part where Dario was thrusting into her from behind, while Salem was fucking her mouth.

"That's it Vannah. Take my cock" Dario moaned, as he pounded into the woman. The woman moaned, as Salem thrust his cock faster into his mouth. "That's my girl, Vannah" Salem added. The two of them spoke a lot as they fucked her, calling her Vannah any chance they got. I paused it, getting the idea of the video.

"We used to hire escorts" Salem spoke up. He looked uncomfortable for the first time since we'd met. He wasn't sure how I was going to take all of this. "We would make them dress up like you, put on the wig and the red lipstick, and we'd have a threesome. They had to respond to your name and act like how we imagined you would have acted with us".

I swallowed deeply, "how often would you do this? Make an escort pretend to be me?"

"At least once a week for the last four years" Dario replied. I made a noise of shock, as I looked back at the paused screen. "I swear, it's not as bad as it sounds" he continued quickly, thinking I was offended. "But we were both in love with a woman we thought we could never have. Those women were the way for us to feel like we were close to you, without actually being close to you".

I turned back to the tablet and pressed the other file. The video started shaky, as a camera lined up between a small gap in a door. It took a moment to focus, before it showed a person getting change. I quickly realised it was me. Again, Enzo must have taken it because it was filmed in the bathroom at the Amalfi villa. I gasped, when I saw it was a video of me showering. I skipped ahead, blushing when I realised that in the video I was masturbating in the shower, biting my lip to stop from moaning. I quickly paused that video.

"These boxes are all about me" I whispered, feeling my heart speed like it was going to beat out of my chest.

"Yes" Salem nodded, "you're all we want, Vannah, all we have ever wanted".

The three of us were quiet, as I slowly put the things back into the boxes and closed the lids. I knelt there, besides the coffee table, for a very long moment. Slowly, I looked up at my two husbands. "The movie of the girl dressed like me".

"We'll get rid of it" Dario replied instantly, going to grab the box.

"No" I whispered, putting my hand on top of his. "I was going to say do it to me".

Salem blinked, "what?"

"The way you fucked the girl dressed like me. Will you fuck me like that?" I looked between them, as my hands shook nervously. I'd never asked for sex before, never instigated anything before. But they wanted me, more than I thought it possible for someone to want me. If they really were obsessed with me, then I had no problems letting myself feel the same for them.

Dario cleared his throat, as Salem grinned like a maniac. I got to my feet, and Dario instantly took me in his arms. "Giovannah Conti, you can have whatever you want from us. You want us to fuck you? Done. You want us to take turns eating you out all night? Happily. Fuck, you want to just go to bed? We'll fight over who gets to spoon you. You get it now?"

Salem cupped the back of my head, making me turn to meet his eyes. "I wasn't fucking around when we talked about having a baby. I am determined, more than ever, to see you pregnant with my kid. I want a kid, sure, but more than that it means it ties you to me forever. You never get to leave me or be without me. That was the deal we made. Dario got to legally marry you, while I got to put my kids inside you".

Dario leant down and ran his tongue over my neck. His mouth stopped by my ear, "now about this threesome. Mrs Conti, we are going to make you cum so hard, that it shakes all this bullshit about not being good enough out of your gorgeous head".

"We're going to fuck you so good, and so hard, you'll never doubt how badly we want you again" Salem agreed. "Because we're yours baby, just like your ours".

I swallowed deeply as I looked at both of them. Finally, I nodded, breathlessly. "You're mine".

CHAPTER THIRTY TWO

Vannah

A hand ran down my spine, making me shiver, as Dario kissed me deeply. Salem chuckled, as he came up behind me, running his hands over the hem of my t-shirt. Guess my ugly pyjamas didn't stop them like it used to with Aldo. Maybe Dario and Salem just wanted me more.

Carefully, Salem slipped his thumbs under the waistband of my pants and pushed them down. They pooled around my ankles, making Salem chuckle as he rubbed himself up against my ass. "She's so perfectly tiny between us, brother" he mused.

Dario also chuckled, as he broke the kiss to cup my chin. "More than perfect" he laughed, griping my face to look at him. "*Our* wife".

"Damn right she is" Salem mused, as I stepped out of my pyjama pants. Dario's hand slipped between my legs, finding me wet already. I couldn't deny it – seeing that video of them had turned me on. Mainly because it made me realise just how much they wanted me. I moaned, as Dario slipped a finger inside me.

Salem chuckled against my back, as he pulled my shirt off – careful over my bad wrist – leaving me naked between them. Salem's head went into my neck, his lips ravishing the area as he cupped my breasts from behind. Dario kissed me deeply as his finger continued to slip in and out of my wet cunt.

"Oh" I moaned, as Dario's thumb brushed against my clit and Salem rolled my nipples between his fingers. "Feels good".

"It's always going to feel good with us, baby" Salem mused, tongue licking my neck. "That I can promise you".

Dario pulled away from me and they guided me over to the couch. I sat down as Dario got on his knees in front of the couch, and then pushed my legs apart. "I was so damn jealous seeing you cum all over Salem's tongue earlier" he smirked, "all I wanted to do was join in". He winked at me, before he dived face first into my crotch.

As Dario put his skilful tongue to work, teasing and sucking on my clit, Salem quickly removed his clothes. His tattooed body was large and solid, his hard cock standing to attention as he moved onto the sofa next to me. "We're gunna fill you up so good baby".

Dario's fingers plunged back into my cunt, as his tongue lapped at my clit. I moaned, a warm flow of desire flowing through my body, as he brought me close. Salem, seeing my orgasm was close, moved onto his knees and brought his cock to my face. "Open up for me baby" he encouraged.

I whimpered, breathless from arousal, as the tip of him pressed against my lips. I opened wide and he slipped his cock into my mouth. He groaned happily, as my tongue ran over his length. My hands gripped his hips, as Dario's tongue picked up speed. I moaned around Salem's erection, my legs beginning to shake.

I sucked on Salem's cock, as Dario brought me to my climax. My screams were muffled, as I came on his face – soaking him with my arousal, my spine arching away from the back of the couch. "Fuck, baby, that's it. Let go" Salem groaned, cupping the back of my head to encouraged my head bobbing. Like Enzo he didn't attempt to choke me with his cock, which just made me more eager to please him.

I rode my orgasm out, until I flopped back against the sofa with a long breath. "Shit" Dario chuckled, wiping his glistening face as he got back to his feet. As he undressed, I turned my attention to Salem's cock in my mouth. My fingers dug into his hips again, as I worked my lips around his length, drawing his pleasure out of him. He groaned and cussed, his hands gripping my head.

"Oh, hey, slow it down baby or I'm gunna cum" he commented, pulling himself from my mouth. A thin line of spit ran down my chin. He leant down and licked it up, before kissing my lips hard. He pulled away, still cupping my face, before turning me away. "Make Dario feel good too, baby". Dario was suddenly naked and on the other side of the couch of me. He stroked his cock, as my mouth opened and he slipped inside. "Good girl" Salem praised me, as I took over sucking Dario's cock.

Dario's cock was slightly longer than Salem's, but there was less girth, so it took me a second to get my gag reflex under control. Once I got into the rhythm of things, I swirled my tongue as I took control. "Oh fuck" he groaned.

There was something very commanding, almost animalistic, about having a man shaking and moaning your name. It was the first time in my life that I felt truly powerful in my life. That I could get these Alpha males to their knees so easily.

I worked Dario's cock for a while, as Salem caressed and brushed his hands over my body. I'd already orgasmed once, so I was extra sensitive to his touch. I squirmed and whimpered, as Dario pulled out of me with a deep shudder. "Too close baby" he chuckled, "but your mouth just feels so damn good".

Salem slipped his arms around me and drew me into a long, hot, kiss. "Ready to take us both, baby?" he asked.

"Yes. I want it" I whispered, voice shaking as much as my hands. I had done that with Enzo and Salem in the casino, but I hadn't asked for it. There was something about being the person to ask for it, that made me extremely nervous. It was scary to admit how much I wanted them.

Dario moved me so that I was sideways on the couch, as Salem continued to kiss me. He positioned me on all fours, as I felt the tip of his erection at my entrance. I broke the kiss with a groan, as Dario slowly slipped inside of me. It took him a matter of seconds to be seated inside me.

Salem cupped my cheek, making me look up at him, as his cock pressed against my lips again. I opened my mouth, swallowing him, as Dario began to thrust slowly into me from behind. "Oh god" I moaned, around Salem's cock, feeling them both filling me up so completely.

They both look up, connecting eyes over me, before they both began to fuck me. Their thrusts were in time as they pumped me up from both ends, groaning and moaning and cussing. "God Vannah, you feel so fucking perfect" Salem moaned, cupping my cheek as I swallowed his veiny cock as far as I could.

"We got our girl, brother, just like we always dreamed" Dario groaned, his balls slapping against my ass. I moaned, my voice blocked, as I felt Dario hit all my tight walls. His hand reached underneath me, his fingers finding my clit as he fucked me. Salem grunted, as he also reached under me and cupped my breasts.

Dario rubbed my clit, as he fucked me harder. "God, baby, you going to cum on my cock? I love it when you squirt on my cock" he groaned. I moaned, almost choking on Salem's dick, as my orgasm slammed into me. Salem pulled his cock out of my mouth, as I screamed through my climax.

"Oh, that's it, baby. That's it" Salem moaned, pinching my nipple harder. My thighs began to shake, as pure euphoria went through my body, as wetness coated my inner thighs and Dario's cock. My mind went blank as nothing but pleasure coursed through my veins.

"Fuck" Dario groaned, before pulling out of me with a hiss. "Gotta switch now". His voice was strained, as the two of them moved around to be on opposite sides of me. "I'm super close, wife" Dario told me, as he brought his glistening cock towards my face.

I opened my mouth, letting his erection rest on my tongue as I tasted myself on his heat. He groaned, as my lips closed around him, as Salem stroked my ass from behind. He dipped, pressing a kiss to my back, before slipping inside me. I cussed, in surprise, the word vibrating around Dario's hard length.

Salem began to fuck me hard, rougher than Dario had, as my other husband worked his erection in between my lips. Once more they got into an equal rhythm, working me from both ends as I panted and squirmed like a bitch in heat. These men were changing the very fabric of who I was – and I loved it.

"Oh fuck, Vannah, baby" Dario grunted, before his orgasm hit. His salty release flooded my mouth, as he threw his head back in bliss. I grunted in shock, before swallowing it down in a few large gulps. He withdrew from my mouth, breathing heavily, as Salem's fingers pressed harder into my hips.

"Almost there baby" he grunted, slamming into me harder. I screamed as another orgasm ripped through me – my third of the night being shorter, but the most intense, as Salem yelled my name as he came.

The three of us then collapsed into a pile on the couch. Both men sat lazily, as my body rested over Salem and my head was perched on Dario's thigh. "Damn, wife, that was better than I even hoped for" Dario mused, brushing strands of hair from my face.

Salem gave a tired chuckle, "surely you can't doubt our devotion to you after that?"

"Hmm" I moaned, tiredness hitting me like a freight train.

Dario laughed, still stroking my head. "Let us catch our breaths and then we'll carry you up to bed".

"As long as you both stay with me tonight".

Salem grinned his maniac grin. "Little V, there is no place else we'd rather be".

CHAPTER THIRTY THREE

Salem

I reached out to touch her, but felt nothing but cold bed sheets. I grunted, eyes opening to see an empty slice of bed beside me – Dario was still in the bed with me, on the other side of the empty area. "A lot weirder without Vannah in this bed, huh?" he mused, running a hand over his scruffy hair.

"Where is she?" I asked, pushing up to sitting.

"Enzo took her out for breakfast about twenty minutes ago" he replied, yawning as he grabbed his phone from the side table. He instantly began typing out a text, as I climbed out the bed and stretched. "Jesus, asshole, cover up your ugly naked ass" Dario yelled at me.

I flipped him the bird over my shoulder, as I left Vannah's room and headed back to mine. I showered and dressed for the day, smiling to myself thinking about my sexy wife, before heading downstairs. My phone buzzed as I began making coffee. "That's Vannah" Dario commented, walking into the kitchen. "She said she's bringing us pastries for breakfast".

"Good" I replied, handing him a coffee before taking my own over and sitting at the kitchen island. I sipped my espresso as Dario fielded calls and texts, occasionally scowling at the screen in annoyance. "Problem?" I asked.

"Fucking Marco" he grumbled, meaning his useless Uncle who was setting Morales up with the FBI.

"I ask again, problem?"

"Nah" he grunted, putting the phone down. "Everything is running smoothly but he just keeps giving me thousands of stupid fucking updates. He's just trying to make himself look good. He'll be emailing me his shitting schedule next".

I smirked, "he's a little bitch and you're a scary bastard". We shared a smile, as we turned out attention back to the coffee. After a few minutes, I sighed heavily. "We need to tell Vannah about our plan".

"No" Dario replied instantly. "She doesn't need to

know all the nitty gritty details. We'll simply explain we're leaving for a few days to deal with the cartel and, for her safety, she'll visit her family for a week or two".

I ran a hand over my beard, the bristles brushing against my hand noisily. "I don't like lying to her, D".

"We're not lying" he growled, "we're just…emitting the bloodier details of the plan. Vannah knows who we are, she grew up in a damn mafia family, but she doesn't need all the gory specifics".

"Dario" I groaned.

"Hey asshole, I don't remember you running to her to explain what happened with Aldo. You're happy to keep that secret from her". His eyes narrowed in challenge, as I physically cringed. He was right, I planned to take that secret to my grave – all three of us did. Not just to spare Vannah the hurt, but because if she found out we'd risk losing her after just getting her.

Knowing I was beaten, and hypocritical, I backed down. He was right, Vannah didn't need to know all the ins and outs. I certainly wouldn't want her to know just how many people I had tortured and killed over the years. She was too kind and sweet to understand.

Vannah may have been born a mafia princess who had become our mafia queen but, like any monarch, she didn't need to know all the bloody and depraved things her soldiers did for her to keep her throne.

I'd gladly kill every fucker on the planet if it kept Vannah safe and happy. And I'd probably enjoy it too.

The front door opened and keys clinked into the bowl in the entrance. A few moments later Enzo appeared, looking tired and stressed, before Vannah came up behind him. She was wearing grey yoga pants and a skin tight shirt, showing off her sexy little body. Carrying iced coffee in one hand and a bag of pastries in the other, she swept into the room.

"Morning" I grinned at her, as Dario opened up the paper bag of breakfast. She walked over and kissed me sweetly in greeting. My hands instantly went to her waist as I held her close. "Got to say, I'm not a fan of waking up to an empty bed".

"It wasn't empty, Dario was there to cuddle if you wanted to spoon" she teased. She moved away giggling, as I slapped her ass for being so cheeky. But I loved seeing her in a happy mood, especially when I knew I had helped contribute to that feeling.

Dario gave me a scowl over his pastry, "you ever try and spoon me, Matusalemme, and I'll kill you in the most painful ways possible and cut off your wonky cock".

I winked at him, "lie all you want, D, but you couldn't keep your eyes of my 'wonky cock' last night".

Vannah giggled, as both her and Enzo sat down with us. Dario put his food down and glared at me. "I like watching the way your cock fucks Vannah's tight wet pussy, doesn't mean I want it anywhere near *me*".

I pulled Vannah's chair closer to me, as I mocked whispered to her. "Guess that just means I have to keep my cock near you at all times". I winked at her, making her giggle again. I pulled her in for a long kiss, tasting the sweet coffee on her lips, before she pulled away. I gave her another wink, before digging into the breakfast she brought us. We silently enjoyed each other's company, as Vannah and Enzo finished their coffee and Dario and I ate breakfast.

"What are the plans today?" Enzo asked, as Dario and I were finishing off the last of our pastries.

Dario wiggled his phone in the air, "Marco is being a pain in my ass".

"And I've got to go knock a few heads together with the Eastern Europeans" I replied with a groan. "Apparently Boris has been letting his business breeze towards the state lines, need to push the bastard back into Arizona".

Dario frowned, "you're going all the way to Arizona?"

I grunted, "yep, gotta do it in person. I sent some guys last time who got them back over the border, but obviously they weren't forceful enough".

Having the most powerful mafia in Nevada meant there were always lower gangs, and cartels, that thought they could muscle their way in. Most of the time a visit from me was enough for them to suddenly decide that Idaho was a rather nice place to be. But occasionally, I had to deliver the message a few times to some determined fuckwits.

"How long will you be gone?" Enzo asked, glancing at Vannah who began gathering dirty plates and cups and carrying them over to the dishwasher. I understood his hint – we still needed to fill her in on the cartel situation.

"Just one night. I'll take a handful of guys with me, drive up and deliver the message tonight, crash in a motel and drive back tomorrow morning".

"Enzo you should go with him" Dario commented. He opened his mouth, before pausing and glancing over at our wife. "Vannah, love, can you give us a few moments". His words had me frowning, hating to exclude her from the conversation even though I knew it was necessary. But Vannah didn't mind, just smiled at us. She pressed a kiss on Dario's cheek when he apologised, before announcing she was off for a bath.

Once she was gone, and we heard the sound of the bath taps running upstairs, the three of us turned back to business. "Boris is a coward and he's shit scared of you" Dario explained, "if he's testing our territory lines, then maybe he is suddenly feeling a sense of security he didn't have before".

I nodded, understanding what he was getting at. "You think the Morales Cartel are working with the

Eastern Europeans?"

"Hmm, doubt it, but they may have heard some things that made Boris think our stronghold is weakening".

"Testing the waters" Enzo grunted.

"Exactly, which is why I want both of you to go. If Boris knows anything about the Morales Cartel, then I want you to get it out of him".

"Sure thing, *boss*" I grinned. Technically Dario was my boss, but mostly I said that sarcastically – after you share a wife, and hours ago were spit-roasting her together, you sort of lose the ability to be anything other than sarcastic when calling him 'boss'.

"What about Giovannah?" Enzo frowned, "I would rather stay with her".

Dario shook his head, "don't worry, I'll keep her with me until you guys get back".

Enzo clearly was still uncomfortable with that, "I don't like leaving her".

Dario rested a hand on his shoulder, "don't worry, brother, I won't let her leave my sight. I'll take her to the office with me and make sure I have security always within fifty feet of her at all times".

"Fine" he sighed, running a hand over his face. "Fuck, I hate that they're targeting her. Us, whatever, who gives a fuck, right? But Giovannah? It's too far".

"Typical cartels" I snorted, shaking my head as I stood up. "They have no honour for children or women. They know the best way to send a message is to kill a family, so of course, they went after Dario's new wife. Like I said, typical cartel bullshit".

Enzo stood up, a very serious look crossing his face. "I won't lose her. Nothing will stand in the way of her belonging to me. I will kill anyone who dares keep Vannah away from me". He paused, glancing at the two of us. "I hope that doesn't include you two".

I narrowed my eyes at him, "watch the threats, Rossi, I have no problem taking this outside".

"No" Dario growled, stopping us declaring a fight before it could happen. "With everything going on, save your anger for Morales. Letting others see you black and blue might make them think the bomb hurt us more than it did. We don't need people thinking you two are injured. You can beat the shit out of Eastern Europeans instead".

I grunted, glancing at my watch. "An hour and then we hit the road".

"I'm driving" Enzo snapped, turning and walking out the door.

"Like hell you are" I yelled, following after him.

As I left the room, I heard Dario muttering to himself. "At least I still have enough post-nut relaxation to deal with these assholes".

"You and me both, brother" I shot back, my frown

turning into a grin as I mentally replayed my night with Vannah again because it instantly made me happy.

CHAPTER THIRTY FOUR

Vannah

I leant my head back against the rim of the bathtub, as the warm water lapped around my body. Grabbing my phone from the side, I put some music on through the speakers embedded inside the large tub. I sighed heavily, happy, as the soft tones of Lana Del Rey played.

A knock came on the bathroom door a few minutes later. I shouted for them to come in and the door opened with a cautious looking Enzo. "Hey" I smiled, and that nervousness vanished at seeing he was invited. I understood Enzo in a way that the others didn't, because I understood his surprise at being wanted.

"You look relaxed" he grinned, closing the door behind him.

I ran my fingers through the water, "you going to join me?" He considered it for a moment, before pulling his clothes off. He paused when it came to his boxers, as usual, but took a deep breath and pushed them down. I scooted forward and he slipped into the tub behind me, allowing me to lean back against his large chest.

All of my husbands were well built men, but Enzo was easily the largest – his entire body solid and he could cover my entire torso with just one of his arms. I felt safe against him. He wrapped his arms around me, sighing as he relaxed with me. "I wish I could keep you safe like this forever" he muttered.

I turned my neck to look up at him, "unfortunately life doesn't work like that".

"I can make it work like that".

"What? By making me a prisoner and you the warden?" I leant my head on his collar bone. "That wouldn't be healthy for either of us".

"But you'd be safe". He rested his chin on top of my head. "I'd do anything to keep you safe".

"I know you would. But I'm not a princess you can lock up in a tower and expect me not to resent you for it. That's not the way things work, Vincenzo". I reached up and traced the scar that ran down his face with my thumb. His jaw tightened, no doubt recalling the horror of the attack that caused all the scars on his body. "You were once locked away from the world and it almost destroyed you".

"I'm not my mother" he frowned, "I would never control you like she used to control me".

"No?"

"Of course not" he snapped, narrowing his eyes at me. "I just want to keep you safe".

"And I'm sure she thought she was keeping you safe, too". I pressed a gentle kiss to the end of the scar on his chin. "You were one of the first people who was ever truly kind to me, Vincenzo, and I know who you really are. But, you can't let your paranoia about my safety get in the way of us living our lives".

"It's not paranoia when people are really trying to hurt you".

I raised an eyebrow, "so this is just a temporary thing while you try and find the cartel that you think is behind all of this? After that's dealt with, you'll suddenly relax and not worry about my safety?" I didn't say it sarcastically, but Enzo didn't reply as he knew that I was being facetious. "You will always find some excuse to coddle me, Enzo, and it's not healthy".

He just grunted in reply, but I could see by the tightness of his lips that he was thinking on what I said. That was fine, I knew it wouldn't be easy getting Enzo to relax – but maybe I had at least sowed the seed.

"Let's talk about something else" I smiled, looking up at him. "Dario told me your birthday is coming up. Apparently one of the other casinos, Conti Raw, has newly built rooms or something so Dario booked it out for the four of us".

Enzo grunted, "I'm not really a celebration sort of person".

I rolled my eyes at him, "don't be a debby downer. Anyway, I was thinking the night before maybe you and I could do something?" I seductively ran my finger up his wet chest. "Maybe have a nice dinner, some drinks, and then book ourself into a nice hotel for the night".

His eyes shone when he realised I was talking about sex. "I'd like that. Just me and you for a night".

"I think it will be good for us to get a little time without Dario and Salem around". I leant forward and kissed him, tasting our morning coffee on his lips. I hummed happily against him, as his large bear paw sized hands gripped my waist. As we kissed, Enzo used his hands on my hips to turn me around so I was straddling him.

His lips were soft and passionate, but I could always feel the small indent in his lips from where the scar ran through – a reminder, no matter how much we fell into our kisses, that Enzo was more damaged than I could ever imagine. So, I let him set the pace.

I could feel his cock hardening beneath me, as I rocked my hips against him. His hands ran up the span of my back, holding me tightly as our tongues tangled together. Enzo was still cautious and a little clumsy, but it felt rustic and him – a man who had no desire to ever do this with anyone until he met me. It made me feel warm inside.

Enzo lifted me slightly, positioning me against his erection. He groaned, as I pushed him between my pussy lips, letting the tip of him press against my clit. My arms wrapped around his neck, as I rubbed myself up and down his cock. "Fuck" he mumbled against my lips.

We both moaned, as his hands moved down and gripped my ass – holding it with strength as he pushed me snuggly against him. Enzo grunted, as his cock slid against my wet pussy and hit against my clit. He held me with strength as we moved against each other. My orgasm building with each press of my clit.

I broke away from the kiss, my head going into his neck as we moved faster. "Shit" I moaned, gripping onto his shoulders, "fuck, I'm so close".

Enzo groaned in my ear, "you gunna cum on my cock, baby?" He moved faster, his fingers digging into my ass harder. I moaned loudly, as the beginning of ultimate pleasure began to spread through my limbs and warm my body.

My orgasm hit, as I threw my head back in a silent

scream, as Enzo's cock continued to slide between my pussy lips. "Oh my god" I breathed, my thighs shaking as I rode out the bliss. As I was coming to the end of my orgasm, Enzo roared like a bear as his own climax hit. He grunted as his cum sprayed his stomach and rubbed a little onto my skin.

I rested my head against Enzo's chest as we caught our breaths, my thighs slowing down from their shaking. "See" he sighed, running his hand up and down my back. "You can't make me feel like this, love you like this, and not expect me to do everything I can to keep you safe. I can't lose this, Giovannah, I *won't* lose this".

I didn't say anything, just grabbed a sponge and cleaned us both up. I wasn't sure what to say – Enzo was hard to rationalise with when it came to my safety. Luckily, the conversation was cut off by the bathroom door opening. I glanced over my shoulder to look at Salem. He grinned at me, his eyes taking in mine and Enzo's intimate position.

"What do you want?" Enzo growled, frowning at Salem.

He shrugged, still grinning like an idiot. "It's like a storm siren".

I blinked, "what?"

"When a storm siren sounds, people go a running. When I hear my girl moaning, I come a running". Salem winked at me, making me roll my eyes but a little blush heated my cheeks. Simply because I hadn't realised I'd been loud enough for him to hear.

I shook my head, "you're all idiots in this house". I moved to climb out of the bathtub and both jumped in to help. Enzo steadied me, using his hands on my hips to lift me out the tub, while Salem wrapped me up in a towel. Just as I was covered up, Dario walked into the room.

He raised an eyebrow at me, "I thought I heard you having some morning fun in here".

Salem chuckled as I glared at him. He shrugged casually, "see, I told you. Storm siren".

CHAPTER THIRTY FIVE

Salem

I wrapped a towel around my waist, as I wiped the condensation of the mirror. My reflection shone in front of me, the stupid smirk of happiness I had been wearing all day lit my face up. I hummed some Led Zeppelin under my breath, as I combed and oiled my beard – a new habit I had gotten into, since Vannah had commented how soft it was and that it smelt good. I had been oiling it twice a day since.

A banging came on the bathroom door, as I continued to comb my beard. I ignored it, making Enzo shout instead. "Get the fuck out of the bathroom, asshole". He banged his fists a little harder. "I need to piss!"

Sighing heavily, I opened the door and came face to face with Enzo. He was dressed in all black, with a murderous look on his face. "You'd think your mood would have been improved with that relaxing bath you had this morning" I grinned.

"Shut the fuck up" Enzo growled, grabbing my arm and shoving me out the bathroom. I laughed at his bad mood, as he slammed the bathroom door behind him. The crappy motel we had checked into only had one bathroom and I had apparently taken too long for Enzo. We decided to get a twin room and maybe that had been a mistake – but, honestly, we were just going to be sleeping in it.

I dressed, as Enzo used the bathroom. I went with dark jeans, black t-shirt and a leather jacket. My boots were my classic 'stomp on your balls' motorcycle boots. Once I was dressed, Enzo came back out and my phone buzzed with a message. I grabbed it, smirking at seeing the text from Dario.

Dario: took V shopping as a little reward for last night. Apparently she is a little less reluctant to spend my money than before!

Under the text, was a picture of Vannah admiring some designer handbags. At the bottom of the image, was Dario's polished shoes beside four or five other shopping bags. I smiled, as Dario had noted Vannah hadn't wanted to spend any of his money when they first got married. And if Dario wanted anything, it was to spoil Vannah like a princess. So, it was good she was letting him treat her like he wanted to do.

I showed the phone to Enzo, as he came out the bathroom, who took a long breath. "She's fine" I told him, knowing his bad mood was due to worry. He hadn't let Vannah out of his sight since the bombing, and barely before that, so I knew he'd be on edge until she was in his sight again.

"It should be me there with her" he grumbled, turning away and grabbing his jacket. "Let's get this bullshit over with".

"You don't get to be with her all the time. That is obsessive and you'd drive her crazy". I gave him a dangerous look, as I strapped my holsters on. "I know you know that, so knock it off. Dario can keep her safe, and so can I, so stop with the Billy Big Balls throwing your cock around. We can all keep her safe, not just you".

Enzo was deathly quiet, as he strapped his guns and just stared at me. Finally, he stopped, before stepping closer – his face inches from mine. His eyes were full of insanity. "I may only have one ball, but it's bigger than both of yours combined. I don't need to throw my cock around because everyone already knows it's the biggest".

He shoved me back, before storming out the motel door. I grinned brightly, as I followed him. "Don't make a challenge like that, man, unless you're ready to drop pants and get out a tape measure".

"Get in the fucking car" Enzo growled, as he climbed into the driver's side of his Porsche. I just laughed as I followed him.

The Eastern European gang worked mainly in Arizona, their organisation starting out as a bunch of strip joints and brothels, before they eased into trafficking and drugs. We monopolized the sex trade in Nevada, but all our escorts were willing and healthy – not like the Eastern Europeans.

They had recruiters in their homelands promising poor young girl's jobs and money in US. They then brought them into the country illegally, unbeknownst to the girls who believed it all to be legit, before they found themselves prisoners to gang members. They were drugged until they became addicted, and then they withheld their next fix until they 'worked with a client'. The girls didn't speak English and were told because they were illegally in the country that the cops wouldn't help them.

It was a disgusting way to do business. A few years back, we tried to close down the operation. But their organisation was just a viper nest, take out one snake and another just slithers out. So, any opportunity to kill some Eastern European bastards, made me practically giddy with glee.

Their boss, Vanya Chilenzakov, worked out of a large strip club in the centre of Phoenix called Satin

Kittens. Vanya, who we nicknamed Boris because it pissed him off, was a cowardly bastard.

Enzo and I queued to get into the club, before getting a drink at the sticky bar. We stood in the dark, eyes taking in the dark and busy club. Scarcely clad dressed girls, with glazed eyes, danced and served throughout the room. One girl, a skinny blonde, saddled up to us. She put her hand on Enzo's arm before I could stop her. "Hey, big daddy, you interested in a dance?"

Enzo growled like a dog, shoving her hand off. "Touch me again, bitch, and I will peel all your skin from your body with my teeth".

I gave an awkward laugh, and slid between them, giving Enzo a shove towards the bar. "Sorry about my friend, his girl just broke up with him so he's nursing a heartbreak". I pulled a fifty from my pocket and handed it to her. "We're good for now, sweetheart, take a break for a bit". I winked at her, as she took the note and disappeared back into the crowd.

I turned back to Enzo and glared at him. "Prick" I shook my head at him.

"I don't need any whores touching me. I've got Giovannah, I have no use for drugged up whores".

"As compassionate as ever, Rossi" I rolled my eyes. Enzo's mood was really beginning to get under my skin. How could I have fun torturing human traffickers when he was being such a buzz kill?

"Let's just go find Boris". He downed the rest of his scotch before heading towards a back room door. I sighed heavily, downed my own drink, before rushing to catch up with him. We headed through the rear door, a quick bullet to the temple of a guard on the inside allowed us to go straight through.

There was a poker game in the back room, with two orcs of gang members outside. They glanced up as we walked over. "Private area, fellas, head back to the main dancefloor" one said, dismissing us with a wave.

"Shut the fuck up" Enzo rolled his eyes, before shooting both between the eyes. They slumped to the ground, barely flat before he was stepping over them.

"Alright then" I muttered. Thankfully we were using silencers – which was less fun but more effective. But, with Enzo's mood and fast trigger finger, I doubted I'd have much fun anyway. With a large kick, Enzo forced the door open. "Subtle" I grumbled, as I followed him into the room with my gun up.

Seven men, most overweight and balding, were sat around the round table playing poker. Half-naked girls – who were definitely girls and not women – were serving the men...in more ways than just bringing them drinks. Before I could even process the scene completely, and before the men could work out what was happening, Enzo was firing off bullets like it was open season.

"Fucking idiot" I hissed at him, but quickly lined my own shoots up. The girls all hit the floor screaming, as we killed the men instantly in a rain of bullets. Blood sprayed the walls, as the six dead bodies slumped to the floor. The only one left alive was the one we needed. The chubby, balding, sweaty bastard was frozen to his chair. His eyes were wide and shocked, as moisture dripped from my brow.

"Don't even think about it". I snapped, as his hand inched towards his jacket. I rounded the table and took the gun from his jacket. I emptied the clip before throwing it onto a pile of poker chips. Grumbling to myself, I ordered Enzo to tie up Vanya as I rounded up the girls in the room. "Come on, no one is going to hurt you". I herded them into an empty bedroom down then corridor, locking them inside once I established they had no phones on them or in the room. We didn't need reinforcements being tipped off.

I then dragged the two bodies of the large bodyguards into the room, so they were out of sight, before locking Enzo and I in the room with Vanya. The Russian mobster was hogtied to a chair and almost shaking in fear. "Hello Boris, didn't heed my last warning about working in Conti territory, huh?" I mused.

Trying to appear brave, he wet his dry lips with his tongue. "My name is not Boris, that is just offensive".

I shrugged, "don't give a fuck about you, Boris, I

give a fuck about Dario Conti and the way you're disrespecting his territory lately".

Before he could speak again, Enzo pulled a large curved knife from under his jacket and held it out to me. It was a beast of a weapon – almost like a small machete rather than a knife, but with the beauty and delicacy of a dagger.

Enzo glanced at his watch, "you have ten minutes to get the information we need". He headed to guard the door. "Have fun…but not too much fun".

I twisted the knife, letting the shiny blade catch the lights. Vanya was trembling like a new born animal. I grinned at him, as I ran the tip of the knife over my tongue. "What my friend doesn't understand, Boris, is that there is no such thing as having too much fun".

I drew back the knife and slashed him – his scream, and blood, making my smile widen and my cock harden.

CHAPTER THIRTY SIX

Dario

Vannah leant back against me, her dark hair laying over my arm as her head rested against my chest. She was sitting in between my legs, as we watched some stupid cooking programme on the TV in my bedroom. My wife was relaxed and it was nice to see her like that.

As she was intently watching her show, my hand smoothed over her arm and carefully let the spaghetti strap of her pyjama shirt slip down. The swell of her breast teased me with a brief showing. My finger traced the path down her arm again, cautiously nudging her shirt down until her perfect nipple flashed an appearance. I inched my hand slowly towards it and--

"Do you think I don't know what you're doing?" Vannah announced, almost making me jump as it pulled me from my concentration.

"What?" I replied innocently, trying to hide my smile. "I'm simply cuddling with my wife and--"

"And trying to get her naked, thinking you're being sneaky when you're just being super obvious".

I leant in and bit her ear lobe, "if I was trying to be obvious about it, I would just do this". I grabbed her top with both hands and pulled. It ripped straight down the middle, revealing her two perfect breasts and the milky skin of her stomach.

"Dario!" she exclaimed. I laughed warmly as she looked at her ruined shirt with a stunned expression. "This was my favourite set of pyjamas".

"Oh, it's a set?" I mused, before ripping the silk shorts down the middle too. She shrieked my name in mock outrage once more as I laughed more. "Come on, Vannah, I improved it".

"Improved them? How? They are unwearable now".

"Now everything I need access too is available to me" I mused, as my hands went down and covered her breasts. She sighed heavily, shaking her head at me like I was a naughty kid she just couldn't discipline. I relaxed her with a nice breast and nipple massage – and with the breathy sounds she was making, she was definitely becoming more relaxed.

One of my hands dipped down and into the slit in her sleep shorts. "Dario" Vannah moaned, as my fingers slipped into her pussy. She was already slightly wet, and I could feel her arousal building as I slipped my fingers in and out of her tight cunt. She groaned again, as my thumb began to rub against her clit.

My phone rang on the side table, but I ignored it. Vannah glanced over at it, but quickly dismissed it as I picked up speed of my fingers. "Fuck" she hissed, as my thumb played with her clit. Her head flopped back against my chest, as my other hand continued to play with her hard nipples. It wasn't long before she was cumming on my hand, making a delicious wet mess as usual, with her back arching against me.

My phone rang again, as Vannah's orgasm slowed to an end. I grunted before snatching it up and answering it. "What?" I grunted, but my hand was still soaked from Vannah's pussy so my phone slipped from my grip. I cussed, caught it, and put it back to my ear.

"What was that?" Salem asked in my ear.

"My hand is wet from being in my wife's pussy and I dropped the phone" I replied.

"Dario!" Vannah screeched in shock, as I heard Salem – and Enzo in the background – chuckling softly. She looked at me in horror as I chuckled.

"It's just Salem, baby" I reassured her.

"Oh". She relaxed instantly against my chest again, as I transferred my phone to the other hand and wiped my wet hand on my shirt that I had taken off earlier in the night.

"You want me to turn this to camera and watch her face as I make her squirt all over my cock?" I mused, as Vannah looked up at me. Heat shot through her eyes at my suggestion, which just made my cock harden more, but she stayed quietly tucked up against me.

Salem laughed, "fuck, I would love that man, but we gotta talk business".

"Damn, right now?"

"Yeah, right fucking now".

"Give me a minute" I mumbled to him, before turning to Vannah. "Just going to take this call in my office baby, why don't you get yourself cleaned up and some new pyjamas and I'll bring us some cocoa up when I come back".

Vannah didn't pause for a moment, "sure". She pressed a kiss to my chest before slipping out the bed and heading into the bathroom. I knew that she understood the dynamics of being part of a mafia family, and she was more than happy to not be included in business, but I still hated feeling like I was dismissing her.

I had a small wet patch on my thigh, from my wife, so I quickly changed into a clean pair of sweatpants before heading down to the office. "Alright, tell me what happened" I sighed heavily, as I sat at the desk and put the phone on speaker mode.

"After a little fun with my knife, Boris became real chatty" Salem told me.

"Shocker" I snorted.

"They heard that our stronghold on Vegas was weakening, so he sent some of his men to test the edge of Nevada to see if that was true. Which, of course, it isn't. But, he hadn't heard anything about the Morales Cartel".

"So, who did he think was testing our stronghold?"

"Well, this is where it gets fucking weird. Apparently he had some FED type sneaking around, and asking questions about his girls. Said the guy was white, dark haired and dressed in a suit".

"Huh that is weird" I frowned, "Davide reported a similar incident to me a month or so back".

"Yeah, I remember" Salem replied. "Unlike us, Boris was around and didn't buy the FED getup. The guy quickly squealed – I'm guessing after our lovely Eastern European friends had him alone for a while. Guy claims he's a mercenary, he was paid to come to Vegas and get the scope on the syndicates in the area to try and understand how they work. Said he was hired by a gang who want to understand our stronghold".

"He said gang and not cartel?"

"Apparently. But, he didn't give any more information than that. FED guy said that he was mainly focused on the Conti enterprise but came to Arizona to check out the competition".

I snorted a laugh, "Boris? Competition for us? That's like saying a goldfish is competition for a shark".

Salem chuckled as well, "I know, I imagine he was bullshitting to try and save his life. Boris killed him though, thinking he was a rival and just lying, but I'm pretty sure he was in fact a mercenary".

"Hired by Morales? Or is this something completely separate?" I rubbed a hand over my eyes, wishing I could go back ten minutes to where I was happy and warm in bed with Vannah.

"Got to be Morales" Enzo commented, speaking up from the first time. "No way anyone else would be stupid enough to try us".

"I agree" I sighed, "we've not been challenged for our territory in over ten years. There is no way that two different syndicates are going to try us at the same time. This is just Morales, or someone in his organisation, trying to see if they can expand their territory once they plan to destroy us".

"Fucking idiots" Salem snorted. "We're going to monitor Boris for the night, make sure that he isn't bullshitting us, before heading back in the morning".

"Sounds good. I'll speak to Vannah tonight and see if

we can get her on a flight tomorrow. The quicker we get this ball rolling, the quicker it's all over" I replied.

Enzo made a noise of annoyance, "I still think I should go with her".

"I have no doubt people are watching us, awaiting our next move. We need to get Vannah out of Vegas, and back with her family, as quietly as possible". There was a moment of silence – Enzo wasn't happy, he never was when it came to Vannah's safety – but there was no more fighting as we'd already ironed out all the kinks as best we could.

We said our goodbyes and hung up. Sighing heavily, I leant back in my seat and stared at my desk for a long while, as I dreaded starting this all going. Grabbing my office phone, I dialled an unfamiliar number.

"Hello?" a deep male voice answered.

"Giovanni" I greeted Vannah's twin brother, "it's Dario. I need to talk to you about Vannah".

CHAPTER THIRTY SEVEN

Vannah

I sat between Salem and Enzo inside a blacked out SUV. Dario was outside the car, checking over the private plane with a pilot he knew personally. After coming to bed, the night before, Dario had told me he was sending me back to New York while they worked to get rid of the Cartel problem they had. I understood the need to get me somewhere safe, but I was nervous about going home. I didn't feel like I was the same person who left a few months ago.

Enzo's hand was firmly on my knee, his knuckles almost white with how tightly he was holding onto me. I could feel his anxiety a mile away. "I'll be back with you soon" I assured him, leaning my head against his shoulder. He sighed heavily, but didn't reply – there was nothing that would ease his tension. But he put a small bracelet in my hands; silver with a citrine gemstone. I kissed him and slipped it on my wrist. "I love it".

Salem reached over and pushed my hair off my other shoulder, giving me a sad smile. "I love you, Vannah. You have to promise me that you'll keep safe and come back to us".

I took both their hands in mine. "I'm truly happy for the first time in my life. Wild horses couldn't keep me away". At my words, Salem leant over and kissed the top of my head.

A knock came on the door – Dario telling us it was time. As the plane's staff got my suitcase from the trunk, both Salem and Enzo gave me lingering and passionate goodbye kisses. Then the door opened and Dario was helping me out. I gave my other husbands one last look, before the car door was shut on them and Dario was walking me over the tarmac.

The plane was small, streamline, and obviously top of the line luxury. Despite certain celebrities, real billionaires didn't have their own planes unless they travelled every few weeks or were passionate aviators. It just wasn't worth the upkeep when you could rent one at extreme short notice or fly first class.

The inside of the plane was plush, with lots of clean

whites and greys, and well-dressed staff who headed to the front of the plane to give us some privacy. I sat down in one of the seats and Dario squatted down beside me. "You'll stay safe, right?" I asked. I didn't know what they planned to do, nor did I want to know, but I knew it was risky if they were sending me away.

Dario gave me a small smile, "don't you worry about me, beautiful, you just enjoy some time with your family and we'll be back to get you in a week or two". He gave me a long, stomach clenching kiss, before resting his forehead against mine. "Nothing is more important to the three of us than you, Vannah. You're our wife, our dream and our sanity".

I gave him a soft smile, "you'll look after them, won't you? Salem and Enzo".

"Of course, they're my brothers". Dario kissed me once more, before he was gone and the door was being closed. Thirty minutes later, we were flying and I was being served steak tartare and champagne.

Six hours later, I was climbing down the plane steps to see my brother leaning up against his Italian sports car texting. He glanced up at seeing me and gave me a smile. He finished his text as I walked towards him, before pocketing his phone. "Hey sis" he grinned, giving me a hug before taking my suitcases from the plane workers.

As I climbed into his car, Gio tipped the plane staff,

before getting into the car. I texted Dario, telling him I was safe and with my brother, as we drove home. Gio and I may have been twins, but we were very different people – so having had time away from each other, we had a lot to chat about. But once those topics were burned through, the sibling bickering started anew.

"Mom is excited to see you" he told me, as we cruised into our childhood hometown. "She's missed you a lot".

"I've missed her as well" I admitted, "I keep meaning to call more than I do…it's just that everything is so different in Vegas than here that I don't want to seem like I'm bragging to her".

Gio raised an eyebrow, "bragging? You think you're better than us now?"

I rolled my eyes, "don't be an asshole and twist my words. I just meant that Mom and I used to have very similar lives when I was married to Aldo, whereas now things are very different and I don't want to seem like I'm bragging to her how new and exciting it is for me".

I knew the conversation wasn't going well, especially when Gio's hands tightened on the steering wheel. "Aldo may have not been the best match for you, Vannah, but he gave you a good life. You lived in a nice house, got to stay home all day and he gave you an allowance higher than I give Maria. If you think Mom has such a bad life, maybe you need to remember how lucky she is to be married to a well-off man like Dad".

"Money isn't everything" I snapped.

"Dario Conti is richer than anyone in our family and he gives you an allowance to spend that money. You would think very differently if he lost all his money and couldn't provide your lifestyle. Marriage is a contract, Vannah, and you weren't exactly an attentive wife to Aldo, you need to consider changing things if you wish to keep Dario interested. You aren't eighteen anymore and--"

"Oh, get off your high horse" I cut him off, making him glare at me. "I don't need you to preach about how lucky I am to have someone marry me after being so used up by Aldo. Not to mention how I'm practically geriatric being twenty-six, not a virgin and not a mother. It's a wonder no one has taken me out to a field and shot me by now, surely that would be kinder than allowing me to live such a miserable life".

"Watch the sarcasm, sis" Gio rolled his eyes at me. "And, yes, you should be grateful that we managed to get you such a good match with Dario Conti *despite* those things. I would have never married a widow".

"Why because we're used up? Our cunts have too much mileage for you?"

"Hey!" he yelled, face reddening with anger. "I don't know what sort of way you talk to your husband, or what sort of language they speak up in Vegas, but you're still a Bianchi woman. And Bianchi women have respect and speak with integrity".

"I'm not a Bianchi woman anymore" I shot back, "I'm a Conti woman now". *A Conti-Galluci-Rossi woman really,* I thought silently and smugly to myself.

I was a different woman than I had been before I left. I had read once that people were just a sum of their experiences and I believed that to be true. Every part of me was thanks to something I had gone through; I was constantly changing as a person. I was different before I married Aldo, and after he died, and I was very different after experience true freedom and liberty with Dario, Salem and Enzo.

"You know what?" I snapped at Gio, when I began to notice familiar houses. "Just drop me off here, I can walk and that way I don't have to spend another second around your arrogant ass". I opened the door as he slowed to turn a corner.

"Dammit" he grumbled, slamming on the breaks and pulling over to the side of the road. "We're like two minutes from Mom and Dad's, don't be a diva".

Ignoring him, I climbed out the car and slammed the door on his exasperated sigh. I could see Gio shaking his head at me as I pulled me suitcase from the trunk and began to walk away. It was only a ten minute walk, and it was a sunny day, but I also knew I should have stayed in the car. The Cartel problems were back in Vegas but Dario would still be furious that I was alone.

Gio's car creeped down the road beside me as I walked, calling for me to get back inside. I considered it for a few seconds, hearing Enzo's disappointed voice in my head, but I didn't. By the time I got to the top of the road, Gio gave up and just drove off. It was only two streets away, so I'd catch up within five minutes.

As I walked, I took notice of how quiet the streets were. They had always been that way growing up, as it was a privately owned neighbourhood, but I noticed it more after experiencing the hustle and bustle of the Vegas Strip by the casinos.

Maybe it was due to the quiet, or my awareness of the danger in Vegas, but I quickly noticed when someone seemed to be following me. Instantly I walked faster, which was hard in heels, as my heart pounded a little faster. The footsteps sped up and fear shot through my body.

"Giovannah?" a voice called out. I span so fast on my heels; I slammed into my suitcase and almost fell. Deep laughter sounded as hands steadied me. I looked up into the familiar face of my 'follower' and blushed like a tomato. "Not a cartel assassin" an amused look crossed Aliza's face, "but what the hell are you thinking walking around out here so exposed?"

"My brothers an asshole" I admitted to her.

"Ah" she smirked, before gesturing to my wrist. "Mr

Rossi put a tracker in your bracelet".

I rolled my eyes, "of course he did".

"You didn't really think they were sending you off to New York without backup did you?" she mused, before we began walking together towards my parent's house. Aliza was technically my bodyguard, but I hadn't needed her much as usually Enzo was with me so she just did 'long distance' bodyguarding where I didn't see her.

From the few times we had chatted, Aliza seemed competent and nice. She was ex-army, having been discharged after several tours in the middle east, and her spouse was currently serving Air Force – who was presently working out of Nellis base – so she'd gone into private security when they'd relocated to Nevada.

Aliza made small talk as we walked, before we reached the top of my parent's drive. "I arrived last night and have scoped the place out. If you have any problems, you have my number, I'll be floating around in the background".

"Thanks Aliza" I smiled, before turning and heading into my parent's house.

.

CHAPTER THIRTY EIGHT

Dario

The pot holes were nothing new, but you didn't feel them in a luxury sports car like you did in a rundown prison truck. Enzo gave me a look of annoyance as the prison truck, that was taking us to county jail, bumbled over the uneven road again and he banged his head on the roof. These weren't made for men over six foot – I was uncomfortably squished and Enzo had at least four inches on me.

Salem, who looked down right gleeful, didn't even seem to notice the journey. He was too excited about getting to the destination and getting his revenge. Luis Morales had been arrested yesterday and – with

Vannah safely with her family – it was time to take our pound of flesh and chop the head of the damn snake in our garden.

When we arrived at the jail, Salem pushed his way out the truck before anyone else. Probably the only motherfucker in the world eager to get thrown in jail. "Watch it, Jones" the county cop snapped, as he tugged Salem back before he could bound to the doors like an eager puppy. 'Jones' was the fake name that Salem had been arrested on – even if the fake charges were going to be dropped in two days, we still didn't need our names connected to this.

The processing into jail was slow and took way too long – made even longer when they had to get tweezers to remove a pocket knife from Salem's asshole. Sometimes I forgot just how crazy my oldest friend was. Mostly he dealt with the enforcing business with others, as I tried to stay as legitimate as I could. But when I did get involved with things like this, it always reminded me just how fucked up Salem was.

"Don't worry, boss, I can skin him alive with my fingernails" Salem grinned, as we were taken through the jail. "I saw it once on the discovery channel and have been waiting for an opportunity to try it".

"Sick motherfucker" Enzo grumbled, dragging behind us like a sulking teenager.

I gave Salem a look, "he's right. You better not show

this side of yourself to Vannah, she'll not want a kid with your crazy genes".

He laughed, "don't worry about me and Vannah. If anything, we're the best suited out of all of us". He shrugged, before moving through the door for a second frisk before entering the general population. Enzo and I exchanged looks, both of us disagreeing and believing *we* were the best suited to Vannah. We were probably all deluded and Vannah would be much better suited to some boring middle management office worker who drove a minivan. But, we were too selfish to ever let her find out if there was anyone else better for her than us.

The three of us separated to find our beds for the next two nights, before the guards left and locked all the external doors. The county jail wasn't overly large, but arrangements had been in place to ensure that we were in the busiest pod along with Morales. Once all the guards were long gone, a familiar face made their way over to me.

My cell mate was reading on the bottom bunk, I nodded my head to the tables in the centre of the pod. "Read out there" I told him. The guy eyed me up and down, his lip curling slightly, before he looked into my eyes. Career criminals can always tell Mafia and he decided that, yeah, reading out at some of the tables was a good idea.

"Boss" Seppe nodded at me, as he walked into my cell. Giuseppe Montorow was married to one of my cousins – we weren't close but he was competent enough when working for the family that I trusted his loyalty. The idiot had been arrested in connection to an art robbery a little while back, and was still awaiting trial, so I had asked him to stick close to Morales once he had arrived.

"You good, cousin?" I asked.

"Eh" he shrugged, "jail is jail and cops are stupid, the charges won't go to trial but because the FBI are involved it's taking too long for the evidence to be thrown out". He rolled his eyes as I nodded along. As much as I had Nevada cops in my pocket, we still had to be careful when government agencies were involved – Seppe was right, he'd never go to trial, but it would be too obvious if he was just released on the local cops say so.

"Morales?"

"Piece of shit" he snorted, "he's not done much since he's turned up. All his cartel buddies have been put in different pods, so he has no backup here". As he spoke, Enzo and Salem came into my cell – both getting head nods of greeting from Seppe who carried on talking to me. "He's in the chapel now, but the service ends in an hour and then he'll be back in here. His cell is that one". He pointed to one on the opposite side of the pod from mine.

"He'll know something is up if he sees us" Enzo commented, crossing his overly large arms over his chest. "We should make sure we're out of the way until he returns from the chapel".

"I'll keep my eye out for him" Seppe agreed, "once he's back in his cell, I'll come get you guys".

With that the four of us split up. I stayed in my cell, as Enzo and Salem made themselves scarce. Seppe took a seat at the table in the middle of the pod, pretending to be writing a letter while watching for Morales. I mostly paced as I waited – so full of energy that I just wanted everything over and Vannah back home.

Our girl had come so far in the few months she'd been my wife. I hoped that with a little bit more time, she'd be fully confident in not only us but herself. Living with a controlling asshole like Aldo for so many years had crushed a lot of her spirit, but there was still fire inside her – she just needed to let it out more often.

An hour and a half passed, before Seppe came and got me – apparently it had taken longer as Morales had also taken his daily phone call after chapel. But, he was back in his cell again. "His cell mate is a kid" he told me, as Enzo and Salem made their way towards us. "Stupid kid but street smart, I'll get him out of there".

He went ahead, as we waited at the top of the stairs to his line of cells. We watched as Seppe, smiling and looking relaxed, popped his head into Morales's cell and spoke to the kid. He invited him for a game of chess, the kid was hesitant – but after a few words of encouragement, the kid agreed. Like Seppe had said, the kid was smart. Once he passed us, the kid nodded to himself and didn't look back – understanding that sometimes things happen in jail and it's best not to get involved.

With that, Morales was ours.

He was laying on his bunk, reading through a bible. Salem stepped into the cell first, practically vibrating with bloodlust, as I followed inside. Enzo pulled the cell door closed and leant against it – his giant frame blocking the view to the rest of the pod. He crossed his arms and glared around, no one would dare come over to him, even if they heard what was going on. Our positions were easily chosen, we didn't even need to discuss it.

Morales glanced up over his bible, his dark eyes full of a blank expression as he took us in. He was a weedy looking man, with golden skin decorated in black tattoos, with the large cartel marking on his neck. He looked skinny, his face almost gaunt and pale.

"Ah, I didn't expect you to turn up to quick" he sighed, carefully shutting his bible, and placing it on the bed. Calmly, he stood up and faced us. "I knew you'd be coming for me, she said you would, but I thought I may have had a few more days".

His calmness was almost eerie. "Oh, you knew we were going to be in the same jail as you, did you?" Salem snorted, eyes glaring into Morales.

"No, I was expecting an interrupted prison van or something to happen when I go to my hearing to be charged" he sighed. "But, I should have known it would be more personal. I heard your collective wife got hurt".

His words turned my blood to ice. "Collective wife?" I asked, my voice coming out like hisses between my clenched teeth.

"She said the three of you had some sort of communal wife". He paused, snorting like a boar. "Stupid and just means you married a whore".

Salem punched him hard. The sound of his eye socket breaking was satisfying, although it must have hurt like hell if the scream from Morales was anything to go by. The sound vibrated through the pod and it went quiet for a moment. Then I heard Seppe yell something and suddenly the TV was double the volume, people's conversations increased and someone began to sing a jail tune very loudly. Snitches get stitches, so best to make sure you can't hear shit.

"Don't you ever speak about my wife again" Salem hissed, standing over Morales. He pulled a small switchblade from his pocket and I frowned.

"Where did you hide that one?"

He quirked a smile at me, "you don't want to know".

"You keep saying 'she'. *She* told you about our wife, *she* told you that we were coming". I leant down and grabbed Morales's chin and jerked his head to me. "Who the fuck are you talking about?"

Blood dripped down his face as he smiled sickly at me. "Huh, look at that. The great Dario Conti himself doesn't even know the enemy he's fighting against". The look of smugness on his face had my stomach turning in knots. Something was wrong, something was really wrong.

I stood back up and glanced at Salem. "Get him to talk".

Salem grinned like a horror movie villain, as he raised his switchblade. "I thought you'd never ask".

Twenty minutes later, Morales was ready to sing like a canary. He was beaten and bruised beyond recognition and his genitals had been skinned and removed. Salem was covered in blood and grinning like a true psychopath.

"Four months ago, this girl came to me".

"Girl? What girl?" I demanded, as Salem propped the dying man up.

"Mercenary woman, refused to give us her name other than Mars. Was some mafia princess from New York. She's been the one pulling the strings".

Salem and I exchanged a look, "this Mars woman, what did she look like?"

Morales groaned, "I'm in so much pain".

"Answer the damn questions and we'll walk away

and someone will get the guards" I snapped. We weren't letting him walk away, but he was too delirious with pain to realise that. "What did this woman look like?"

"Tall, manly, kind of butch" he groaned. "My gang was breaking up. We were just not getting the money like we used to…your fucking fault". He snarled up at me and Salem pressed into one of his stab wounds making him whimper. "This woman came to us, said she wanted to hire some of my people".

"To what? Kill our wife?"

"No" Morales shook his head, his eyes going glassy as shock approached. "Mars wanted to pay her back and destroy her life".

"Pay her back?" Salem frowned, "pay her back for what?"

Morales didn't say anything, just slowly smiled. "She said this would happen. That you'd come for me". He coughed up a mouthful of blood, "she said this would happen".

"Focus" I snarled, but Morales just laughed and sprayed more blood from his mouth.

"You don't get it do you?" he laughed manically, his eyes frosting over as he began slipping away. "She planned this all. She knew you'd come for me and when you did she'd destroy the one thing you care about most".

My heart skipped a beat, "and what the hell is that?"

Morales smiled one last time, "your marriage". Then he took his last breath.

†

I pulled every string and favour I had, but nothing could be done in time. Someone was out to get Vannah and we couldn't get out of jail for at least thirty six hours.

We played right into this unknown enemy's hands. Vannah was in trouble and we had no way to contact her or get to her.

CHAPTER THIRTY NINE

Vannah

Before, when I was married to Aldo, I was so jealous of Maria. Gio's wife, Maria, was three years younger than me and seemed to have the life I wanted. Like me, she'd had a nice house and a rich husband, but unlike me she'd had no trouble having babies. My niece was born only eleven months after they married, and my nephew eighteen months later.

But sitting there, watching Maria – heavily pregnant – juggling two young children fighting, I realised that I wasn't jealous anymore. I noticed things about Maria that I hadn't before; the circles under her eyes, the way Gio walked past her struggling and didn't help and the way she made herself small and unnoticeable in the room of men.

After the large Sunday lunch we'd had, after a lengthy church service, everyone began to disappear. My father left for business with some of my uncles, as I stood at the window watching Maria struggle to get the kids into their car seats, while being unsteady on her feet, while Gio texted on his phone and didn't help.

I knew that no matter the dynamic of my husbands and I, that they would never let me struggle like that. Aldo would have, as like everyone else around my father he believed that child raising was the woman's job. Even though Salem was planning to father the children, I knew that neither Enzo or Dario would be able to resist some sort of fatherly role in their lives.

"She's going to pop that third kid out any day now" my mother said, coming up behind me to clean up the last of the mess made. She looked over my shoulder at where I was watching Maria and Gio.

"He's not going to be like that" I blurted out, "my husband I mean. He'll be a hands-on parent". I shook my head as Gio snapped for Maria to hurry up, but still didn't give her any help. I turned away from the window, not watching anymore. "Was Dad like that? When we were kids? I have such warm memories of him but I don't remember him doing much of the actual child raising".

My mother looked away, busying herself. "You have

to understand, Vannah, that both your father and Gio are very busy men and--"

"Bullshit" I cut her off, making her give me a hard look in warning. "If he wanted to he could. All of them could give a little bit more time to their families if they wanted". I grabbed some of the last plates and followed my mother into the kitchen. We silently cleaned for a while, before I turned to her with a sigh. "I'm sorry, Mamma".

She raised an eyebrow at me, "for what?"

"Last year when I caught you with Santo. How I acted, the things I said...I was wrong" I admitted, looking away from her. A year ago, I had caught my mother kissing Santo, a lower member who was assigned to watch over her, and I had been very mean and judgemental towards her. It mainly came off the back of me being cheated on, again, by Aldo and having no one to vent my anger too. So, when I realised my mother was also cheating on her husband, I'd spewed my venom at her.

My mother blushed, "you had every right to say those things, Giovannah. My actions were despicable".

"You were lonely" I said softly. She looked up at me, her blue eyes glistening with tears as she reached up and pushed her blonde hair behind her ears nervously. "I get it, really I do. I was so lonely with Aldo and I was so damn miserable. I think if someone had showed me attention, damn if someone had even just been kind to me, I would have done the same thing. I don't blame you for what happened and I'm sorry I was mean about it".

She was quiet for a long moment, before taking a shaky breath. "Santo is the only man who ever seemed to see me. To him I'm a person, not just an object told what to do and where to be. I know it's wrong, what I'm doing, but he is the only thing that makes me feel human most days".

"So maybe you should be with him" I commented. She looked up at me in shock and confusion. "Why don't you come back with me to Vegas? Spend a few weeks and think things through. And if you want to stay, and maybe with Santo, then Dario and I can help with that".

My mother was quiet for a long while, before giving me a watery smile. "Maybe I could just come with you first. Just to...think things through. Leaving your father, it would be a big problem for everyone. Your father isn't the kind of person you just divorce".

"Don't worry about that. Dario can sort everything out if he needs too" I told her truthfully. And I knew that if I asked any of my husbands to help my mother out then they would.

"You seem to be happy" she commented, "you seem free and content. Is there...I don't mean to presume, but is it Dario that is making you this happy...or someone else? You seem so understanding of me and Santo that I can't help but wondering maybe it's a different man that is making you so happy".

It was my turn to blush softly, "it is Dario...but it's also his two top enforcers, Salem and Enzo". My mother's eyes widened in shock. "But it's not an affair. Dario knows...it's an open situation".

"And he has other girls then?"

"No" I shook my head, "Dario is my husband and Salem is my husband and Enzo, is also, my husband. Apparently they all wanted to marry me and the only way for them to agree was for them to share me. I'm exclusive with them and they are exclusive to just me".

"Oh well, it's definitely...unorthodox" my mother admitted carefully, "but you seem happy and with how horrible Aldo treated you, it's about time you had some happiness".

Before I could say anything else, a noise sounded outside the back door. I frowned as I moved to the window to look, but didn't see anything. Then the sound of a sliding van door and I craned my next to try and see around the side of the house, but again saw nothing. But I wasn't too worried, Aliza was out there somewhere.

"So, what do you say?" I smiled, turning back to my mother. "Should I get Dario to find a nice penthouse for you to rent for a few weeks in Vegas, to see if you like it?"

My mother opened her mouth to answer, before

the sound of shattering glass vibrated through the room. I ducked in reaction, cussing in shock and confusion. I glanced at the window behind me, to see one of the panes of glass had a hole in it. "What the hell?" I frowned, before turning to my mother.

There was a moment of pause, as she just looked at me before she fell. Her eyes were wide, shocked, before the life left them and every part of her soul left her body. The shock of her body crashing to the floor jerked me out of my momentarily confusion. I dived towards her, grabbing her just after she hit the floor.

I looked at her, at her empty blue eyes, and tried to understand what had happened. There was a bullet hole right in the middle of her forehead. But it didn't look real...there was only a single trickle of blood and the hole was so small. "Mamma?" I squeaked, refusing to acknowledge what was happening. She'd just been shot, been killed, by a bullet through the window. "No" I whispered.

The back door flew open and suddenly there was people in the kitchen but I couldn't take my eyes of my mother's dead body. How was that possible? How could that have happened? My eyes must have been tricking me, they must have.

Hands suddenly grabbed me from behind, snapping me out of my grief and shock. I tried to fight as they pulled me to my feet as if I weighed nothing. "Shut her up" an unfamiliar male voice said, as I screamed out for help – hoping that Aliza or a neighbour would hear me. A large gloved hand covered my mouth, shutting me up, as I whipped my head around.

Four large men, dressed in black with balaclavas over their faces, surrounded me. I didn't feel fear, just pure adrenaline. I bit into the hand over my mouth, making the man cuss at me as he moved his hand away. "Bitch" he hissed; his voice clipped with a slightly Hispanic accent. Cartel. They'd obviously followed me from Vegas.

I screamed again, making one of them punch me in the face. The world span and I instantly shut up as the pain stunned me into silence. I opened my mouth again and got another punch. Blood filled my mouth as my vision spotted. "Get her out of here" one of them hissed.

My world moved slowly as I was carried out the house, my brain too sluggish from the punches to work out what had happened. I was taken through the yard, past Aliza who was laying on the ground, and to a van. Without care I was thrown into the back. My already pounding head hit the floor of the van, making my vision spot further and my stomach twist.

"Call Mars, let her know we're on our way" one of the them said, seconds before my world went dark.

CHAPTER FORTY

Vannah

The first thing that happened when I woke up was vomiting. Hard, acidic, bile burnt its way up my throat. I tried to double over, but I couldn't do more than turn my head to stop it spraying all over my lap. I still wasn't safe from splashing, but most of it hit the cold concrete floor.

Once I was able to clear my mind, and my stomach, the kidnapping came back to me in a flash. I glanced around, my head pounding from the face punches I'd received. I was tied to a wooden chair, the harsh rope constricting my hands and feet – tied tight enough that my fingers and toes were moveable but slowly going numb.

The entire room, which seemed to be an abandoned warehouse, was dark and grey – the floor a dirty chipped concrete and exposed metal beams in the roof. I seemed to be alone, but there was a projector on a wheeled in stand to my left. It took a few moments for my mind to clear, before I glanced at my wrist and cussed. My bracelet, which Enzo had put a tracker in, was missing.

"That tracker was so obvious it was insulting" a voice commented from behind me. I tried to turn in my seat, to find the owner of the familiar feminine voice but couldn't see far enough. "Yellow" she mused, "that is his colour isn't it? Three different colours and gemstones for each of your husbands, right?"

"Who are you?" I demanded, voice hoarse and strained. I recognised the voice, but it couldn't be possible. It absolutely couldn't be possible.

She continued as if I hadn't spoken. "Blue sapphire for Dario Conti, green emerald for Matusalemme Galluci and yellow citrine for Vincenzo Rossi". A soft laugh, "it's almost sickening how much those fucking idiots planned their lives for you".

The sound of boot falls echoed, coming closer behind me, as my heart beat a tattoo against my chest. The steps were heavy and dominant. That solidifying the fear in my body just from hearing the familiar voice. "Patty?" I asked, voice barely a squeak.

"Oh, you do remember me then, little sister? I thought you had totally forgotten" she laughed, before moving to stand in front of me. A sob broke from my mouth at seeing her. My half-sister Patrizia had been dead for over ten years...and yet there she stood in front of me. Not a ghost, not a hallucination, but real and solid and aged.

Patty was twenty-three when I thought she had died, but eleven years had passed and it showed on her – making me not doubt that she was real. Patty was tall, almost five eleven, with a stocky build and melon breasts. Her brown hair was pulled back in a bun and she wore all black, with holsters attached to both thighs.

Around her neck was a chain with three identical wedding rings. My necklace; my husband's wedding rings. I had seen her steal my necklace, but I had been injured and convinced myself I had been delusional. But there she stood, very much alive, wearing my necklace like a medal of achievement over me.

"How are you alive?" I asked, tears leaking from my eyes.

"Oh, don't cry for me, little sister. After all, you're the one who shot me". She gave me a manic grin, the look transforming her face from angry to down right terrifying. Patty had always been dangerous, but I had never realised how truly unhinged she had been.

I looked away from her, "I didn't have a choice, Patty. It was me or you, you would have done the same thing".

She snorted, crossing her arms over her chest. "I wouldn't have done the same thing. When I shoot someone, I always finish the job".

Patrizia was not a classic beauty and father struggled to find her a marriage – it didn't help that she didn't want one and scared every potential suitor off. She wanted to be a mafia worker, not a princess – so our father gave her a compromise. She would concede to a marriage, registry office and no dress, and he would let her work for the family. She agreed.

The first time I met her husband, Frank Emilio, he cornered me in the bathroom and told me he was glad he'd get to see me a bit more. I was fifteen and he was thirty two. Every time after that he tried to touch me or put his hands on me. Three months after they were together, Patty picked me up from school and told me there was a family emergency.

But rather than driving me home, she took me to a seedy motel and made me a sexual pawn in their relationship. Frank and Patty hadn't consummated their marriage yet, as apparently they weren't attracted to each other. Somehow my father found out and wasn't happy – as he said it wasn't part of the deal they made.

Frank agreed to have sex with Patty, but he wanted me to 'get him started'. My psychopathic sister went along with this. Patty had brought me to that motel in order for her husband to rape me, to get him 'hard enough' to sleep with her.

However, it didn't happen quite like that.

Frank tried to take advantage of me, but he was high on cocaine and I was crying and shouting for help. He couldn't get an erection. He didn't blame me, instead he blamed Patty. The two of them fought and Patty shot, and killed, Frank. She then realised that she had fucked up and my father wouldn't forgive her for what she had done.

I realised she was going to kill me before she even made the decision too. I grabbed Frank's gun, which he'd left on the bed, and pulled it on Patty before she could even unholster hers. I shot her, in the stomach, and watched her fall in a pool of her own blood. I watched her cuss and scream revenge at me until she took her last breath.

Or, what I thought was her last breath.

I had called my father, who had come to the motel and cleared everything up. He'd told me that I had killed Patrizia but he wasn't angry with me. Three years later, he used the excuse that I had blood on my hands that he couldn't find me a decent man who wanted a killer wife. That was the reason he married me off to Aldo – because of what I did to Patty.

"I'm sorry I hurt you, Patty" I admitted, looking at

my sister who was very much alive. "That was the one and only time I have shot a gun. I didn't aim, didn't plan, I just shot. I'm glad you're alive".

Patty gave an exaggerated groan and dramatically threw her hands up into the air. "You are the literal worst person in the world" she screamed dramatically. She laughed at me, shaking her head in what was almost disappointment. "The one and only good thing you have done in your life was stand up and shoot me. And now you're glad I'm alive. Don't you get it, little sister, I am behind every bad thing that has happened in your life".

"That's not true".

"Actually, it is. I told father I would come back and kill you unless you suffered for what you did to me".

I blinked in shock, "wait...father knows you're alive?"

"Of course, he's known since that day in the motel. He took me a hospital and when I was better, he gave me a new identity and bank account and sent me to a mercenary agency for work".

I frowned in confusion, "I'm so confused".

"Alright, let me break this down for you, little sister" Patty sneered condescendingly at me. "Father doesn't have the balls to kill his first born little girl, so he let me live. But I have enough on him that he knows he has to do what I say. I said that the only way I'll leave him, and you, alone was if he followed some rules. You shot me, so I ruined your life".

"How?"

"I made him marry you to Aldo, I had your doctor dosing you up with contraception so you couldn't get pregnant and I even paid prostitutes to give Aldo an STI. It was fun seeing you so damn miserable". Her eyes glistened which made me cry harder.

"You hate me that much?" I sobbed, "you really hate me that much".

"Yes" Patty shrugged. "And then I went away on an assignment with the mercenaries and when I get back? What do I find out? That Aldo is dead and you're about to marry some handsome rich man who genuinely loves you". She shook her head, "not on my watch, sister".

"You tried to shoot me at the wedding".

"No" she laughed, "I mean, well, yes. But I never planned to kill you, it was just the start. While you were preparing to marry Dario, I was doing my research. I learnt that it was even worse than I imagined. Not only did one handsome rich man want to make your life amazing, three of them did! And I just couldn't have that".

"So why not just kill me?" I hissed, anger solidifying in my veins as I realised just how much of my life Patty had taken from me.

She grinned, "because I knew that was too easy. I could have killed *them*, but again too easy. Instead, we had some fun together and I let you fall in love with them".

"Why?" I cried, "why let me fall in love with them and then bring me here to kill me?"

"Kill you?" Patty laughed, "oh no, little sister, you're not here to die. You're here to have your whole new happy world destroyed".

With that she walked over to the projector and turned it on. And what I saw...she was right, it ruined all the happiness I thought I had had.

CHAPTER FORTY ONE

Vannah

The projector started and showed a slightly grainy CCTV of my old house with Aldo. It started with me cleaning in the kitchen as Aldo poured himself a glass of ice water. I was wearing pyjamas and Aldo was wearing a silk robe that didn't close all the way over his large beer belly. I had forgotten how unattractive he was, and how much I used to hate having him on top of me.

"I'm tired, I'm going to bed" Aldo informed me – his voice clear through the video. He walked over and kissed the top of my head, before taking his water and leaving the room. As I was cleaning, I took a glass of orange juice from the side and stopped to take a sip. As I drank, a noise sounded off camera and I put my drink down and disappeared from the frame.

I realised then what the video was about. That was the night Aldo died.

I had heard a noise at the front of the house and went to check it out. A second after I walked off screen, the back door from the yard opened and a man dressed all in black, his face covered, slipped inside. I gasped in shock and confusion as I watched. The man paused, glancing in the direction I had gone, before taking a syringe from his pocket.

I watched as the balaclava covered man injected clear liquid into my orange juice, quickly mixed it with the needle, before slipping back out into the yard. I walked back into the frame, having no care or fear, and picked my orange juice back up.

The camera changed to one in the lounge and time had obviously skipped, as I was passed out on the couch. My half drunk spiked orange juice on the coffee table. I assumed that the man had spiked me with a sedative – which made sense since I knew that I had slept through Aldo's heart attack that killed him.

I watched the video, my heart pounding as three men also covered head to toe in black walked into the room. But, when they were together, I knew who they were. Enzo's large size was obvious, even with his face obscured and the way Salem silently moved was classic for him. My new husbands had been in my house the night my old husband had died.

"Aldo didn't have a heart attack, did he?" I whispered.

"Clever girl" Patty laughed. I continued watching as Salem knelt next to me and affectionately ran his finger over my cheek. They all paused for a moment, looking at me, before heading upstairs towards the bedroom.

The screen cut to a third camera, one hidden in the main bedroom. I silently watched as Dario and Salem eased into the room and Enzo stood in the doorway. They looked at each other, before Dario crept up to Aldo's sleeping form and put a hand over his mouth. Aldo's eyes popped open in shock, but he froze when he felt Dario put a gun to his head.

"What do you want? Who sent you?" Aldo demanded, trying to look beyond the balaclava of his assailant. They were silent as Salem pulled a second syringe from his pocket and uncapped it. As Dario kept Aldo still with a gun to his temple, Salem pulled Aldo's sock off his left foot and injected the needle between two of his toes.

The three of them stayed silent as they watched Aldo begin to sweat and convulse. Dario and Salem stepped back and watched as Aldo clutched his chest and struggled to breathe. Finally, he fell from the bed, dead. Aldo had died from a heart attack – my father had ensured he'd had an autopsy done – but it was brought on by something Salem had given him. Salem put his other sock back on and the three of them left the room.

The camera came back to the sitting room, where I was still passed out on the couch. It was Dario who came over to me the second time, pressing a gentle kiss to the top of my head. Then he turned to Enzo. "Do it now".

Salem whipped his head between the two of them, "do what?" Enzo pulled a third syringe of drugs from his pocket and moved towards me as he uncapped it. Salem moved in front of him. "Wow no. We've given her enough sedative, any more and it could put her in danger".

"This isn't a sedative" Enzo replied, pushing him out the way.

"Then what the hell is it?" Salem snapped, once more moving into his path.

Enzo didn't reply, so Dario walked over and placed his hand on Salem's shoulder. Salem let Dario move him out the way. "It's a mifepristone and misoprostol" he explained and I gasped loudly.

"No" I whispered, tears falling harder than ever from my eyes.

"Oh yeah" Patty laughed, as we watched Enzo slide

up my shirt and inject me in the hip. Dario was speaking quietly to Salem, who was shaking his head. I couldn't see their facial expressions, because of the coverings, but I could tell that Salem wasn't happy with what was happening.

Patty stopped the projection and moved back in front of me. "They killed Aldo, but you don't care about that. But they killed your unborn baby". She tutted, shaking her head but she looked happy. "The men you love, your husbands, betrayed you. I bet you've even let them all fuck you at the same time, haven't you little sister? They were probably laughing behind your back, knowing that while you grieved your miscarriage it was actually a chemical abortion".

I couldn't say anything because I couldn't feel anything. I had trusted them and confided in them how hard it was being married to Aldo. And the entire time they had been behind his death and my miscarriage. I truly felt alone for the first time in a long time.

Patty had made it her life mission that I was constantly miserable and my husbands had taken away maybe the only thing that would have given me a good life. Patty had taken my happiness; they'd taken my child.

"What now?" I asked, looking up at my evil older sister. "You killed my mother, you ruined my marriages and you've destroyed my entire life. Is it enough yet?"

Patty sighed, shaking her head. "We've only just started, little sister". She walked forward and grabbed my face, her fingers digging into my cheeks. I screamed, as she pressed on my facial injuries from where her goons had beaten me earlier. "You destroyed my entire life for the past thirty four years, I've only had fun with you for the last eleven years. It's never going to be enough".

I looked up to her, physical and emotional pain filling my entire body. "Just kill me".

Patty let go of my face and smoothed over my crazed hair – her touch almost affectionate and motherly, despite her eyes full of hate. "I'm not going to kill you, Giovannah, that's just too merciful".

She turned and walked out the room, returning a few minutes later with a box. In the distance I could hear low male conversation and the sound of running engines. "You'll be seeing me soon, little sister, don't worry". Patty opened the box and pulled out my tracker bracelet.

"I'm sure someone will be along soon for you, Mrs Conti" she winked, dropping the bracelet by my feet.

She left and a few moments later car doors closed and they drove away, leaving me alone and broken.

Looking down at the bracelet my heart felt cold. My husbands had lied and betrayed me...I wasn't even sure I wanted them to rescue me. Maybe it would be best just to never be found and never have to feel this pain again.

Because when I saw them again – Dario, Salem and Enzo – I knew that it would just hurt even more. They claimed to love me, but they'd only hurt me.

And I was done with hurt.

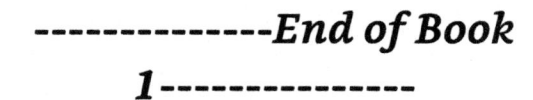

--------------End of Book 1--------------

BLOOD STONES:
CITRINE

The next book in the Blood Stones series will be released soon. Citrine will pick up directly from the end of Sapphire and will continue the story of the Conti Harem.

ABOUT THE AUTHOR

Bunny Brooks

Bunny lives in a world of handsome billionaires, deranged but protective serial killers, sword wielding timetravelling knights, Alpha Werewolves seeking their mates and criminals who would forsake everything for their one true love...
Then she puts her pen down and reenters the normal world with her own family, job and pets. Not quite as thrilling but equally as exciting.

Printed in Great Britain
by Amazon